THE ARCH
AND
THE BUTTERFLY

THE ARCH
AND
THE BUTTERFLY

MOHAMMED ACHAARI

Translated by
Aida Bamia

دار بلومزبري - مؤسسة قطر للنشر
BLOOMSBURY
QATAR FOUNDATION
PUBLISHING

مؤسسة قطر
Qatar Foundation

First published in English in 2014 by
Bloomsbury Qatar Foundation Publishing
Qatar Foundation
PO Box 5825
Doha
Qatar
www.bqfp.com.qa

First published in Arabic in 2010 as *Al Qaws wal Farasha* by
al Markaz Al Thaqafi Al Arabi

ISBN 9789992179055

Printed and bound by CPI Group (UK) Ltd, Croydon CR0 4YY

Whatever does not belong to me wholly and eternally
Means nothing to me.

Hölderlin

The Dilemma According to Al-Firsiwi

I

As soon as I read the letter, its single line written in a nervous hand, a cold shiver ran through me. I shrank into myself so far that I did not know how to stop the shock overwhelming me. When, after a gargantuan effort, I finally regained control of myself, I found nothing. I had become a different person, stepping for the first time into a wasteland. In this desolate new place, I began assimilating things without sensation, finding them all alike. I felt no trace of pain or pleasure or beauty. My only desire was to make my inner self react. My only weakness was that I could not make it do so.

I had been getting ready to leave the house when I had found the letter that someone had slipped under the door. It contained the following message: 'Rejoice, Abu Yacine. God has honoured you with your son's martyrdom.' Then the phone rang and I heard the voice of a man with a northern Moroccan accent. He repeated the same cold sentence, accompanied by ready-made phrases of condolence.

I placed the letter on the table, only to watch my wife lift it to her face and read and reread it, losing her balance, like an animal being slaughtered, before giving a shattering cry and falling to the floor.

My only son, who had been doing so brilliantly at one of France's most prestigious engineering schools, had chosen to go to Afghanistan and join the ranks of the *mujahideen* until the day he would meet God. He had met Him soon after arriving, in unexplained circumstances, before he had turned twenty.

I carried my wife, dragging myself with her, to our bed. At no point during those moments did I feel any piercing pain from the tragedy. I knew it had happened, but it did not touch me. I observed it spreading slowly before me like an oil slick. I watched my wife's collapse as if it were merely something physical, until I understood that she had embraced the boundless tragedy. It was as if she were taking her revenge for our long years of emotional austerity.

I sat staring at my fingers, toying with the letter, and looked every now and then at Yacine's photograph that hung in the living room. I saw his childish, innocent, delicate, cruel, sweet face. Scenes from his short life passed before me, starting with the day my wife, getting out of bed and lifting up her hair, announced that after the long, gentle intercourse of the previous night, she was sure an egg had been fertilised. Then Yacine crying in the doctor's hands. All the growing up that followed, and the fears, joys and anxieties experienced along the way. The ferocious quarrels over his clothes, his eating habits, his education, his games and his comings and goings. The moment at the railway station when he took the train to the airport and then to Paris and then to darkness. His first and last letter, in which he wrote: '*My studies are much easier than I expected, and the city is much harsher than I expected. I believe I'm living my first love story, a little later than the average for us Al-Firsiwis. I'm not sure I'm the best son, and I'm not sure you're the best parents, either. Don't send money till I ask. From this distance I could almost say I love you. I am, however, apprehensive.*'

4

I listened for hours as a senior police officer questioned my wife and me about the letter and the phone call. We answered, with mindless incomprehension, questions related to Yacine's friends, his habits, his books, his music, his films, his sports club and his favourite mosque. We felt as if we were reconstructing an entire life to be presented as a stiff corpse to the officer, who could think of nothing better than to ask me, 'Do you approve of the way he died? Sorry, I mean, did you sympathise with his cause? Sorry, sorry, you didn't know. Neither of you knew anything. Are you upset about what's happened?'

I said, sincerely, 'No, I'm not upset.'

From the moment I received the news, I was filled with a fury that made it impossible for me to grieve and feel pain. Had I had the opportunity to meet Yacine at that moment, I would have killed him. How could he do such a vile, cruel, contemptuous, humiliating thing to me? How could he push me over the precipice on whose edge I had stood all my life? When did the poisoned seed take root? Before he was born or after? When he was a small child or as a teenager? Did he play with hands dripping with blood that we did not see? Had we spent our lives walking behind a funeral bier?

My life seemed like an appalling mistake. It would have been impossible for all this to happen unless I had spent all those years going in the wrong direction. In the weeks following, this conviction made me think daily about decisions that would correct some of that overarching mistake. Whenever I sensed this was impossible, I was overcome by a strange feeling that my body had departed and I remained suspended between an absent person and another who observed him curiously, and I was undecided which of the two to choose.

★

WHAT HAPPENED to me after Yacine's death was very much like losing one's voice. I was unable to convey anything to others, be it an idea, a comment or a joke. I sometimes answered questions I was asked, all the while wondering what another person would have answered had those questions been put to him. I was totally incapable of conveying anything related to feelings, simply because I could not feel anything any more.

Like the light fading into the darkness of night, that same condition gradually progressed from the realm of feelings and emotions into the material world. I completely lost my sense of smell. Losing my sense of smell was not the result of poor health or progressive deterioration. It struck suddenly, without forewarning. Normally on my way to the office, I could recognise people's features and their histories just from the way they smelled. But soon after Yacine's death, as I was passing by the Experimental Gardens, I noticed that my system for picking people out had not been working since I had left Bourgogne Square. I felt that a cold, solid mass had inserted itself between the world and me.

I spent the rest of the day doing things that would prove this loss to be fleeting. I drank every kind of hot and cold drink served in Rabat's bars. I devoured dozens of dishes. I drenched myself from every bottle of perfume at hand. I drew close to every creature I met on the way, hoping to find in their wake vestiges of fragrance or a stray scent. I sat for hours in my favourite, the Steamboat. I left it, exhausted and oppressed, to take what remained of the night back to the home whose covert violence I had endured for a quarter of a century. I stopped by the wall on the railway bridge and spent ages staring at the metallic sheen of the tracks, indifferent as to whether another train would pass. Then I emptied my stomach in one go and felt that I had also vomited out the man I had been until that day.

Yet all that complex chemistry had no smell.

From then on I stopped listening to music and watching films, and rarely went to exhibitions or museums. I had to attend receptions as part of my work, and I would spend a long time listening to people's chatter while trying to remember the taste of the wine I had had a passion for in my youth. I could only locate it in my imagination, something distinct from the liquids I was drinking, which I could differentiate merely by their colour or temperature.

During this time of my life, having already turned fifty, I also became convinced that there was a woman I had known and somehow lost. I made a huge effort to remember her, but to no avail. I could only recollect that something intense had brought us together, that I had made exhaustive efforts to win her over, and that I had endured many disappointments as a result. In particular, I remembered that I had never stopped chasing her. I did not recall the details, only my ensuing state of mind. I grew obsessed with picturing her face and finding a way to reach her. The more I tried and failed, the more obsessed I became with her, although this had no impact on my emotions, as if I were being impelled by a clockwork mechanism separate from my existence.

I believe that this searching endowed me with a mysterious charm that I interpreted as the energy of a mind seeking a woman who has slipped away. I acquired an extraordinary ability to seduce women without, however, experiencing any particular pleasure in doing so. As soon as I had exchanged a couple of words with a woman, I would feel I had become hostage to a love story that I had absolutely nothing to do with, and from which I would have to try very hard to extricate myself later on. Almost invariably, that meant leaving some of my scalp behind. I took no pride nor found any satisfaction in any of this. I thought long and hard about the matter, and devised a solid plan to avoid falling into traps of this kind. Deep inside, I was amused by this absurd situation that made me lose all restraint, after having spent a chaste quarter of a century with the same woman— my wife, Bahia Mahdi, who I had met one winter morning in the 1970s, married the same evening, and realised before midnight that I had made a fatal, and irreversible, mistake.

Before I lost my sense of smell, I could tell important details about the life of every woman I met based solely on the mix of scents I picked up. I could pinpoint her ambivalences, and their gradations. I would, for example, know roughly her age and the colour of her skin, the cosmetics she used, and the kind of hair she had. I could intuit the last dishes she had cooked. Sometimes I would know that a woman had just had sex, and whether she was very, or not at all, satisfied. All of this without seeing her.

My new situation compelled me to use my hands to become acquainted with these details. This required inordinate finesse and effort to avoid the rudeness and roughness of touch, and was not without mishap.

It goes without saying that this natural inclination to become acquainted through smell was not purely technical, but emotional as well. The drive behind this skill was a kind of abstract passion whose substance was nameless and featureless. It was a feeling similar to a passion for mathematics: something impalpable that traverses remote regions of an intense mind, where intelligence alone decides what must or must not be true. My sex life, with all that this expression implies in terms of adventure and upheaval, had been very poor; in my few prior experiences, the woman's move from fantasy to the bedroom had been irreversible and tragic. I should point out that this displacement did not happen when I married Bahia. Rather, Bahia and I took up permanent residence in a state of incomprehension, which, no matter how hard I tried, I could never move away from.

When I first lost the sense of pleasure, I fought it by displaying an ability for pure, refined technique, and my accomplishments became an expression of pleasure that I did not truly experience. I became mad about cooking, acquired an encyclopedic knowledge of wines, and completed one of the most important artistic studies of Roman sculpture. I wrote *Letters to My Beloved*, a collection of reflections on love and despair related to the woman I had lost and whose love I recalled without being able to recall her. The reflections appeared serially in the newspaper where I worked, before being published in a book that one critic considered the most important work on love since al-Hazm's eleventh-century *The Ring of the Dove*.

In all those achievements I attained the intended result – the total illusion that I could feel the tiniest and most complex pleasures, those connected in their essence with aesthetic perception, not only of actual forms of beauty, but also of all that came before. I grew convinced that what mattered most regarding pleasure was capturing the details of its formation, or, to be precise, making it eternal on an infinite trajectory. For example, the most important aspect in the appreciation of any wine is not the sensory experience of the seasoned taster, but the complex chemistry that contributed to that result. The pleasure lies in the sun and rain, in the bounty of the earth, then in the fruit and, finally, in the magical liquid derived from it.

Once I reached this conviction, I became more amenable to life and more copiously productive. I wrote a daily column,

9

published a literary work in parts, and penned features and investigative pieces every month. I wrote an art review every week for a specialist journal. I had begun a new life, which had nothing to do with the drab years I had spent writing boring reviews of the free books mailed to me daily. This new life was a real renaissance that helped me return to my true self, pay attention to my wellbeing, reconnect with my old friends and put a minimum of order and rigour into my professional and private lives. The transformation confused my wife, who was unsure of how to react to the sudden changes. She considered my talk about the loss of my ability to enjoy life nothing more than a mask, behind which I hid my shame at seeking pleasure despite all that had happened to us.

I told my friends that I did not like anything at all, and I almost told them that I did not like anyone, either. I do not remember when all this began, and I cannot tell if it happened to me all at once or in timid steps, until that ill-fated moment when it reached its peak. I only remember the feeling that stayed with me for a long time as a result of what happened: no one owes anyone anything. In this world, no matter how strong and intimate your relationships, you face your fate alone, isolated, and with an instinctive inclination towards depression and self-pity. No one ever achieves happiness because of others, no matter how close and dear they are. Any moment of happiness, intense or tenuous, can only be achieved internally.

I resigned myself to accepting what befell me as a kind of incomplete death. Whenever I remembered myself in a state of enjoyment, fondness, savouring or admiration, it was as if I were recalling someone who had passed away, and I had to accept whatever was left of me before joining him. Only then would we become the way we had been, one person, with the hands of our clocks resuming their normal rotation. For that reason I did not resist or seek treatment, but organised myself according to the expectations of a man who loved life, and I set the rudder of this confiscated existence without dictating conditions on anyone.

I HAD lived a relatively quiet life until then. Though I had a complex relationship with my father, my mother had died tragically, and had spent several years in Qenitra's central prison without knowing why, I felt my life consisted of connected parts leading painlessly from one to the other.

I had first joined an extreme leftist group while living in Frankfurt, Germany, which led me to a Moroccan leftist group that had split from the Communist Party. I rapidly grew tired of the effort required of me to adopt extreme positions, so I joined a moderate leftist party. But an old comrade had kept my name in his diary, which led to my arrest, followed by a trial not a single word of which I understood, and finally to a prison sentence that consumed three years of my life for nothing.

While most of my friends at university threw themselves into amazing love stories, I simply ended a terse conversation one day with a colleague with the question: 'Could you possibly marry me?'

Clearly nervous, she had replied, 'Why not? As long as you're asking without even smiling!'

I discovered the morning after the wedding that I was in total harmony with Bahia, as if we were two identical beings or two machines running on the same programme. We loved, with identical degrees of intensity, the same foods and drinks, and the same music, films, paintings and cities. We had similar inclinations in our sexual desires, and in meeting them, down to the tiniest detail. All this existed in a sort of complete technical harmony, where there was no room for dysfunction or emotional confusion, apprehension or surprise. A harmony that began and ended with movements determined from time immemorial. All that was left in the end were the invisible ashes of momentary flames, volcanic ashes from ancient times, cold and petrified, only awakened from their timeless slumber by our slow breathing.

I was taken aback by this disturbing compatibility, and even more despairingly so by the absolute certainty that I would never love her. The moment I reached this certainty, our relationship settled into a permanent state of tension. Bahia considered me to be satisfied with the minimum in everything. This upset her and put her in a bad mood most of the time. I, on the other hand, saw her as a regrettable mistake that continually jabbed me and made me feel like I had lost out.

Yacine's death accelerated the collapse in our relationship, with all the rage, fights, murderous thoughts and feelings of guilt this entailed. Bahia felt I had not grieved at all for our tragic loss. That was not true: I knew exactly what Yacine's death meant in the context of events related to the Taliban. I imagined him awash in his own blood, lying somewhere after a raid or clash and waiting for someone to pick him up off the dusty road. I wondered whether he thought of me before he died and if he remained determined to go all the way, or if he experienced last-minute regret and thus spoiled the glory of martyrdom. I was unable to picture him even for a second under the ground or revelling in the shade of Paradise. Yet I did not fall victim to unbearable grief, and one day I even surprised myself with a deep conviction that Yacine was still alive. Nothing provided incontrovertible proof that news of his death had come from Afghanistan. The letter had been written in Morocco and the call could have come from anywhere. I imagined that the story was only intended as camouflage and that Yacine would show up later to carry out terrorist operations here, free of the stigma of his previous identity.

I shared those ideas with Bahia. In an effort to explain what was happening to me, I told her that parents who had penetrating emotional insight were not fooled by such tricks. Their hearts guided them to the truth and led them to reject false grief. But my wife lost her mind and organised a mourning ceremony, where she displayed all manner of hysterical behaviour, because, she argued, I was both denying Yacine's death and making of him a future butcher. As far as I was concerned, I had come close to believing that behind this story was a certain miracle that might bring Yacine back into my life as a newborn. I then realised that if such a miracle occurred, it would hand him over to a destiny just as brutal as this one. I remembered once more the letter and found nothing to disprove it.

One day I asked Bahia, 'Why don't we build a tomb for Yacine? It would be the best thing to bring us together.'

She looked at me sternly and said, as she went on gathering objects from the bedroom, 'Each one of us must build a tomb for the other, bury him alive, and pour all the earth of this world over him. Only that could unite us, do you understand?'

I could have left the house for good, but I did not. If I had, the total and complete loss would never have happened.

2

OF ALL MY FRIENDSHIPS, I only kept up two – with Ahmad Majd and Ibrahim al-Khayati. I had a theory about this: at our age, we did not have the time or energy to make new friends. My friendship with them nevertheless proved to be problematic as they both treated me with a kind of paternalism that made them interfere in the tiniest details of my life. This was particularly so during the disturbance I went through, when I was convinced that the best way to get rid of a person you disliked was to replace him with someone else. But we really ought to do that with ourselves before doing it with others. At that stage, I had no illusions about my true losses. I came to realise that the real loss was not what had come to pass, but rather our feeling of helplessness at having failed to act. I had read – I no longer recalled where – that at birth we had unlimited possibilities for different lives, but by the time we died the only possibility left was the one that had come true. It was not so much that we had missed out on options – since they were not available to us at any time during our lives – but that we had tragically lost the possibility of being different to what we were.

Ibrahim al-Khayati dreaded my fits and tried to stop me from driving by putting a driver at my disposal whenever I needed. He never understood that the attacks did not take me by surprise, but rather took hold of me gradually like a slow dimming. They began with something resembling depression, then I would lose the desire to do something specific, even if I were in dire need of it. I would be hungry without appetite for a definite dish; I would go to the Steamboat and not know what to order for my thirst; my innards would groan with an animal desire that I did not know how to satisfy. The situation was like going on strike against life for two or three days, after which I would awaken to a kind of existential burnout that gripped me in a new attack. I could prevent losing consciousness in the physical sense either by speaking or by moving my limbs.

Early one summer morning during this delicate period, I walked along Al-Nasr Street, and then crossed the Experimental Gardens and Bourgogne Square, to attend a meeting of the party – one of those meetings that you secretly wished had been cancelled without your knowledge. I endured its atmosphere of despondence for half the day, and then decided to leave. This was not for any valid reason that I could have defended, not even because of Yacine, who had sprung from the loins of a pure socialist and died in the arms of the fundamentalists. I left because I could no longer bear the language used in those gatherings: the repetition of clichéd sentences that lacked any hint of imagination or witty sarcasm or sincere feelings – and even lacked good grammar. I felt crushed under the weight of the lifelessness being expressed, which exposed a different, and more dangerous, kind of death.

I left the hall quickly and did not look back, until I found myself crossing the Experimental Gardens for a second time and exchanging subtle smiles with women and men who were killing time there on a Sunday in the temple of sport.

The following day I went to the offices of a well-known independent newspaper and without much effort convinced the editor-in-chief to hire me. On my first day, I approached the job as I would territory that had surrendered, and immediately started writing my daily column, imagining with no little malice the splash it would make on the gossip exchange the next day.

My wife paid no attention whatsoever to the stories that circulated about my presumed love affairs. She knew that I met many women in journalistic and artistic circles, but she also knew that, beyond the game of seduction and the pleasure of company, I did not understand much about women, and my chronic timidity did not help when it came to going further. Neither had we ever experienced the anxieties of jealousy and suspicion, or a tendency to control one another. My trips did not raise any questions for her, and the only time we had a quarrel over this issue had been years earlier in the car at the start of a holiday. We had been talking about Ahmad Majd and the story doing the rounds about his ex-wife and her relationship with a well-known architect in the capital. I had been expressing my disapproval at how public they were about the affair, when Bahia had lost her temper and begun defending the woman's right to live as she pleased. I had asked if this meant that marital infidelity should also be considered a virtue.

'Yes,' my wife had said. 'It's the pinnacle of virtue because it leads to a moment of truth, while the pretence of faithfulness is nothing but a vulgar lie.'

I had remained silent, knowing that she did not believe what she was saying but had said it only to provoke me, when she had added nervously, 'Even vis-à-vis God, a person is purer while experiencing this moment of truth.'

'Has this happened to you?' I had asked.

'Do you think I would tell you if it had?' she had replied.

We had spent the rest of the drive between Rabat and Agadir in a poisonous, destructive argument about who had done what, without gaining anything except a hollow, senseless jealousy that had nothing to do with us personally, yet which awakened feelings of outrage, affront and hatred. Meanwhile Yacine had been fussing in the back seat with his electronic games, shouting every now and then for us to tone it down.

Once I became firm friends with Fatima Badri, however, Bahia began to pay attention to everything connected to the women in my life. She viewed with antagonism all my new clothes and books, the films I saw and the music I listened to, convinced that a woman, and most probably Fatima, had ushered me towards them.

Bahia did not understand – from my explanations or of her own accord – that the falling away of my own sensation of things and the absence of any pleasure in what I consumed was what pushed me towards the unfamiliar in my life. The person I had been disliked Andalusian music, but since it was all the same whether I listened to that or jazz, I accepted what I had disliked before, seeking a modicum of pleasure to jolt me here and there. Perhaps I simply did not know what I wanted, which was also true of my romantic conquests, if we could call them such, which did not reflect a sudden flightiness or a delayed adolescence on my part. I was, despite myself, thrust into stories I did not help spin together, nor was I a real player at any stage of their development. It was as if the death of my senses had transformed me into a black hole that swallowed every particle of light that approached it. I was aware, every time this happened, that the total darkness controlling my inner self lent me this attraction. I therefore organised my affairs in a very strict manner to allow me to navigate within the limits of what I could see in this dark hubbub.

When Fatima became a large part of my life, it was the culmination of an old acquaintance. I had known her distantly because of our shared profession and passion for the theatre. She had once directed one of my modest texts for the Casablanca Players. Our relationship changed on a scorching afternoon in a restaurant on the beach. On my way back from the restroom, I glimpsed the cook putting a giant crab into boiling water and saw the steam rising from the pot take on a pinkish tinge. I expected to be swamped by this putrid cloud. My body over-reacted and I fainted. After I lost my sense of smell, I acquired an extraordinary capacity to imagine aromas, and even to be strongly and, at times, disproportionately affected by them. The unfortunate incident led me to share a delicious lunch with the woman – Fatima – for whom the crab was boiled. I watched Fatima struggle to use pincers and a scalpel to extract the pieces of white meat lodged beneath the carapace of the boiled creature, which she then devoured with gusto. The exertion quickened her breathing and made her chew in a way that sounded like staccato panting as she toyed with the long legs of the shellfish, sucking them with her eyes closed, holding the ends with her slender white fingers and hardly touching the horny pink shell.

She asked if the smell would cause me to faint again, and I told her that I didn't smell in the first place. My answer did not seem to surprise her, and she commented without interrupting her battle, 'I also imagine scents. I can even smell them on TV and at the cinema.'

I laughed, but she insisted that she was not joking.

After that, I described to her in great detail the situation of a man who has lost his sense of smell. It was not, of course, to do with losing the memory of smell, because the scents we smell even once, starting with that of our mother and on to that of death, would never be forgotten. Taste remains, but requires more time for the tongue to register a substance and send a clear signal to the brain, which in turn deciphers the code and transmits a readable message to the sense of taste.

I said to Fatima, 'Do you know that this handicap has positive aspects? There are so many things that invade our nostrils without our permission and force us to retain stinky smells for ever!'

I then confessed that the most annoying thing was not being able to recognise people from their smell. It was an unrivalled pleasure to first encounter the fragrance and then sense it was in motion, eating up its distance from me, then drawing closer or moving away, freely. It would offer me the encounter I had expected or one I had not expected; it had given me an exceptional opportunity to pack a whole woman with all her details into that wonderful moment. Sometimes it seemed to me that this inability was utter deprivation, so I would try to heighten other senses to overcome it. I would use my fingers alone, with the concentration of a mathematician, to recognise a body that did not invade my being with its scent. Less than a week after losing my sense of smell, I could distinguish scents by the colours and shapes I attributed to them. Tobacco had a brown, cylindrical scent and fish a rectangular yellow one, tea was a crimson-coloured square and coffee a blue semicircle.

Fatima dipped her fingers into a bowl of lemon water and said, 'Why don't we sleep together this afternoon and see what happens after?'

I was stunned into silence.

'Listen,' she added. 'I don't want us to tie ourselves down in a complicated affair. It'll be sex only. We can have fun and then go our separate ways. Do you understand?'

'Yes, I understand, but why me in particular?'

19

'Because you won't be able to smell the fish factory I've turned into after this meal!'

But I did not have sex with Fatima. I had drinks at her place and we talked a lot. We read dozens of pages of haiku and a whole book about Scorpios. I then left the sad building where she lived, feeling good about the world.

Fatima settled into many aspects of my life, as if she had entered it years earlier. She knew how to chat with me without expecting anything in return. She talked about the theatre, the press, and the man she was still waiting for on some quayside. She came to the house with invitations for concerts and exhibitions and tried to convince Bahia to join her. Whenever she was persuaded, they went off together and I would stay at home on the large black sofa, planning indifferently for a future that did not interest me.

I would be unable to define the kind of relationship I had with Fatima. I only knew that it was essential. I knew this with a certain cold feeling, taking into account that she too had good reasons to consider me highly essential. I trusted her reasons, even if I could not pretend that the world would be out of kilter were she not around. I would simply feel that the machine was not running right. It would be like reading a message on the dashboard of a car telling me that my internal guidance system was amiss.

Bahia and I never discussed Fatima, although she did sometimes glean information about her by asking seemingly innocent questions. Only once did Bahia follow a dead-end. It happened when Fatima went to the US and asked Bahia to send her the serialised *Letters to My Beloved* as they became available. Bahia did not say anything that betrayed her feelings, but I felt her frustration when I heard her, one morning while I was in the bathroom, send the requested fax, loudly enunciating the US hotel phone number to draw my attention.

This was followed by total silence until I heard her read aloud: '*I nearly drew your real face yesterday evening. Ever since I began drawing your face to reflect my feelings, I was never this moved. It was something like the pulse of an adolescent who sees his beloved suddenly appear on the balcony he has been watching. The situation lasted only a few seconds and I could not recapture it. I am unable, as you well know, to recall anything. All that remains in memory is the feeling of loss, but the content is swallowed by darkness. Nevertheless, the partial appearance of your face had an amazing effect on my whole being, and I almost remembered our first kiss and the sentence that preceded me to your lips. I do not know any more if I talked about love, or the heat or the dream. I do not know any more whether a single letter remained attached to my tongue. I remember it mixed with a full lip; whose lip was it? Mixed with burning breaths; who was kissing whom? Was it in a strange room? Yes, yes. It was in a hotel room you could not leave, while I was in the lobby waiting for you. I still am. But you had locked the door, placed a second pillow over your head, and switched off everything, including the fiery kiss that was followed by total darkness. I would like to tell you something, but I wish I knew what. Come out from behind this mute curtain, I am on the balcony where I have always been. If you were to pass by the garden now, I would simply stretch out my arm, which would lengthen and lift you higher and higher, until you rested, once more, between your lips and the sentence that precedes me.*'

Silence returned to the room. I poked my head outside the bathroom and looked at Bahia apprehensively. She was sitting down, holding the paper in both hands and smiling, the smile of someone who understands and does not understand at the same time. When she turned her head and saw me staring at her, she quickly folded the paper and said in an irritated tone, 'What wonderful bullshit!'

3

IBRAHIM AL-KHAYATI BECAME THE cornerstone of my relationship with the world for different reasons. When I was a member of the party organisation, he was both close to us and distant at the same time. He financed our cultural magazine and helped run it without seeking some of the minor glories that went with the territory. He was not affected by the arrests of the 1970s, but remained our strongest supporter. Generally, there was nothing in the practical part of my life that did not include Ibrahim. I could almost say that I never took a decision that needed insight without Ibrahim being a key factor.

It was natural, therefore, that he was the third person to read the letter on Yacine's death, and then, as a lawyer, that he represent Bahia and me in the subsequent investigation into Al-Qaeda's activities in Morocco. Since the letter had been delivered locally, it suggested that the group that had received the news was a local organisation. It also implied that Yacine had been in touch with this organisation before he left, and might even have been sent by that same organisation to Afghanistan. This clearly meant that other members of a sleeper cell were awaiting orders to depart or participate in attacks on home soil.

When a Fes group was arrested following the assassination of a French tourist, it was believed that someone from that group had brought the letter to my house. From the moment Ibrahim started providing me with information about Yacine's direct links with flesh-and-blood terrorists – fellow citizens, not phantoms from Kandahar – I fell victim to destructive anxiety. I could not bear the idea that Yacine had joined Al-Qaeda while he was living with us, mad about electronic games, annoyed at our political discussions, always ready to poke fun at us and everything else. The possibility of that deception made me doubt everything. Ibrahim tried to make me stop believing that Yacine had deceived me, insisting that every one of us proceeds towards our fate unable to distinguish the things we use to deceive ourselves from those others use to deceive us.

In the early years of our acquaintance, Ibrahim had been the thread that bound our group. He had served as a romantic go-between, capable of solving the most complex love-related problems, particularly since the great esteem he enjoyed among women made them confide their secrets and stories in him. He was not known to have had a special relationship with a woman, and it was rumoured that he was gay. This did not upset him, and he did not deny it. He would bring his friend Abdelhadi, an 'aytah artist who sang at the Marsawi nightclub in Casablanca, to our soirées; both were welcomed with smiles that soon faded into a tolerant complicity that Ibrahim's sparkling yet modest personality inspired. After a brilliant education in Rabat and Paris, Ibrahim had been able to set up a large law firm dealing in financial and corporate cases. He amassed a huge fortune that had allowed him to support a large number of painters, sculptors and actors.

Ibrahim chose to live with his mother, an extremely bright, traditional woman with multiple talents, and he was affluent enough to indulge his natural inclination to live in a house with open, complex spaces. We were very close. He was an avid reader, and there was not a book I read that he had not recommended.

Ibrahim would experience three serious traumas over as many years. The first was the suicide of Abdelhadi. He felt that the world had collapsed under his feet, and that he would keep endlessly plunging until he lost contact with everything around him. He felt he would continue falling, not quite touching something akin to the ground, until the void swallowed him anew. The reason for that feeling, as he explained to me later – after Yacine's death – was not the death in itself, but his having failed to see it coming. He had not even once registered the suffering of someone close to him.

Ibrahim and Abdelhadi had created a kind of social accommodation that made it possible for them to coexist without serious compromises and without gratuitous stubbornness. Ibrahim arranged an independent life for his friend; he married him to a relative of his, and celebrated the birth of his twins, Essam and Mahdi, with boundless joy. Their relationship remained intimate and warm despite the sadness that resulted from the sensible arrangement of a life that defied organisation. Late at night, Ibrahim would swing by the club where Abdelhadi performed. He would sit in a discreet corner, soaring up to the heavens with his friend's beautiful voice, amazed by the depth of the sadness revealed by a man who normally did not stop laughing and joking. As soon as he opened his mouth to sing, it was as if a dark breath filled with past tragedies rose within him and he would withdraw into the far regions of his inner self. At the end of his performance, Abdelhadi would stride across the hall filled with his fans, laughing resonantly, and walk towards Ibrahim's table to spend the interval with him. They would make small talk, commenting briefly and elegantly on clothes, skincare products and seasonal dishes. They would talk about the twins and their mother Haniya, always silent and busy with the housework with a devotion that bordered on the religious. They exchanged tender words about absence and missing each other, and fixed or failed to agree on a date for an upcoming soirée. The following day Abdelhadi would stop by Ibrahim's house and sit with his mother by the back door of the kitchen that overlooked the garden and tell her that artichokes were available at the central market. If Ibrahim's name should come up, his face would light up, as if his blood were talking, not his tongue.

How could such apparent contentedness explode one day, to leave a hanged man dangling, and Abdelhadi of all people?

I, in turn, tried to convince Ibrahim that Abdelhadi would have done what he had done in any case, regardless of the simple or complicated nature of their relationship. He seemed to accept this, but his look was one of dark despair.

The second trauma occurred when Ibrahim was the victim of a vicious attack that almost cost him his life. He had left the commercial court building in Casablanca when two men stopped him. One said that he wanted to talk to him about an important and urgent matter, while the other wrapped his arm around his waist and pulled him forcefully towards him, saying, 'An important *personal* matter.' He was not fearful or concerned until he felt something sharp against his side. Things happened very quickly, but as Ibrahim attempted to shake free of the man, something cold pierced his stomach. Before he hit the asphalt like a heavy weight, something solid smashed into his face and another object caught his chest and head. As he was being kicked and stamped upon, he felt he was being shoved towards a thick fog which turned into darkness, stars and vivid colours. He heard someone ask for a stick, and the stick touched him or pierced him, he could not tell which. Soon he heard roaring laughter and had a distant impression that his whole body was coated in a stickiness that bit by bit turned into a confused consciousness within an extremely white and rainless cloud.

Ibrahim spent five weeks in hospital. All of us – his mother, Haniya and the twins, Ahmad Majd, Fatima, and myself – visited him every day, monitoring his condition that was critical until he had been through six operations. While he was in a coma, a leading newspaper published his photo under the headline: *Lawyer Ibrahim al-Khayati Target of Assassination Attempt by Anti-Homosexual Group.* When Ibrahim recovered, the police questioned him at length about his sexual orientation. He strenuously confirmed that he was straight, as he had done when interviewed after Abdelhadi's suicide.

Ibrahim's mother, who constantly repeated that she knew him best because she had given birth to him, had a stroke of genius. She sat on his hospital bed one evening and spent a long time staring into her wounded son's eyes. She began laying out her plan for Ibrahim in veiled words and tear-filled sentences. Ibrahim responded with an appeasing gesture and a few words. 'OK, I agree. Don't torture yourself. I completely understand. I agree.'

'What are you agreeing to, my son? I haven't said everything yet.' Finally she spat it out. 'I want you to marry Haniya, so that Essam and Mahdi can be looked after by you. That'll put a stop to all the gossip and give me peace of mind before I die.'

Ibrahim knew full well what awaited him. He signalled his acceptance with a wave of the hand and gave his mother permission to act as she saw fit. He felt that the arrangement fitted in totally with everything else. There was no better way to avenge

Abdelhadi's suicide, and there was nothing in his life that did not reveal to him, on a daily basis, that step by step he was drawing nearer to this destiny, submitting to the inevitable.

When, months later, the door closed behind Ibrahim and Haniya for the first time, he was nervous and embarrassed. He almost choked on his feelings, until he turned towards her. She was sitting on the edge of the bed, her face angled slightly towards the wall. His heartbeat quickened because in her isolation, she looked like Abdelhadi in the melancholy of his song.

Casablanca was still joking about their marriage when Ibrahim received another terrible shock, the death of his mother, which hurt him like a painful amputation. The morning she died, he was awakened by the cries of Haniya, Essam and Mahdi shouting, 'May God have mercy on the Hajja!'

'What are you doing in the garden? Why don't you keep still so I can understand?' he asked.

Haniya then stood before him and told him his mother had been playing with Essam and Mahdi in the garden and collapsed. She now lay dead, her head in the water of the swimming pool and her body stretched on the lawn. 'Listen, invoke God's name. Your mother has passed away.'

Ibrahim said impatiently, 'No one dies like that. Mother's playing, she's just playing!'

When he raised her head from the blue of the swimming pool, she seemed to smile. He got ready for her to jump to her feet cackling with laughter, as she would do to amuse the twins, unconcerned that she was stiff and cold. At that point, Haniya and the maids, wailing loudly, came and picked her up. They carried her to her room and laid her carefully out on the bed, as though they had long been trained for this.

Ibrahim buried his face in his hands and relived, as if standing under a gentle shower of rain, the details of the life they had been through together: her milk, her fears for him, her tears, her devastation at the loss of his father, her silence, her games, her happiness, her misery, her presence on the edge of his bed until he went to sleep, her stories, her dreams, and her skills at fighting poverty and time. He remained in that position until Haniya reminded him angrily that death was a believer's duty and if life were meant to last, it would have lasted for Prophet Mohammed. Ibrahim replied, distressed, 'But Prophet Mohammed is not my mother!'

After the funeral rites were over, Ibrahim entered a black box where he lost his ability to reconcile with life. He turned inward and dwelled on his conviction of the futility of a life of delusions. This was before he submitted to the resignation that dominated the scene and impacted our whole generation, a mixture of dervish tendencies, secular Sufism and new-age spirituality. I was at his side during that difficult period and took advantage of his spiritual predisposition to reveal that I was meeting Yacine as a child who talked to me about everything, as if he had not crossed to the other side. Ibrahim accepted and approved my experience, confirming that souls meet in total freedom independent of our ephemeral bodies. Whenever the police called us to resume the investigation with new information related to terrorist organisations, Ibrahim, in all seriousness, begged me not to tell Yacine, as there was no need to bother souls with what we did or did not do.

4

I MET LAYLA FOR THE first time one quiet morning in the
lobby of the Hilton. She was absorbed in a book as people
came in and out of the hotel with their luggage and I approached
to make sure it was her. Sensing my presence, she lifted her head
but did not give me a chance to talk or introduce myself and
burst out saying, 'You must be the journalist who's covering
Saramago. It's great, really great, that you've come early. It's a
good omen to meet a journalist who arrives early. An interview? A newspaper interview with Saramago? Forget it! He's
the type who believes that what he writes is all he needs to say.
There's no point insisting. Hold on, use a hunting technique.
Track the prey then pounce. Or maybe he'll decide on his own
to grant you an interview. Try and talk to him; cajole him or
trick him. You must have read his books – or at least I hope
you've read them. I don't think it's possible to talk to a person
like him about anything else. He doesn't talk much about the
weather! I'm reading *The Gospel According to Jesus Christ* for the
thousandth time. Believe me, out of all the books I've read,
there isn't one I enjoyed more. You know what? The subject of
the book doesn't matter at all. How Jesus was born, how he
grew up and faced life's questions, how he met God and how

he met death. The story isn't like in the Gospels, but as Jesus might have lived it. What are the Gospels anyway? Are they the book, or Jesus as he lived or might have lived? None of this matters at all. What matters is the prose, the way words and sentences become more important than the narrative, a purity that gives you the sense of beauty in the abstract, without subject matter, or it's its own subject matter. Do you understand that?'

I had been straining to interrupt her dense stream of words and finally managed to get a word in. 'Yes, yes, I understand completely. I've also read *Blindness* for personal reasons to do with my father, but it depressed me so much that I stopped reading for a few months.'

She was nervously gathering her belongings when she said, 'Have you spotted him? He's just stepped out of the elevator. There he is. Look at his movements. I swear, the slowness has nothing to do with age or anything else – quick, let's head over – it's a deliberation of the mind – this way's better, come on – a pause over every detail. One must have extraordinary ability to do that. To think that I spend most of my time fighting details. What idiocy!

'Mr Saramago, please, don't make us run after you. This is the journalist I told you about. I don't know his name yet. Let's make his acquaintance together.'

I heard myself pronounce my name, Youssef al-Firsiwi. I noticed that it had a strange impact on the woman whom I had not taken my eyes off from the moment she started talking.

On our way to Fes, I said to Saramago, 'When all is said and done, *The Gospel According to Jesus Christ* and the revealed Gospels are two sides of the same coin. Imagination is needed in both narratives, and fiction is needed in both cases.'

He smiled and shook his head in a way that did not reveal whether he agreed or disagreed. At that point Layla said, 'The novel is open to multiple interpretations, including the ones present in the revelation. As for the revelation, it accepts only its own narrative.'

Saramago laughed but did not comment. We all looked in the direction of the green fields that had been startled by the November rain. We agreed, with varying degrees of sincerity, that it was a beautiful morning. Layla then announced that she would eat the pastries she had brought with her, and asked whether we would like some. Neither Saramago nor I wanted one. Nor did he want to discuss literature. He asked me about the Sahara and the negotiations with the separatists, and whether Morocco was moving towards real democracy or whether there were those who longed for rule with an iron fist. He asked about the strength of the religious movement, what interest groups there were and where the opposite interests lay.

I offered lukewarm responses because I was annoyed with the inquisition and did not have answers.

'Your conversation is ruining my mood,' said Layla. 'I don't understand how the same person could write with such sensitivity about Jesus's relationship with his mother, with Mary Magdalene, and with Satan, and yet lose valuable time talking about the Sahrawi people's right to self-determination. Do you know what people do in the desert, Mr Saramago? They roam the wilderness, eat, perform their ablutions and compose poetry in the style of pre-Islamic times. They fatten up their women, and screw while talking aloud lest the children hear them. Do you think they would dance for joy if they heard you cared about their self-determination?'

We laughed, and then Layla said, 'What truly amazes me is the magical power that you and those like you have to express what we all know in detail but are unable to express, simply because we lack the magical means you have. I feel infuriated sometimes because you're saying exactly what I've felt for ages, but could not describe with precision until I read it. I don't know what you think, but, personally, I consider precision to be the ideal form of beauty.'

Her voice from the back seat seemed to strike my shoulders and neck, jolting me out of my recent lifelessness. I felt the words were addressed to me in a kind of unintended consolation. Precision in science, nature and art – without the distortion of emotion – really did embody the concept of beauty.

Consider the compatible and incompatible elements needed to add flavour to a piece of raw fish. We do not want one flavour to overpower the others, or any flavour to be hidden, delayed or premature. We want the saltiness to peak at a specific moment, before the spices but after lemon by a fraction of a second. Then comes the waning of the substance and the lingering aftertaste of all these elements, along with an additional element, the time the aftertaste takes to permeate the farthest reaches of our body. The aftertaste fades, leaving behind another trace of a trace, then another trace of the trace of a trace, and so on. This precision in making and then unmaking something, in its emergence and evanescence, can give birth to the pleasure we seek to eternalise in total despair, attempting to move it from the realm of the senses to the realm of perception, from incoherence to coherence. All the while we are aware of the tremendous tragedy latent in beauty, because outside this mental precision, beauty can only be fleeting.

Having pinpointed this matter under Layla's inspiration, I expected to feel deliriously happy, but instead was assailed by a depression similar to the one I had experienced in previous panic attacks. I fought it off, while the conversation in the back seat continued and I could hear Layla's voice and Saramago's mumblings on and off.

'I confess,' said Layla, 'that at first I found your novel a variation on an old theme, then your writing made me feel that devils are the mirrors of prophets, and that good, in order to be good, must subsume the burning heat of evil. It doesn't matter what the subject is, because we're not looking to be persuaded while reading the novel. You made the Christ in your book throw off the mantle of revelation, only for him to don it again as a shepherd, a fisherman, a lover and a prophet. He suffered, desired, feared and performed miracles, then proceeded towards his crucifixion where he found no one in the end but Satan himself to collect the drops of his blood in the clay bowl that cleaved from the ground at the moment Christ cleaved from nothingness. That's the life that became a Gospel, isn't it?'

'Hmm-m-m,' mumbled Saramago.

'What I mean is there's a constant ambivalence in the subject of revelation. Who reveals to whom!'

'Hmm-m-m.'

'Do you mean yes or no?'

'Hmm-m-m.'

'It's yes and no then! No problem. Believe me, writing matters more than all the Gospels. It's not a question of belief. I'm a believer myself. I tried very hard for years to be an atheist, but I failed.'

Saramago chuckled.

'I'm not bothered by your laughter. I believe in God and He loves me. I'm sure of it!'

A whispered conversation followed that I could not make out. I dozed off and the conversation passed me by. I then felt that my whole body was hurting and that the blue sky, the ripening earth and the rain-washed light were nothing but tricks to hide my unhappiness.

When we reached the hotel I could not get out of the car, and no one asked me why. My limbs were numb and I regretted having come along. I was busy wondering whether we did not all need to rewrite our life stories and free them from the violence of the single reading. In my case, I thought what my life story would have been if I had not lost Yacine, and how Yacine would have remained alive if I had not been what I was. I woke up and saw Layla's face. She had opened the car door and was leaning towards me, anxious and concerned.

'Are you all right? Do you want us to take you to a doctor? Can you walk? My God, what happened?'

I had the impression she was far away, although I felt her breath on my face. Her features changed continuously, from those of a woman I knew to those of an unknown woman, and then to a woman I remembered.

'It's terrible that we left the car without noticing you weren't feeling well!' she said.

'No, no. I'm fine. Sometimes I fade like this. I'm sorry.'

'But we went up to our rooms, and this dolt of a driver went to have a coffee and a cigarette by the pool. Nobody noticed that you were still in the car. Scary!'

'No need to exaggerate. Has it been long?'

'Almost an hour. You must hate me!'

'I'm very sorry, but I'm unable to hate you.'

As we entered the hotel lobby, I felt that I had recovered and my spirits were high. I was able to forget why I was there, and look forward to other things that were impossible to predict.

I took a long bath and then went down to the restaurant to find Layla waiting for me at a table for two. Saramago did not wish to leave his room. This must have pleased me, or my facial expression must have implied it, but Layla was sad. She might even have been crying before I arrived, but I did not know why. She soon regained her vitality and burst out talking. Her joyful outpouring of words and energetic rush of ideas and images projected happiness, as if she were dancing with her sentences.

I said to her, 'He doesn't know what he's missing by retreating into a tête-à-tête with his old man's memory!'

She laughed, but her laughter was like a cold blast blowing across our table. I contemplated her again in confusion and saw a frisson pass over her face. I looked down, and before I lifted my gaze, she said that a few years before, she and a friend had lived in the same apartment building as me in the Ibn Sina quarter. She said, 'I used to see you every day and it made me furious that you never showed even the slightest interest in my humble self!'

This was how dinner led to a strange intersection of two dormant memories.

I did not remember having met a woman who looked like her in the building where I had lived. If I had seen her, it probably would have been on the stairs or in the courtyard. Then again, I might have met her in another life and lost her the way I had lost many other people. I might have loved her for a short or a long time but could no longer remember. I might have waited a whole lifetime for her, but she never came or came and did not find me.

Now here she was before me in another life, and I had nothing to entertain her with but fanciful conversation about a desperate effort to build a vast edifice, a castle with a thousand doors and endless halls, rooms within rooms, a palace made of words and visions inhabited by our forgotten desires, our fears, our apprehension at returning to our small huts, where there was no possibility of contradiction between what was and what could have been.

Layla said, 'I may have been in love with you then. But you didn't know, and I didn't exactly know either. You gave off the impression of being very absent-minded, as if you were going up and down the stairs while walking on another planet.'

'That's if it actually was me going up and down the stairs.'

She responded firmly, 'I'm sure of it. There was a dim light in your eyes, which is still there now. I can't mistake it.'

I remembered that during that particular time I was neither dimmed nor depressed. I was at the peak of my delusions and convinced that things responded to us if we wanted them to. From the lofty heights of the current moment, that time seemed lively, exuberant and eminently manageable. It also seemed to me that a being like Layla would exist in all times, and my relationship with her could take the form of a structure relegated to the past. Why not? Aren't the relationships that we miss also real possibilities for a connection of a different kind? Isn't every relationship one chance among others? It is not self-evident that we pick the best one. I put this to Layla, and she replied, 'It isn't self-evident that we'll pick the worst, either.'

'Ultimately,' I said, 'I'm pretty certain that every one of us, and not only Saramago's Christ, has one divine biography and another one that springs from the tortuous paths of one's life.'

I continued, 'I don't understand why you're so enamoured of a run-of-the-mill novel, beautiful but still run-of-the-mill.' As soon as I finished the sentence, her face darkened. We spent a long time trying to extricate ourselves from this sudden disagreement. Finally, after a few shaky attempts, she returned to her ebullient self.

'Listen,' she said. 'We all know that from the moment Satan refused to bow to Adam, he's been carrying out, as much as he can, his threat to tempt human beings at every pass, pushing them towards sin and perdition. Then suddenly, as we read this book, we discover another side to Satan, as if with time and as a result of all the tragedies he caused or that were committed behind his back, he has changed, adopting a kindly wisdom completely unrelated to the menace that caused him to fall from paradise.'

'We wouldn't have needed the novel to assert that!'

'But the novel did create the exciting idea that prophets, in a kind of alignment of opposites, see themselves mirrored in devils. Because managing the affairs of humanity makes this alliance necessary in order to maintain the world's wavering balance between good and evil.

'According to the story, once Jesus was in his mother's womb, the archangel appeared in the shape of a beggar and told Mary, "The child is manifest in his mother's eyes as soon as she becomes pregnant with him." From that moment on the archangel would accompany Christ until his death. He would accompany him as if he were his avatar, his other voice imbued with certainty and doubt, pleasure and guilt. More than that, Christ would submit to a kind of initiation at the hands of the archangel; years spent herding sheep, before he departed for his destiny.'

'But you said,' I told Layla, 'that what mattered most for you in the novel was the style and not Christ's earthly form, the writing of a new Gospel according to another Jesus.'

'Yes. It is, after all, a personal matter. It seemed to me that this arrangement answered some of my questions, and that basic things in my personal life totally conformed to some of the images I picked up on in the book. This transformed it, in a somewhat exaggerated manner, into my personal gospel. For example, when I became pregnant with my daughter I felt a vast emptiness. This upset me and even tortured me, because I didn't appreciate the feeling of emptiness when I was filled – concretely not figuratively. When I read in the novel that Mary had the same feelings when she was pregnant with Jesus, the author's interpretation made me jump out of my seat. He claimed that the emptiness was in everything around her. I found that amazingly convincing.'

Layla ate a large plate of tomatoes with white cheese, basil and olive oil. She then ate a plate of duck liver *à la française*. She ate with appetite and did not stop talking. I had slices of smoked salmon with onion and lemon and a thick piece of meat, without at any moment being able to tell them apart, because I lacked sufficient concentration. When we were ready to leave the restaurant, Layla's face was flushed. She put her hands to her cheeks and said, 'Look, I'm burning up!'

I said without touching my cheeks, 'Me too!'

As we stepped out of the elevator, I was looking at her as if she were walking on the fourth-floor landing in Ibn Sina. I was still looking at her stimulating body with its slight dip to the right as she walked, when she turned and said, 'It's as if we were crossing the landing on our old floor.'

I was about to tell her I was thinking exactly the same, when she added, 'Maybe you were thinking the same thing.'

At that moment I made my move, having lost all hope of keeping up with her. She was intensely and precisely present, and I was certain that her presence there and then could not be a passing coincidence, but was a powerful sign from destiny.

I took in her allure without being overcome by what lay at its core, or even by the possibilities it promised. I could not at that moment determine where our nervous steps along the dark corridor would lead us, since we could not read our room numbers. Then I found myself carrying her, and yet not carrying her, proceeding along an endless corridor. I felt her arms around my neck like two cold branches. I sat her on the edge of the bed and cupped my hands around her face, watching her with her eyes closed but without receiving any inner message, as if I were touching a being from a distant past.

'Kiss me, I beg you,' she said.

It was not her. She was not the one who had crossed the landing in my apartment building, and not the one I had carried and not carried. She was a girl from years past, whom I once found shivering on a rainy day under a bare willow tree, soaking wet and almost blue from cold and fear. I had not been able to follow what she was saying through her delirium, but I had understood that she had run there from the bus stop in a rainstorm and had no strength left. 'I stopped here under the tree because my whole body was soaked and my limbs were numb.'

'But the tree's totally bare. It's also soaked through and its branches have gone stiff!'

'I didn't notice. Really, I didn't. I was waiting to drop dead and I preferred that that happen to me while standing here, where my friend would find me when she came back!'

I had spent a long time trying to dry her hair, her face and her limbs with little success. Still shivering, she had said, 'I think I'd better take a hot bath and change my clothes.'

I had helped her remove her wet clothes and get into the hot water. I had massaged her body, her whole body, from the top of her head to her pale, slender toes. My fingers had detected vitality creeping back into her from the first touch. I had gone along with her body's repressed frenzy, as if my whole body had become a movement that pierced her pulse. I was doing what I was doing not because I had found her in such a state, but because I would have surely done it, whatever the circumstances, to fulfil a mysterious desire for it to happen with the gentleness with which it did, and as an expression of another possibility for our existence, different from the one derived from planned desires, a possibility accompanied by impossibility and oblivion.

In one of the parts of *Letters to My Beloved*, I wrote:

You were sitting on the edge of the bed when I touched you. I cupped your delicate face in my hands; I cannot remember if it was burning hot or cold and damp. I simply remember that it almost vanished between my big hands and only your lips pulsated in this picture as they said, 'Kiss me, I beg you.' I do not remember kissing you. I do not remember what happened between us that distant afternoon. I do not remember your face. I remember carrying you up the stairs of a building, or in a sparsely furnished apartment between the bed and the bathroom, and noticing that a painting on the wall was not straight, its deep blackness slashed by an impetuous yellow. I said, 'I will come back later to straighten the painting. It looks wrong tilted like that, because the streak of light across it hits too hard.'

You said, without being angry or sharp, 'Je me fiche du tableau.'

When did this happen? I no longer remember a thing. Did it happen in Ibn Sina or in a room in some hotel? I no longer remember if it was when we were going out, before that or years later. What happened when I carried you and set you on the edge of the bed, or when I set you down and carried you, and then carried you and did not carry you? Did I really put you in a warm bath and massage the toes of your small feet? Impossible! I could not have done it! But where have all these images that waver between certainty and illusion, between remembrance and visualisation, come from? How would I settle on one of these and find peace? How would I know that you never existed before this day, or that you were always here, in this dark corner of my memory? And why is it not you who speaks? Why do you not return, knowing, contrary to what I claimed, that I love you more than anything in the world? Did you really know? How would I know?

I write to you full of sadness, because of the letter you sent me last year that I found in my desk and had not read. That was because I could not remember your name which was written on the back of the envelope, or the city from which you sent the letter. I slipped it between the pages of a book and forgot where I had put it. When I came across it months later and recognised its origin, I feared it would contain news that would make me die of sadness because I had not read it. So I threw it in the fireplace without regret, because I forgot what I did with it. Now I do remember it in a way I cannot fathom. I remember the whole story linked somehow with you standing wet under the bare willow tree! If you do read my letter today, I beg you to send me a sign, telling me that you do not bear a grudge against me for burning the letter.

The morning after my dinner with Layla, I woke up exhausted and spent a long time in a haze looking for the day's schedule. When I found it, I pulled myself together and went straight to the shower.

As I was leaving the room I found an envelope slipped under the door. There was a blank sheet of paper in it. My heart beat hard and I understood that the matter was related to something I was expecting, but no longer knew what. When I saw Layla and her guest at the breakfast table, I wished to separate them as soon as possible in order to free her from this legendary companion. Layla was cheery and unruffled while our eminent guest had his face in a bowl of fruit, which he chewed with deliberation while his teary eyes scanned the faces and furniture in the restaurant, as if he were expecting to meet someone.

I exchanged an intense look with Layla and felt an inner lucidity, the lucidity of a person not bothered by anything any more. I told myself as I submitted to the serenity that came from this lucidity that I might have reached the last station of my life, where I would put my suitcase down on the platform like any traveller, not knowing, out of extreme fatigue, whether I had arrived or was about to depart.

At a certain moment in life a person gets detached from his path and becomes a scrap of paper hanging in the air. At that moment he rids himself of the pressures of the path and is able to join any adventure wholeheartedly, because he is not required to justify anything any more or to provide any conclusive evidence of anything. He has freed himself of the future, as if he had died a very long time ago. What he experiences now is nothing except what his immaculate corpse remembers of that shoreless future.

Layla stood up suddenly and startled me. She apologised, saying, 'Were you lost in thought?'

'I was sitting on my suitcase on this vast platform.'

We were on our way to the historical city of Walili when Layla announced that she hated ruins. I told her that ruins had a soul, contrary to buildings. But she stood her ground and claimed that the most beautiful ruins were those we saw around us every day in the form of fallen dreams.

I told her, 'But what you're saying is only a poetic image. Ruins are ossified souls we extract from the bowels of the earth.'

She replied sarcastically, 'And what you're saying now is an exact science and not a poetic image!'

Saramago laughed for the first time since the start of our trip, which annoyed me. We spent the distance between Fes and Zarhun via Zakkutah each absorbed in our own world.

I was thinking about my father, Al-Firsiwi, who, in the waning years of his life, was working as a blind guide among the ruins of Walili. How would I introduce him? How would he receive Layla, and how could I escape his raving if he decided once more to play his favourite game?

Layla was in the back seat, talking about Jesus's adventure in the boat during the storm on the waters. She seemed to be making an affected effort to separate holy genius from literary genius, insisting once more that the miraculous in its literary form had a realistic dimension that gave it an astonishing beauty which was absent from the religious version. It was probably due to the fact that religious faith was the basis for experiencing the miracle, an aspect that was not derived from the text. Layla, despite her insistence, did not succeed in pulling the writer out of his silence, which gave me the impression that she was talking to herself and that the writer had not come with us in the first place, but only his novel, for us to use as a pretext to weave a text according to our own narrative.

I was thinking about the ruins that my father roamed every day, ruins that had nothing to do with the Romans but concerned him personally. I thought about how he endured the humiliation of this end. He would show off his fluent German, deliberately pronouncing every letter separately and stressing their tonal variations. He would introduce biting comments about the city that had led him to these ruins, in cruel revenge for his glory days. He would be in his rickety boat, facing storms he could not see that pulled him into a crushing tornado which he rowed towards with his voice.

As we approached the city, Layla was narrating the scene of the boat caught in the divine presence, while Jesus rowed, as if this action still had meaning compared with the gravity of the encounter. Man remains bound to his body even when that body becomes meaningless, having just met God at the height of his loss and despair.

This preoccupation with the novel had driven me to despair. I suddenly turned to the back seat and said, 'Mr Saramago, would you like to know my humble opinion of your novel?'

He replied immediately, 'No, no, no. Not at all. Don't bother yourself. I absolutely don't want to know your opinion.'

At that point I pulled myself together, took my mobile out of my jacket pocket and called Fatima. I told her that I was in my old ruins, in the house of Juba and Bacchus and others, amid the earthy scent that no longer welcomed me, part of the cloudy landscape of all those forgotten columns, arches, temples, olive presses and houses.

She responded every now and then with 'Oh' and whenever she was about to start talking, I would interrupt her with something similar to my father's delirium. 'I will once again enter the palace of ruins,' I told her. 'Everyone in this world imagines he can rescue something under the ruins.'

'I imagine that too. Do you want me to join you there?' she asked.

'No, no, I'll be back this evening. If you want, we'll start a new dig together!'

'I'll prepare the site,' she replied.

When I ended the call a heavy silence reigned in the car. The avenue of olive trees that led to Wadi Khumman welcomed us as it had invaders and transients, without emotion or any particular disposition.

At the outhouse to the historical site, my father was saying goodbye to a mass of German tourists amidst roars of laughter and warm handshakes. As soon as we stepped out of the car, speaking in our soft voices, he came over, perceiving that we were a new group. When he got close to us he recited his

44

favourite line from the Qur'an: 'Do not think me senile, I do indeed scent the presence of Youssef.'

Fighting back my emotions, I said, 'I'm Youssef, this is Layla, and this is José Saramago. You are still alive and kicking I see.'

'Of course, of course! Who can escape life? You cannot go backwards and you cannot flee forwards. Life – as you know, my son – is a real dilemma. Is that not so, Mr . . . ? Who did you say he was, Youssef?'

'Saramago.'

Listening to Layla's translation and showing true engagement for the first time, Saramago said, 'Yes, yes, it's a real dilemma!'

The Cornerstone of the Sacred Mausoleum

I

O N A COLD, DRY October morning in the early 1970s, two months after returning from Germany, Mohammed al-Firsiwi visited the holy shrine of Moulay Idriss I. He was accompanied by three *faqihs* from the village of Bu Mandara, but Al-Firsiwi himself supervised the recitation of the Qur'anic verses for the repose of the moulay's soul and sought his bless- ings before he left with his small retinue. Al-Firsiwi then went straight to the old quarter's central market, where an auction was being held for the rental contract on the Hall of Oil, which everybody was convinced would go, as it did every year, to someone connected to the Idriss dynasty.

By noon, however, to the shock of those present and absent, it had gone to Al-Firsiwi, son of Bu Mandara and scion of the rural folk, whose individual and collective submission to the contempt of the Idriss dynasty had lasted since their arrival in the region. This historic event was merely a prelude: hardly a week after that earth-shattering deal, Al-Firsiwi bought the city's only petrol station (manually pumped), the Al-Ghali mansion, Qatirah's house, and seven rundown houses in the Hufra, Tazka and Khaybar quarters. He was paving the way for his rural kin to enter the city as conquerors.

Barely a year had passed before the Idrissis and those referred to as the wealthy burghers of Fes – traders in cloth, foodstuffs and grain – had become mere servants in the nouveau-riche network led by Mohammed al-Firsiwi. According to his admirers, he spoke seven languages. He owned an impressive Mercedes, and argued sharply with his German wife when they drove through the city. The young boys who watched this amazing sight wondered whether the Christian woman, in spite of her blue eyes, went to the toilet and performed her bodily functions like other human beings.

According to the eyewitnesses who ventured as far as the Apollo cinema in the city of Meknes, whenever Al-Firsiwi and his wife sat in a café and ordered tea, a large number of women wrapped in their woollen gowns, indolent men and nervous children would crowd the pavement opposite. They would push and shove, making a terrible noise just to watch the bumpkin who combed his hair with brilliantine and his wife with painted lips and bare legs.

Over time public curiosity waned, replaced by stories about the dazzling rise of this strongly built man with the piercing look who did not leave his enemies even a tiny margin for manoeuvre. After only three years, Al-Firsiwi was able to add to his regional empire the olive groves that extended from the foot of the Bani Ammar hills to the edge of the Bu Riyah plain. Only the waqf lands escaped his control, though he rented many acres, acquiring them annually through auctions in which no one dared compete with him. Nearly everyone with a cow, a sheep or a goat in Bu Mandara and every other village in the area went into partnership with him. He intuited the future importance of carob – which at that time had no value on the market – and bought up the lands where it grew, which spread over Bab al-Rumela and the whole of the

Zarhoun Mountain. He and a partner set up a carob processing plant in Fes and he was given the nickname of 'Carob Hajj'.

The country folk who had been an oppressed minority became masters of the region. Some of their notables even married noble Idrissi women, and began to receive visitors and the official delegation for the festivities of Moulay Idriss I. They cornered the market in animals for sacrifice, candles and sweets. Some of those who extended their building activities also expanded their control to supervise the chanting and spinning sessions of the dervishes, despite all the worries they would endure as a result. They would implore their Creator to put a quick end to the howling of those soft-headed creatures who repeated poems and songs whose only intelligible words were 'Praise to the Prophet'.

Then it occurred to Al-Firsiwi to embark on a new adventure: he founded the Zaytoun Hotel on the plateau overlooking the ruins of Walili. He spent almost five years building this spectacular landmark; he fought fierce battles for the land, then for water and electricity, and finally to pave the road that led to the plateau, until the hotel became like a balcony overlooking the monumental ruins of Walili, where every day the sun set behind the columns of the temple and the triumphal arch of Caracalla.

At this point of his achievements, his wife Diotima sat on the throne of the reception desk located in a legendary hall, decorated with mosaics in Roman style portraying Al-Firsiwi's grandfather among the nymphs of Al-Ain al-Tahiya; Ben Abd al-Karim surrendering to the French officers; and Al-Firsiwi himself struggling with scaly forest snakes. The corners of the mosaic were decorated with carvings that imitated in a naïve fashion Juba II, Bacchus and others.

Al-Firsiwi had to fight with the authorities for five more years to obtain a licence to sell alcohol despite the hotel's proximity to the tomb of the founder of the Moroccan state. He got what he wanted in exchange for sweeteners and bribes that surpassed the cost of the hotel itself.

Once the consumption of alcohol was no longer confined to foreign guests, but spread to the local people, their tongues started to tell endless stories, the likes of which this meek country had never heard before. Thus began the ill-fated phase of Al-Firsiwi's life. Public opinion never doubted that the main reason for this rapid and total decline was the Cantina bar and the depravity and debauchery that came with it, all at the feet of the holy leader. The folk imagination invented stories about foreign and Muslim drunkards who ended their soirées in the Roman baths where they swapped female partners and practised sodomy in the moonlight. There was talk about the smuggling of various kinds of drink from the Cantina to surrounding villages. And people soon devised a miracle fit for the situation. They made Moulay Rashid, Idriss's faithful servant, go out at night and obstruct the path of the drunks as they crossed the cemetery on their way from the hotel bar to the town. He whipped them severely with jagged branches from wild olive trees, leaving permanent marks on their backs, their sides and their legs.

Al-Firsiwi's bad luck began with years of drought, which stopped the olive trees from bearing fruit for successive seasons. Then the price of carob collapsed, making the cost of gathering it more than the proceeds of selling it. And finally came the years of pox.

To this day no one knows how it happened. One morning the customers of an ancient bath-house in the old quarter saw a man squatting near the hot water cistern, howling and writhing hysterically from the pain of the inflamed pustules covering his body. Someone volunteered to pour hot water over him.

The man went on his way, and a day later small pustules filled with a colourless liquid began to appear on the bodies of men, women and children from different quarters. As soon as the pustules appeared on the skin, more followed. Hardly a week had passed before the markets, schools and mosques of the city and surrounding villages were filled with alarming groups of distraught people. Not talking to one another and not knowing where they were going, they walked with their hands inside their clothing, scratching their skin, which was covered with a hard inflamed crust, their mouths open wide in pain and pleasure.

Men, women and children would go on to the streets and the alleys, uncover their backs and scratch them against the walls of the city until they bled; or they would use implements such as vegetable peelers, washing-up scourers, wool carders or door scrubbers, and sit, one behind the other, and begin a dismal collective scratch that brought tears to their eyes.

Almost every day, hordes of the poxed left their neighbourhoods and crossed the inner market, not distracted by anything, heading straight towards Khaybar Plaza, where authorities had installed large pumps to spray their bodies as they stood behind plastic shower curtains. They returned reeking of sulphur and went to sleep until the relentless inflammation of the pustules stabbed them with pain yet again.

The city was officially quarantined. Foreign tourists stopped coming to stay at the Zaytoun Hotel, which turned the Cantina into a cheap bar frequented every night by the legions of the poxed, who drank and chatted till the break of dawn. They fell asleep to the collective moans of pleasure and pain from the nonstop scratching, which opened the door to exquisite intoxication, until, from the depths of this rapture, rose the agony caused by nails digging into pustular skin.

During this period the inhabitants of the nearby village of Fertassa took advantage of the misfortune that had befallen Al-Firsiwi – especially after his wife Diotima's suicide and the bankruptcy of a number of his projects – and damaged some of the canals that carried water from the spring to the Zaytoun Hotel. A legal battle ensued and Al-Firsiwi was forced to sell much of his property to pay off those willing to side with him in the dispute.

Then suddenly and much to everyone's surprise, Al-Firsiwi married one of the hotel maids. She had rough brothers who terrorised the inhabitants of Fertassa. Things calmed down and people understood that Al-Firsiwi had put the hotel in his new wife's name. Though this news spread, he did not comment, content with beaming sarcastic smiles at the drunks chatting about him.

Then Al-Firsiwi sold the petrol station and announced the bankruptcy of the modern mills of al-Mishkah. One Friday morning in May 1982, the authorities closed the Zaytoun Hotel, while a mass demonstration of thousands of the poxed shouted anti-government slogans, criticising the authorities for doing nothing to alleviate their suffering except spraying them with burning yellow liquid. The demonstration turned violent, with the trashing of shops and public buildings, before heading for the tomb complex where a protest sit-in was declared.

People wondered whether all this was to protest against the closing of the Cantina, that infested place, by the authorities. The answer they received from the victims was that they objected to the closing down of the city, not the Cantina.

On 9 May 1982, the statue of Bacchus was stolen from the entrance to Walili, where it had stood for decades. The figure was small with a lightly tanned complexion, an adolescent posed standing with his weight on his right leg and his left leg stretched slightly behind, and his left arm, broken at the wrist, slightly away from his body. The thieves had had to pull the statue off its plinth, leaving some of the toes of the right foot behind, which was all that remained of the beautiful sculpture.

Contrary to all expectations, the investigation into the crime led to the arrest of the director of the site, then two tourist guides, and finally Mohammed al-Firsiwi, who everyone had seen constantly excavating the site for something, though no one knew what.

2

I AM YOUSSEF AL-FIRSIWI AND that is my father. My mother
was a refined German woman who found no better end to
her stormy life than suicide. It happened on a day spent hunting quail and rabbit in the woods with my father. Close to
sundown, she packed away the game, the gear, the clothes, the
picnic basket and the cans of drink with the careful attention
that drove my father crazy. She then sat in the front seat, put on
her safety belt and turned on her tape recorder to listen to
Beethoven.

On the way back she asked my father to go via the mountain
road, the first section of which overlooks the city while the rest
overlooks the ruins. She said meekly that she wanted to watch
the sunset. Contrary to habit, Al-Firsiwi complied without arguing or bickering. More than once after the incident, he would say
that only divine will could have so blinded him that he failed to
notice that this was the first time in her life she had made such a
request. He had never stood with her on a peak or in a valley to
watch God's sun rise, set or do anything else, he would say.

My mother asked Al-Firsiwi to stop the car at the last bend
before the descent to Walili. They both got out, and she said,
'The sun's going.'

'One day it will go and never come back, or it will rise in the west and never set,' Al-Firsiwi said.

'Why are you talking nonsense?' my mother asked as she walked to the back of the car.

'Because that will be the day the world ends! When we won't need money, energy or weapons. All of us, regardless of who we are, will need only one thing.'

My mother was opening the boot of the car, so he repeated his last sentence without looking at her. 'We will need only one thing!'

'Which would be what?'

'Shade, my dear. Shade!' said my father.

There was total silence, and Al-Firsiwi thought he had dumbfounded my mother with his unbeatable peasant genius. At that moment he relived his relationship with Diotima, from their first encounter in a Düsseldorf post office, in its smallest details. He thought of confessing his love for her, there and then, because, as he later admitted, 'I had never said those words to her. It's not our habit, us peasants, to pay attention to such nonsense.'

When my father turned around to proclaim this welling up of feeling, Diotima was not where he expected. He heard the gunshot as if it came from underneath the car. In a panic, he rushed towards the sound and found my almost headless mother stretched out opposite the tomb of Moulay Idriss I, not far from the Roman ruins where a desolate sun had set moments before. Despite all I observed of my father's breakdown, despair, suffering and anger, to this day I do not know why I imagine with great conviction and in anguish that he had killed her. To this day I cannot recall that event without being inclined to maintain that Al-Firsiwi had planned his crime with a devilish attention to detail that made it possible for him to escape human justice. As for divine punishment, according to my maternal uncle, he incurred it in this life. His huge material losses kept accumulating, and he descended into bankruptcy and vindictiveness before drowning in total obscurity.

I was greatly distressed by the incident that took my mother's life, and I haven't gotten over it to this day. I lived for over a year with a maternal uncle who worked at the German embassy in Rabat, and I shared my doubts with him. I told him that Al-Firsiwi hated my mother, and might even have killed her. He, in turn, informed the German authorities of all the details I gave him, and a long investigation ensued. It did not lead to anything, but it made my father believe that I had, without any doubt, inherited the seed of evil from the Germanic blood that infected my pure Moroccan blood. I ended up living in a care home in Frankfurt, where I spent my drab adolescent years convinced that I would never be able to restore my relationship with my father and his country.

But being categorical about anything related to human nature is always reckless. As the years sped by, the sharp impetuosity that made me believe that my mother's blood – contrary to Al-Firsiwi's claim – was a gift from heaven melted away. Deep inside I had been ashamed of my peasant blood, which would undoubtedly corrupt the accumulated genetic capital that the German nation had spent long centuries investing in before I received my miraculous share.

It was my discovery of the Rif, its language, its places, its history and its people, in the heart of Frankfurt that took me back to the country I had left. I returned overflowing with forgiveness for Al-Firsiwi, his new wife and a half-sister who loved nothing more than contemplating my blue eyes and declaring them a glorious link with the civilised world. But after months in prison, the closure of his hotel and the myriad court cases, Al-Firsiwi had become a difficult man to deal with. After he went almost totally blind, he grew hot tempered, ready to engage in violent fights for the simplest of reasons. This made me consider him an integral part of my difficult return. I tried to spare him from becoming engaged in a new, tragic role, and I attempted to immerse myself gradually into his world without receiving from him the keys to that world.

Of all his ordeals, Al-Firsiwi's arrest in what became known as the Bacchus case was the nearest thing to a personal mythology. On its account, he spent six months in prison and was subjected to torture during interrogation (which he could never face talking about) before the court acquitted him.

My father said that being found innocent was prima facie evidence of the justice system's stupidity. He backed those words with a thousand arguments that incriminated him and proved his amazing success in pulling off a masterful theft that no one could solve. It was an honest robbery which he had not undertaken for monetary gain, but simply to humiliate the Romans and their modern allies.

'So,' I said, 'what people say about you having stolen Bacchus and selling it to a rich German to ward off bankruptcy is a plausible explanation?'

'Bullshit!' replied my father. 'Did I steal it? Yes I did. But sell it? No! I'm not a dealer in idols.'

'What did you do with it?'

'I buried it!'

'Oh, Firsiwi, there's no bigger idiot than you. Bacchus had been buried for centuries until French archaeologists and German prisoners of war came and excavated the city from the depths of the earth, and excavated Bacchus from the depths of the city. Then you come and steal it only to bury it again!'

'Yes. And if I could have, I would have buried all of Walili and Zarhoun too!' He added, laughing, 'I buried it in the courtyard of an obscure mosque. I can just imagine the puzzlement of archaeologists in a few centuries' time asking themselves what Bacchus, the Roman god of wine, was doing in the courtyard of the twenty-first century mosque of the Muslims of Zarhoun!'

Al-Firsiwi obtained a permit to work as an accredited tour guide for the ancient city of Walili thanks to his being found innocent of the Bacchus theft and his profound knowledge of Walili's history and archaeology. He had painstakingly read ancient and modern texts and dig reports in search of – or so he claimed – a direct or indirect cause, foreknown to God, that had pushed him to undertake the robbery. Or to be unjustly and vindictively accused of having committed the robbery, as stated in the court's verdict of innocence.

Al-Firsiwi's personal path – the lives of his ancestors, the catastrophic years of Bu Mandara, the German period that culminated in his marriage to the beautiful post-office employee and his recent glories in the city of the founder of the Moroccan dynasty – did not qualify him to encounter the people and places of the site. How had it been possible for a person who witnessed the downfall of the Rif during war and famine and the death of Bu Mandara from poverty and immigration to end up in the ruins of Walili as a guide to a place that had died centuries ago?

Based on those questions, Al-Firsiwi had developed a theory that immigration was a worm that gnawed at the soul. Ever since he had opened his eyes in Bu Mandara, he had witnessed people tortured by the place they had left behind in the countryside, tortured by the place that was dying in their arms and tortured by the places they dreamed about emigrating to. He himself had spent ten years digging in the rock to immigrate to Germany, and when he finally arrived one snowy morning, he sat on a bench at the railway station trying to recall for the thousandth time the name of the city he was heading for. Disslutet, Disselcorf, Disselboot, Disselcokhat, Dissel, Düsseldorf. By God, it was Düsseldorf where Hamady Burro would receive him with the intention of marrying him to his spinster sister whose bones had dried out from the cold. He could wait, Al-Firsiwi thought suddenly. When he got his papers and hid them safely in his military coat, everyone would hear about the escapades of Al-Firsiwi resounding in the skies of Disselbone, Dissoltozt, Dissolbuf, Düsseldorf, yes Düsseldorf! It was enough for him to pronounce the name of that city three times to give him a monstrous erection.

Immigration was a dormant worm; it sucked and slept. When did it awaken? Al-Firsiwi believed it awakened when things settled down, when the winds were favourable, when the sails were full and the boat was gliding along. When Al-Firsiwi reached the highest heights, buying and selling and, after spending ten years at night-school, translating in the courts, buying property and earning as much as he could, and married the German Shajarat al-Durr!

That was when the worm awakened and whispered in his ear: Do you want to ruin your health for the sake of this race? Do you want your son to grow up as a Christian while all his ancestors, as far back as Abraham, carry the Qur'an in their hearts? Do you want to let the Sherifs humiliate the remaining members of your tribe? Do you want the city that contains relics of the prophets to become a den of sodomites, drug addicts and beggars?

The worm kept on whispering to him, day after day, and Al-Firsiwi put his trust in God and organised his reverse immigration. Diotima, who had kept the notebook of her grandfather who participated in Walili's excavations with other German prisoners, also embraced the worm.

There they were, my friend, in the vastness of the *zawiya*, climbing from the courtyard of the tomb in the inner market to the courtyard of Khaybar where the municipal office was located. They went from one to the other, writing contracts, training brokers, bribing the weak and distracting the malicious.

Diotima embraced the new place like a forsaken paradise, sleeping with her grandfather's secrets near the earth that he turned with his fingers, quietly cajoling the buried secrets, as if he had never crawled on his stomach in combat. Diotima wanted to take root in the blue mountain, and nurtured institutions in the city to help women, vaccinate children, improve education for girls and raise health awareness. She would go to the nearby villages and spend all her day visiting clusters of houses, where the inhabitants slept with their cows and goats and defecated behind their brick ovens while dogs and giant rats stole away the still-warm excrement from under them. There she supported projects for waste processing, fighting epidemics, treating spring water, collecting plastic and preserving the region's orchards. Year after year, projects were born and died: new goat stock would arrive from the Iberian Peninsula, solar energy from charitable organisations in Germany, compost pits for waste that decomposed naturally. No matter who benefited, no matter who vandalised, no matter who resisted, Diotima failed to understand that this land would never accept the transplantation of her roots.

Finally she gave up and sat cross-legged on the throne in the reception hall of the Zaytoun Hotel, succumbing to a crushing sadness that erased all signs of benevolence from her face. The ardour she had lavished on the geography of the place, its produce and its crippled people had not provided her with so much as one drop of human affection. Whether recipients of her bounty or not, not a single heart held a trace of fondness, gratitude, recognition or appreciation for her. She was rowing upstream in a river of disgust and hatred that people expressed in various ways, from turning their heads away to invoking God's help. Even when she was helping the civil protection teams in the city during the campaign to cure the pox that had spread in the region, some of the afflicted deliberately shook hands with her with excessive warmth, having scratched their skin for hours until their fingers and nails were covered with pus and scabs, in the hope of seeing this Christian woman contaminated. Whenever they saw her safe and healthy, mixing the powder with water and helping to treat the women, their anger grew, and they poured all their rage on the Germanic race that had produced both exceptionally resistant human beings and steel.

Even Al-Firsiwi, who revealed a kind of human purity that was almost romantic at the beginning of his relationship with Diotima, very quickly lost that purity as he pursued deals and projects, and planned tricks for the honest people and their allies. He would comment on the matter whenever he saw pity in his wife's eyes for the spite that had being growing within him for ages. 'Don't worry,' he would say. 'We engage in the exchange of hatred necessary for our psychological and physical wellbeing! If you encounter a Rifi who doesn't hate the Sherifs, it's a sure sign that he's from a long line of bastards, and vice versa! Despite that there are no dead, injured or war wounded among us!'

At the start of their relationship, Al-Firsiwi was still capable of upholding the virtues of uprightness, seriousness, honesty and devotion as basic dimensions in his life. They gave his personality a certain gallantry, a mixture of haughtiness, shyness and modesty. He even made love with a certain distance and strictness, with a concern for perfection, accuracy and precision. It became a source of confused pleasure where there was no room for play, seduction or adventure. They were fast, trembling pleasures that almost resembled incestuous love.

But after Al-Firsiwi and Diotima spent time in this storm, it all disappeared to be replaced by a pure aversion that rejected the needs of the body and the impetuosity of the soul. It was an aversion that combined regret and despair, and a feeling that they were bound together in a downward spiral. Whenever one sought safety, his or her nerves and random actions quickened the rapid push to the very bottom.

This repressed aversion gave them immense energy that made it possible for them to go on living together, with a daily concern for improvising something that united them and led them to the end of the day in such an extreme state of fatigue that they were unable to even look at each other.

My mother made sure to teach me everything she knew: the German language, the difference between poisonous and edible mushrooms and the basics of music and watercolours, but she never talked to me about Al-Firsiwi. Therefore, everything I said or will say about their relationship is solely my personal assumption and does not implicate anyone but me.

Our family consisted of closed squares. One included my mother and me; another, tightly closed, included Al-Firsiwi and Diotima, and another, looser square was where we all gathered, or where I met Al-Firsiwi face to face.

As far as I was concerned, my mother largely succeeded in purifying our relationship of all surplus emotional contaminants. Her maternal attitude had almost no external demonstration; the most she manifested was a minimal smile and a quick touch of the hand. This sensory remove never involved a feeling of abandonment or neglect. Her daily presence and her eagerness to reach the best in me embodied the depth of her maternal feelings and reinforced my conviction that she was an exceptional mother.

When I went to Germany I hated my father and the country that had killed my mother. I longed to establish a life as far away as possible from an atmosphere charged with mystery and dormant intrigues. I spent the first years delighted by this accommodation, free of all nostalgia for any person or place, until I met a Rifi association and found through them another connection that led me to the left-wing group. One day, as I was thinking about the future of the revolution, I decided that my true place was in the field, in the midst of the people who would rise from their ashes and get rid of the thieves and the murderers.

And so it went, at least as far as I was concerned.

Dreamers and Others

I

YACINE, SIMPLY BY BEING killed, became an eternal child. He transformed into a being who would accompany me, emerging from his dark world whenever he wanted, and with whom I would share the details of my daily life. He would sit at my table or on my shoulders, or he would nudge me unexpectedly to pass on a piece of news or a comment in confidence. Sometimes he would sit on the edge of my bed to greet me with a rowdy discussion as I woke up. In his daily appearances Yacine was no more than one year old, yet his voice was that of the young man who had bid me goodbye at the railway station. I would talk with him for hours as I crossed Rabat from Bab Tamesna to the edge of the river, passing through Al-Nasr Street, Moulay Youssef Street, Alawite Square, and then the flower market, all the way to Al-Jazaïr Street and the offices of the newspaper where I worked.

Lots of people – who obviously could not see him – noticed me caught up in conversation and spread the rumour that I had begun talking to myself, and that it must have been because of Yacine. They did not know how right they were. Together Yacine and I commented on the roadworks we came across as we walked, or the demonstrations, or the beautiful women.

Sometimes we delved into our old issues and talked about revolutions, betrayals and the death of illusions.

I sat down in the Garden Café an hour before my appointment with Layla. I told Yacine that I wanted to jot down some ideas for my weekly piece. He laughed at this and made fun of my belated attention to the importance of love, but I did not respond to his sarcasm. I noted down that in the next column I had to talk about a film I could no longer remember apart from a dance connected to it that I imagined I had danced with Layla. I could not remember whether it had been in a dream or at a noisy nightclub on the beach. I also wanted to mention a violent incident I witnessed that conveyed the nature of the film. Once near the Alhambra cinema, on the outskirts of Yacoub al-Mansour neighbourhood, I had seen a man in a white car running someone over and killing him. Though I remembered the brutal nature of the accident, I didn't recall the specific details.

Huge cranes, bulldozers and cement mixers passed in front of the café, blocking the street and filling it with a buzz of activity. Yacine wondered if they were looking for buried treasure beneath the capital. I explained to him why large projects were underway in Rabat, why new neighbourhoods, plazas, tourist areas, museums and galleries were being built. This sudden change, I said, might be because the new king felt he was a native of this city and he had to rid it of the bleakness of a rustic suburb. Yacine argued that people needed food and medicine, not a beautiful capital.

I blamed the Taliban for his comment and tried to rectify the matter by stressing the need to produce as much beauty as possible, that being the only way to overcome despair. He laughed again and reminded me of the long soirées at the homes of Ibrahim al-Khayati, Ahmad Majd and others, with

70

their overwrought discussions that held out no hope for the future without a break from the past.

'What's happened to you lot?' Yacine wondered.

I repeated the question as if asking myself, 'What's happened to us?'

Yacine asked again, 'How did you come to believe that the future would be like a tramp's trousers, made up of different coloured patches from various times?'

I told him, 'We were talking about this city, not a utopia!'

Yacine believed that once the amusement park, the new roads, the furnished flats, the up-market hotels, the restaurants, the cafés, the cinemas and arcades were ready, Bou Regreg Park would be raided by the Zuhair and Zamur tribes, just like in the past. People would shut up their shops after the late afternoon prayer, as they had done in those far-off days in fear of incursions.

I laughed at the idea, but then replied seriously. 'On the contrary, the park will become a source of not-so-tragic stories, a hotbed for love, adventure, wealth and bankruptcy, nights out for celebrities and parties for high society, a hiding place for wasters and drifters, and those in search of something known or unknown. The river itself will be transformed into a fish that goes to sleep at the crack of dawn!'

'In that case,' said Yacine, 'the inhabitants of Rabat won't need to go to Marrakech in pursuit of a fleeting moment of freedom.'

'Not to Marrakech or Casablanca. We'll put a final stop to Ibrahim al-Khayati's claim that having dinner in Rabat is like having dinner at a bus station.'

'But all the inhabitants of Rabat – I mean the rich ones – have bought houses in Marrakech,' remarked Yacine.

'They will sell them when they receive orders to move straight back to the capital.'

'Even that is by order!' Yacine exclaimed.

'Yes. And all the gossip will also be instructed to migrate to the capital.'

'Never. That's impossible. Marrakech couldn't survive without gossip. You know what? I had a friend in Paris who said that once the tales of Jemaa al-Fnaa had almost faded into oblivion, Marrakech devised modern stories, a kind of *One Thousand and One Nights* played out in sports centres, nightclubs and discos. So with or without orders, Marrakech will never relinquish her throne, even if you were to rebuild Baghdad on the bank of the river!'

'I didn't know you were such a fanatic.'

'Between you and me,' he said, 'Rabat is nothing but an old Andalusian hag, extremely fair skinned but sagging. No amount of embellishment can help her.'

'Do you hate her so much?'

'I neither love her nor hate her. I only find her "forward", as my mother would say.'

'As for me,' I explained, 'I find her fascinating, mysterious and dreamy, and she also has a river. I don't like cities without rivers, as if they were cities that don't cry. I don't like Marrakech: always acting like a child and laughing for no reason!'

'Shame! How can a writer dislike Marrakech?' wondered Yacine.

'Guess what? The writer Abu Idris has a theory on the subject. He says that Marrakech is anti-writing, that she's a city for old people.'

'I'm going to tell you something that might upset you,' said Yacine.

'Say it, anyway.'

'It seems to me that you've changed for the worse.'

'What does that mean?' I asked.

'It means you're brimming with a harsh bitterness. You're not fooled by any of life's tricks any more. Don't you expect anything miraculous? How can you bear life in such clarity?'

'I don't make any special effort. It's life that puts up with me!' I said.

'But you've always lived with troubles, doubts, mistakes and blind conviction. I mean, weren't all those things just masks?'

'Yes, most of the time. Back then, I believed we had to resist despair by any means.'

'And now?' he asked.

'Now, to some extent, I've become reconciled to despair. Those who have boundless hopes make me more despairing than those in despair.'

'It seems like I'll never understand you,' said Yacine.

'No one can understand anyone,' I replied.

At that moment, Layla arrived, her voice preceding her physical presence.

'It looks like you're talking to yourself!' she said.

'No, I was talking to Yacine!'

Her face darkened and she mumbled, 'I'm sorry for interrupting you.'

She sat facing me. We looked at each other as if waiting for Yacine to leave. Once he had left, Layla began talking on the phone. I studied her face as she gave curt answers to end the conversation. Her whole face beamed with an inward smile, causing me unbearable pain because I would be unable to make her feel that way. Perhaps that pain cast its shadows over my gaze, for she asked me anxiously, 'What's wrong? Is everything all right?'

'Yes, almost everything.'

Then I talked to her about the inner smile, and we came up with an amusing theory about having to create a sort of sieve in our internal spiritual space to sift the necessary in life (even if painful) from the useless (even if highly tempting). This process of sifting was the most eloquent expression of our balance, our strength and our mental and physical health. Without consulting us or even our being aware, our ultimate gratification, our most refined pleasure and our secret chemistry produced this inner smile. As the product of this marvellous sieve, this smile would be an aura around our bodies and souls, granting us luminous protection and invincibility in the face of life's obstacles.

We talked at length about this subject in a kind of race for words and thoughts. We hardly knew who was saying what. Layla was directing this exercise in order to make me feel the need to arrange a space I controlled all by myself, without leaving any margin, however small, for others' interference. That space, like the living space of any creature in this world, would allow me to differentiate between need and desire, because, according to Layla, the matter depended on this particular capacity.

'Look at yourself,' she told me. 'You're a perfectly healthy machine! All the mechanisms necessary for you to function are working. There's nothing wrong with any of your systems, yet you've broken down and are in paralysis.'

We also talked about Bahia. I gave her an idea of our situation following Yacine's death. I told her that deep down Bahia considered me responsible for what had happened and hated me for it. I hated her, too, for thinking that. Bahia believed Yacine had inherited the germ of rebellion from me and paid the price vicariously for my own political involvement and my neglect of the organisation. She would have preferred to see me settle this account personally, rather than making Yacine believe in my dreams, only to then find himself obliged to save me from the humiliation of my dreams' disintegration by convincing me that extremism was the solution and that getting into bed with the enemy was not an option.

'My God, it really is complicated!' said Layla. 'How is it possible to think like that? Life isn't a succession of acts of revenge and the settling of scores. No generation can live the illusions of another generation. Plus, in the end, Yacine isn't the tragic hero his mother claims. He's just an extremist who met his death. And with the Taliban to top it off!'

Hurt, I said to her, 'Please. Don't talk about him like that.'

She squeezed my hand in apology, and looked closely into my eyes. 'This relationship will destroy you – if it didn't do so already ages ago. Save your skin! You can't stake what's left of your life on reckless hatred. Do you understand?'

To qualify matters, I said, 'No, no, no. It is not as dangerous as all that. I'm at sufficient remove from all those things. The hatred I talked to you about doesn't touch me from within. To tell you the truth, I'm not interested in what's happening, or what will or won't ever happen. I live totally detached from those things, even when I say that I hate her. I'm only using a word that suits the situation but does not express something I feel.' I then seized this opportunity to tell Layla that I felt nothing, absolutely nothing.

She fell silent for a short while and then suggested we go to a Japanese restaurant. I agreed immediately. There, using a plate of sushi, I was able to explain what I meant. Raw flesh in particular eloquently embodied my non-feeling for things. Raw meat did not suggest food with a fabricated identity, but rather was an authentic food in its primitive form, before culture interfered to suggest it be used in a certain way and with accompanying substances. Cooked dishes were, first and foremost, a creation of scent. Raw dishes, however, were a liberation from history for the benefit of the ingredient. As a result, eating became a relationship with elements that were independent of each other, and not a relationship with flavour, as centuries of culture's trickery had made it.

Layla did not seem interested by the topic and preferred to confront me firmly. She insisted that sushi was not something primitive, as I claimed, and that there was a huge difference between a man devouring a fish he had just pulled out of a river and a man enjoying sushi in a Japanese restaurant. 'What you are devouring now is called sushi, not fish,' she said.

I busied myself finishing off what was left on my plate, avoiding further discussion of the subject until her voice broke my concentration.

'When you say you don't feel anything, do you mean, for example, that you can't fall in love?' she asked.

'The issue is probably more complicated than that.'

'Can you or can't you?'

'Yes and no,' I said.

'How?'

'There are many elements to love that I only know about through memory. Everything related to emotions, passion, fear, yearning, regret, guilt, seduction and tenderness.'

'What about desire?' Layla asked.

'Desire in its actual form, yes, but not its course. For example, I am totally incapable of feeling the onset of desire, and its subsequent progress by means of words, movements and suggestions. I just know in my brain that the time has come. At that point I resort to memory to enjoy the culmination of desire.'

'Do you mean to say that pleasure is unrelated to what your body's doing?' she asked.

'No, not at all. I mean that in order for me to enjoy what my body's doing, I must connect its hardware – in operation at that moment – with the bank of emotions found in the hard disk.'

Her eyes welled with tears. 'That's so horrible! What kind of pain is that? What an ordeal!'

I tried to make light of the situation and pretended that the matter required only additional effort on my part for me to obtain some pleasure; and I might, after all, achieve better results due to this effort.

She smiled through her tears and asked suddenly, 'And us?'

'What?'

'What shall we do with our life?'

'In the immediate future, we go to your flat and lock ourselves in until we find an exceptional love story.'

'No, no. You're mixing up the immediate and the long term. We can only lock ourselves in until my daughter returns from school!'

And so it was.

We went straight to her bedroom, and when I paused to look at the titles of the books carefully arranged on black shelves near the bed, she pulled me away, saying, 'Forget the books. We don't have much time.'

I imagined her body's fragrance, or I remembered it, I don't exactly know, right at the moment our lips met and I took in her tongue, reluctantly at first and then compliantly. I imagined her scent when she raised her arms to free her breasts, and as I explored the details of her pale skin, moving from cold, shivering areas to warm, pulsating ones. I imagined her smell as I pulled her to me and released her, when she lay prone, when she turned over, when she spread open and when she curled up, when she turned away and drew back, when she resisted and then yielded and shuddered. I imagined her fragrance in the movement of her fingers, and when she quieted, swooned, moaned and said, 'Yes, like that, yes. Exactly what you did, never do it with another woman, I beg of you. I forbid you to do it with another woman.' She was silent, and then burst out, 'Yes. Now. Please say you love me.' She cried and then was spent.

At every moment, I imagined her body's fragrance – or recalled its memory. I did not say 'I love you'. I remembered the fence of the garden leading to the Ibn Sina apartment, the acacia tree, the scent of a summer night, and the advent of dawn after a silent return from the Beach nightclub. I remembered the woman and the short black dress around her feet, her hands holding the garden fence and the magic of her back illuminated by lamplight. I remembered her fragrance, hers out of all the sleeping or vigilant, seen or unseen creatures that surrounded us; a fragrance redolent of water, vegetation, soil and fruit; the fragrance of her face, the expression of her face that in a flash of anger turned it into a metallic scent, dry and stinging. For she had bent down and pulled up her dress from around her feet up the length of her legs, her thighs and her chest, all the way to the curve of her shoulders. Then she turned around and told me, through her angry expression and her messy hair, 'You must leave at once. I never want to see you again.'

In such way, a fragrance cached in the box of miracles leads us to a timeless pleasure that moves through our body, shaking its withered branches and scattering their leaves to the wind. But we know neither who enjoys what nor who seduces whom.

I asked her, 'Can I stay a little?'

'Of course, you have to stay, even if you didn't say I love you!'

'But you asked me to leave immediately.'

Panic stricken she continued, 'Impossible! Did I really say that?'

'Yes you did, and you also said: "I never want to see you again!"'

'They seem like my words, but I was in no state to say them.'

'Perhaps you said them at another time or in another life. To me or, hopefully, to another man.'

'You could have said I love you even without feeling it.' she said, 'Just like you would say anything else. Would it have hurt you to say it?'

'I did not see a need for it. I figured that such a powerful sentence ought to be said in a different setting.'

She explained herself. 'You should know that I feel insulted if it is not said to me while making love.'

'You're exaggerating.'

'Anyhow, given you're a man who claims not to feel, the sex was still the best thing to have happened to me in years.'

'It's worthy of two persons living a great love story,' I said.

'True!' she said pensively.

She then stretched her body over mine, took my face between her hands and said, 'I like the way you do it!'

I was absorbed in contemplating her face, with the attitude of someone without a care in the world, when she suddenly got up in a panic. 'My daughter's school has ended! You must leave right now.'

I got up ponderously, but she pounced on me with my clothes. She tidied up the room, got dressed, helped me get dressed and leapt around until I found myself at the lift door. She was laughing and told me, having calmed down a little, 'What a miracle! A charming man!'

I walked slowly down the street on my way to the bus stop, then it occurred to me to keep walking. When I left Bourgogne Square and turned right to enter the dreamy street housing the Ecole Normale Supérieur, Yacine poked me with his little finger and asked, 'Is she a new love story?'

'I love no one,' I replied sharply.

He answered immediately, 'Easy, easy now. I'm not partisan here. You could even consider me a neutral bystander. In the best case scenario, I can help you ask good questions.'

'What I need most is good answers,' I said.

'I know, but the dead don't have answers!'

'Too bad. Tell me, how did you figure out it was a new love story?'

'When a man is on his way to the bus stop, then decides to walk, and does this as if he were compressing the distance between him and a woman he was just with, there are grounds to ask whether he hasn't fallen in love!'

'What definitive proofs!'

'You're making fun of the matter to cover it up.' he said, 'But as you were walking, I heard you say, "Me too, I like the way you do it."'

'I said that while I was alone?'

'Yes, quite a few times!'

'I think I'm suffering from a kind of asynchronicity. I should have said that in reply to something that was said to me fifteen minutes before – not because that's what I feel, but only to provide a decent answer.'

'I don't know an illness with that name, but you have strange illnesses. Who knows? Since there was a space of time between what was said to you and what you said in reply, there might be an interval between your falling in love and your being aware that you've fallen in love.'

'You've either said more than necessary or you haven't said enough!'

'I'm only trying to understand what you called asynchronicity,' he explained.

'But you've put your finger on something that tortures me.'

'Such as?'

'Such as the feeling that I'm belatedly living the scenes of an old affair.'

'Do you mean that you loved this woman in another life?'

'Don't be stupid. It's just an affair set in two times.'

'Love in instalments!'

'Or something like that.'

That evening I wrote in *Letters to My Beloved*:

I am waiting for you. All I do is wait for you. I am neither in a hurry nor discouraged. I am not sure of anything and I am neither suspicious nor in despair. The fact is that I am waiting for you and I feel that this gives my life meaning, though I do not know what it means to give one's life meaning. I waited for you as if you were still in the summer nightclub, while I was in the desolate square. Why did you stay there and why did I leave? Are you still dancing with someone we met there? You were extremely moved to see him and you said that he was one of your dearest friends. I imagine that you are still angry with me because of the funny way I danced to the soundtrack of Pulp Fiction. *I intended it to be an awful, funny dance to spoil the artistry of your dance. But you insisted that we do it perfectly, the way Travolta and Uma Thurman did it in the film, including maintaining the right distance to allow you to pass your fingers before your eyes and face. It was the other person who provoked me, his muscles moving in a blind mirroring. Only you were close to the soul of the dance, even if I was busy performing that insolent mockery. There was something sarcastic in the film as* well, but I can't remember it any more. *Travolta* only danced with his body, but you – I mean Uma Thurman – danced with her soul. She was saying, 'I want to win a prize this evening!' But what she meant was, 'I want to win you.' And you, to whom were you saying that?

Here we are now, in the desolate square, in the garden adjacent to the entrance of the building. Here we are storming the dawn with our nudity; here you are taking away what is left of my caution and placing it on the stones of the wall where you press your open hands and form with the white contours of your body a wound in the night. Then you vanish, leaving no trace of you in the ashes surrounding me.

2

I JOLTED BAHIA OUT OF her afternoon nap, jeopardising the quiet of the afternoon. Ahmad Majd wanted to talk to her about an urgent matter related to a lawsuit her family had initiated over land near the capital. She sat up in bed and, after much grumbling, snatched the telephone from my hand – as if we were fighting over it – and placed it directly to her ear.

Whenever conversation revolved around the land whose ownership the government had expropriated from my wife and her brothers, the atmosphere became charged. Dialogue among the siblings, between the lawyer and the siblings, and among all those involved in the matter, became impossible. No one had a solution for it.

For more than fifty years, successive generations of my wife's family had lived with dreams of the unexploited wealth lying in a piece of real estate that stretched along the bank of the Bou Regreg, from its mouth to the edge of Akkrach. They had no rivals except the *awqaf* with their huge properties and a few old-established families from Salé who owned scattered lots.

When the Akkrach rubbish dump settled in that romantic spot of the neglected capital, with its waste, its fires, its smoke and its foul smells, the value of the land went through the floor.

The only ones who endured in this rotten hell that stretched along the river were potters with their kilns, a few farmers who grew contaminated vegetables and, slightly later, some villages that sprang up around the dump. Their inhabitants came from the wasteland of Zaeer, the village of Oulad Moussa and the hills of Akkrach, and from the slums along the river. All this happened in an area of Rabat with the most unique and natural beauty. Meanwhile, Rabat's middle classes, with their lack of imagination, expanded on the plain leading to Zaeer Road and fought a stupid war over the sea and the river at the same time.

Then came the new era, and in the stream of token projects launched under its banner, the government created the Bou Regreg Basin Development Agency, which quickly became the aesthetic branch of plans to restructure the capital. Dreams of unexploited treasure came to life for a new generation: that of my wife and her siblings. They carefully calculated their acres and the anticipated price of a single square foot, and found that their family, which had survived for decades on the breadline, living off the respectability and superiority of old-established families, had become rich under the new dispensation. But the prices did not move up or down because, in the blink of an eye, the self-same land completely evaporated. The Agency seized it, just as it had all other plots of land, to use for a city of dreams.

After every telephone conversation with our friend Ahmad Majd, my wife would speak angrily about how she failed to understand all the bragging over democracy and modernity in a country that did not have the slightest respect for the individual and his property. I would tell her, for the sake of bickering, 'Your family slept on top of this treasure for decades without ever offering any of it to its children or its country. Now that the nation has decided to revive this wealth and

84

lavish it on the people, you suddenly see flaws in the rule of justice and law.'

Bahia would reply by blaming this presumed modernity first and foremost. Then, veering off the point, she would hint at the plaudits for absolute power with which we on the traditional left intoxicated ourselves while collectively humiliating the nation.

I would reply sarcastically. 'Why are you singling out the traditional left, my dear? Is there any louder cheering than that of the new left?'

Mostly, she did not reply, lest her words reach our friend Ahmad Majd, who, after gradually infiltrating into public life, did not miss an opportunity to tout his decisive role in taking major decisions in the highest circles, especially those concerning sensitive subjects related to human rights and secret talks with the Polisario. All that generated an energy for cynicism in me, and I fell victim to its dark side for several weeks.

I had not talked with Bahia about the disputed land during the years of our relationship. I had vaguely understood from her father, who died suddenly, that he owned swathes of the banks of the Bou Regreg, like many other families who considered these marshlands as nominal riches that meant little to them. But after the formation of the Agency and the ensuing conflict, we nervously broached the subject, because the expedited expropriation made Bahia feel she was the victim of an injustice. It made her believe she was pursued by a strange destiny, and if she won this battle something fundamental in her life would change. When I would tell her that the worst thing was that the question of this wealth – the real estate, potential income and endless speculation – would end her life, she would snap that the worst that could happen at the end of a person's life was that they would settle for so little. In other words, accepting that what we had obtained was the best we could get. She would then add, 'Who told you that I want to end my life?'

My wife's family had lived in Salé for generations. None of them left its walls and it never occurred to one of them to go and live somewhere else, far from the city's holy tombs and great mosque. Only one member of the family – no one knew what had got into him – decided to repeat the experience of paradise lost in the family history. In the midst of unprecedented emotional uproar, he emigrated to the opposite bank of the Bou Regreg, a mere fifteen minutes away from his paradise. As soon as evening fell he would set the table of nostalgia in his house of exile and lament Salé and its people, bewailing its ephemeral blessings. With every drink, his nostalgia grew more intense and he vented his anger on the parasitic growth of neighbourhoods around the city. The scion of Andalusia was reduced to a minority lost among the riff-raff, like a single tidy strand in the midst of tousled hair. That man was my wife's father, a professor of modern linguistics at Mohammed V University, whose fear of poverty, nostalgia for Salé and grief over the decline of the Arabic language cost him his life.

At night he used to ask his wife to set the table and then he would take a very formal tour in his car, in the end turning his back to the lights of his tranquil city beyond the river. When he entered his house he always recited half a line from Al-Mutanabbi: *Seeing is a vexation to the life of man.*

When I told him once that the meaning was incomplete without the second half of the line, he replied immediately, 'It's more than complete!'

'Just like that, without explanation?'

'Yes, absolutely like that, because the whole of vexation is to see,' he replied.

This elegant man who studied in Paris and contributed to the modernisation of the Moroccan university could not accept what he referred to as the downfall of independent Morocco. He could not stomach the mismatched construction in his historical city, the deterioration of the Moroccan teaching system, the change of values and the overarching race for wealth. He could not tolerate the disintegration of the Arabic language and the rise of the nouveaux riche, the retailers, the alcohol sellers and the speculators who had become the city's notables and big-shots. He could not stand the fact that Salé had become a mere drop in the ocean, an eloquent symbol of the tragic eclipse and waning away that had taken his generation by surprise.

Hajj al-Touhami would spend the whole day shouting nonstop, as if he wanted to organise through shouting the chaos unfolding around him. Only then would he sleep soundly, satisfied with himself because he had done his duty. Until one day he went to sleep and never woke up.

Bahia never understood the state's motive for punishing this gentle-hearted man by depriving his children of their lawful inheritance. With all the strength she possessed, she tried to make me embrace the cause at a time when I had no enthusiasm whatsoever for any cause. I used to answer her in exaggerated fashion, 'Don't you see that even Palestine doesn't move me any more? Not that, not the fall of Baghdad, not Hezbollah; not a usurped land or a downtrodden people. All that and more no longer inspires me to take to the street and raise my voice! So, my dear, how do you expect me to make your stolen land on the banks of the Bou Regreg a cause for which I would rally support?'

My reply undoubtedly hurt her. She would remain silent for a long time, as if suppressing her voice was a sign of everything else being blocked.

One day she said to me, as if talking to herself, 'You don't know that I spent a whole day with Yacine before he left. We roamed over this piece of land and imagined building stables for horses, swimming pools, moorings, small white rooms and playgrounds for children.'

'But he preferred to do that in Paradise, on riverbanks that no one can expropriate!' I replied.

Then something terrible, and unexpected, happened. She started shouting, slapping her face, tearing her clothes and pulling her hair until her hands were full of it. In this dreadful display of grief, her voice came loud, sharp and deranged.

'I'm talking to you about Yacine, my son, my soul, my own flesh and blood, my son, your son. Your *son*, not a cat run over by a car. Why do you kill him like that? Why do you tear him away from me with your sarcasm? Go, go away. I don't want anything from you. I don't want a lawsuit. I don't want the land. I don't want, I don't, I don't, I don't . . .'

I was pacing the room, not knowing what to do. I did not approach her. I was gripped by a dread that paralysed my ability to act. I could not speak, get upset or ask forgiveness. I submitted to a kind of bemusement that made me look in equanimity at all that was collapsing around me. I considered my condition, which had become a means to cause pain, making it possible for me to provoke unbearable suffering in my wife with lethal spontaneity. It was also possible for her, in her agony, to torture me without any guilt feelings, as if by inflicting on me the most grievous losses, anticipated or not, she were only fulfilling my wishes.

Every Saturday for months after this incident Bahia hosted her siblings, Ahmad Majd and Fatima for a family lunch, during which they discussed the court case and the conciliation sessions that the lawyer organised with a great deal of political savvy. I participated in body, but did not utter a word. Whenever Bahia noticed my presence, she motioned to me with a delicate movement of her head as a sign that she had forgotten what had occurred and that I could contribute. But that was like stuffing a snowball down my throat. I would blush, my vision would blur, and I would end up in the bathroom, where I would spend a long time getting rid of my stomach cramps.

During one of those 'land luncheons', as we called them, Ahmad Majd talked at length about the project that would take more than ten years to complete. It included a tourism zone, piers for entertainment, a tunnel under the Qasbah of the Udayas and the renovation of Chella. This would be in addition to shopping areas, up-market residential neighbourhoods, major hotels, restaurants, amusement parks, cafés, cultural and artistic organisations and sports grounds. All this would transform the river and its mouth into a new lively focal point for the capital.

Bahia said that she hoped the project would help integrate the two banks and put an end to decades of imbalance between them. Ahmad Majd confirmed, with the assurance of someone who knew the ins and outs of things, that this would be the case, and that the project philosophy rested on a vision to turn the river into a means for integration rather than a barrier dividing Salé and Rabat. At this point a verbal battle broke out between Fatima and Ahmad Majd about the management of the project and how political authorities had imposed it on the city. Fatima argued that huge interests had grown around the project even before it had begun, and that the land confiscation was a true scandal. But Ahmad Majd affirmed that the matter depended on a policy of 'voluntaryism' that stepped over traditional obstacles and points of resistance.

As for me, if there was anything that put me off and put an end to any desire I might have had to argue, it was talk of 'effectuality' and 'implementality'. As soon as anyone uttered them, I headed to the balcony. I then heard Bahia declare, quite movingly, that Yacine had dreamed of placing a giant steel arch across the river at its mouth. He thought the arch would give the impression that the river ran through the fingers of the two cities.

As if feeling the approach of a poetic diversion he would not be able to handle, Ahmad Majd returned quickly to the subject and insisted on a reconciliation based on his earlier suggestion, which had been turned down by Bahia and her siblings. This consisted of compensation for the lands that had become registered property, and delaying the decision regarding the other lands until the completion of the registration process. The compensation would be of two types: one monetary, the amount to be agreed upon with the specialist bureau delegated by the Agency; and one in kind, in the form of concessions in the commercial and entertainment zones.

Bahia and her siblings insisted on completing the sale of all the confiscated land at market price. Every time Bahia repeated this opinion, Ahmad Majd became upset and, after a staged pause, begged her to consider the matter carefully. 'Think with me, Bahia. How can the Agency buy your land at market price when it distributes the plots for free to foreign investors to encourage them to invest on the land of your fortune-blessed ancestors?'

Ahmad Majd managed to breech the united front of the heirs when he convinced the youngest brother to agree to his solution. He continued to work on the matter, offering enticing advantages and highlighting the risks in getting involved in legal procedures of unpredictable outcome.

Debate over procedures and solutions went on for more than a year without any significant result. Work was in full swing to finish the harbours, the pavements, the tourist and leisure facilities, the new lagoon and the artificial island. The hoardings announcing those projects lined the roads that surrounded the river. Every time a new phase of the project was launched, the press conferences multiplied. Television promoted the projects with amazing computer-generated images that fired the imagination of the inhabitants of the two banks, thus feeding their historical disputes with modern ammunition.

Which of the two banks of the river would reap the proceeds of this historic change? Would the project exact revenge for the centuries of Salé's decline? Would it save Rabat from turning into a village at night? Ahmad Majd brought many such questions from his private late-night meetings with the elite to our tense lunchtime gatherings. He frequently took advantage of our curiosity to advocate his theories regarding the symbolic significance of a tunnel for cars under the Qasbah of the Udayas and the preparations for a concourse linking the Grand Gate, La'lu prison, and the Arcade of the Consuls, so creating the Montmartre of the capital. But he sighed over the cemetery nestled in the heart of the area. He wondered how a nation could choose to bury its dead in the most beautiful spot worthy of the living.

I said with exaggerated anger, 'Let me remind you that it is the martyrs' cemetery. There lie Allal ben Abdallah, Allal al-Fassi, Abderrahim Bouabid, Al-Hussain al-Khadar, Abdelfattah Sabatah, and thousands of people, great and small.'

Ahmad Majd added, 'Al-Dulaimi, Al-Basri, and hundreds of killers like them are also buried there!'

I objected, saying, 'You have no right to mix them in this way. The dead cannot be jumbled, even when buried in the same grave. Only the dead deserve this spot, one that overlooks the beach and allows a direct connection between their darkness and the *Mare Tenebrosum*, the Atlantic.'

I then felt that I had better get away from this painful issue and I withdrew within myself. Still I listened, amused by the lengthy discussions over the issue of uniting the two banks with a tramway. The lines would transport more than fifty million passengers a year and seed the two cities with more than fifty stations.

I liked the idea of the stations and said to myself that a city did not truly become a city until it had many stations where appointments, relationships and faces (feasible and impossible) could multiply. At that moment I heard Fatima ask loudly, 'Do you think that the tram will unite the two banks?'

'Yes, among other things,' I said.

'How strange. You all think about inclusion with the mentality of a seamstress.'

'What's strange is your inability to grasp the meaning of these great transformations,' I told her.

'Grasp all you want, my boy. Grasp, and good health to you,' she said. After a short period of silence, she added, as if talking to herself, 'There was a time when Sidi ben Achir, Sidi al-Arabi ben Assayeh and Sidi Abdallah ben Hassoun could unite sixty tribes in a heartbeat!'

I neither disagreed with her words nor expressed enthusiasm for them. I went back to reflecting on what Ahmad Majd had said about the tunnel. He was right about the hill having witnessed the first surge of the Moors into the region; tunnelling under it would be like tunnelling under the region's origins.

We would reclaim the sea from the fear that had clung to us for centuries. We would head straight to it, without climbing up to look down on it. We would break the habit of going around the mountain whenever it stood in the way. Now, we would not circumvent it nor would it circumvent us. We would pass under its dense body and then raise it above the headlights of our cars. We would leave the Qasbah suspended above the beach with no defensive role or task, an elevation with no meaning except for the smells and stories swirling in its alley-ways. It would observe from on high the queues of cars entering the tunnel and then coming out at the other end. Gone was the Qasbah that Rabat long shrouded in its memory, preferring to relinquish it to the poor and foreigners who did not fear humidity and considered the stench of the sea a gift from heaven. Now, another hill would rise like an icon over the hubbub of the city; it would overlook amusement parks, hotels and nightclubs; it would forget there was a time when it saw only pirates.

Fatima said, 'Imagine the Qasbah collapsing during the digging of the tunnel!'

Ahmad laughed. 'Do you think cowboys will be digging the tunnel? A multinational company will execute the project, backed by a consulting firm run by a world-famous engineer.'

'Even so, accidents of this kind can happen to the biggest companies and the best engineers!'

'I bet you're wishing for the Qasbah to fall.'

'That's not fair,' she said. 'I just expect the worst from anything surrounded by great enthusiasm.' She fell silent, perhaps hurt by Ahmad's sarcasm. It reminded me of the game of musical chairs we played in our youth. Whenever Fatima, myself and some of our friends called for a certain realism in the activities of the left, Ahmad Majd and his friends in the new left made fun of what they called our reformist tendencies, which turned their back on radical revolutionary solutions and accepted halfway ones. They would repeat to us Guevara's words: 'Be realistic, demand the impossible!' But when Ahmad and his friends became super realists, believing in the ability of enlightened modern powers to change the world without wasting time on political games, we were the ones to accuse them of weakness and making humiliating concessions. For years we traded recriminations, unaware of the huge losses we all incurred as a result.

For a few months Bahia persisted in her stubborn efforts to be involved in the heart of the project. She hoped to receive a parcel of the developed land. Ahmad Majd, on the other hand, kept trying hard to convince her to accept compensation that would put an end to the dispute. But Bahia, for various reasons, considered her involvement in this venture an exceptional opportunity to return in some way to life. She might have been inwardly convinced that the years lost searching for ambiguous dreams and the agony caused by Yacine's death would all be rewarded by her involvement in a project that would transform the city and pump life back into its arteries. The material real- isation of this transformation would provide her with the opportunity to tell herself and the world: 'You know what? The new face of the city is also my face!'

3

ONE DAY BAHIA WOKE up smiling and favourably disposed, for reasons unknown to me. While I was making coffee she surprised me with a question she had never asked before.

'Can I ask your opinion on an idea that crossed my mind last night?'

'Since when did you trust my judgement?' I asked her.

'I don't trust your judgement, but I know how much you love crazy ideas. So I thought you might be able to help me.'

I put my cup of coffee on the table and looked at her for the first time since she had started talking.

Her face was radiant, a touch pale but filled with kindness. I felt I was scrutinising her features for the first time in years and rediscovering that she had them. I felt a certain tenderness towards her. I was probably moved by my awareness of the heartlessness of the situation of living permanently with someone unseen or not even looked at.

'So what is this idea that has woken us up today in this strange mood?' I asked her.

She replied impetuously, 'I'm thinking of devoting part of the land to a humanitarian and artistic project!'

She spread the plans on the table and started explaining.

'Leave aside the main part of the project, the quays, the lagoon, the island, the amusement park and so on. All of those are, if you like, the aristocratic elements of the new space. Let's leave the façade, the part for show, to them. We'll only ask for limited plots in those parts. But here, far from all that noise, at the far end of the bank, near where the Akkrach rubbish dump used to be, we'll ask for whatever is left of our share in the land.'

'What will you do in that blighted area?' I asked.

'We'll resettle the people who lived off the rubbish.'

'Then what?' I asked.

'Rehabilitate the dump.'

'Rehabilitate what?' I asked.

'The dump, yes, the dump,' she insisted.

I laughed like I had not laughed in years. But Bahia did not move. She carried on poring over the plans and proceeded matter-of-factly to say, 'Yes, give the landfill its dignity back. Why are you laughing like that? Don't you know that millions of tons of garbage have been piled up in this beautiful place over the years, turning it into one of Akkrach's hills? It has poisoned the ground water and the river. The smoke of its fires, intended or accidental, blanketed the banks of the two cities. It has ruined the health of generations of Salé's inhabitants, causing asthma, rashes and chronic infections. It's a record of the events and transformations having to do with what the city spews out.'

'And that's why you want to rehabilitate the dump?' I asked her.

'It's not for the concept of the dump,' she explained, 'but for its concrete body. It would be unnatural if we erased this hill from geography and memory in a kind of naïve clean up. It wasn't just a rubbish dump, but a source of life, a way of life. Imagine the number of men, women and children who have spent their entire lives searching through its entrails for something to survive on. Imagine all the people for whom the dump was the first thing they saw and the first thing they heard, and whose nostrils were never filled with another smell. All those who collected their toys from there, playing with obvious things and others less obvious: rusting computers, dismantled objects, remnants of things, medical waste, human limbs dumped by the university hospital; then the surprise of a complete doll, and cars and toys still in their boxes, because the city rejects its surplus and, at times, cannot distinguish between what it throws into its forgotten cupboards or into its rubbish dumps.

'Imagine all this crowd tanned by the sun and the grime, those who were born there and spent all their lives on, under or inside the dump. They don't know any other space and think that life can only exist in a dump, and that the rubbish piling up around them comes from another planet. Imagine all the people who built their huts and their dreams there. Imagine the situation when they are told, "The dump has moved. Follow it to the new location."

'But the dump wasn't just a rubbish dump. It was a hill and a bank on a river. OK, a stinking bank, but still a bank by a river in flow covered with reeds blown by the wind, and a large market for vegetables, fruit and meat. It was also home to love stories, good and bad marriages, grudges, small tortures, the dead and the buried. They cannot be told to go away because we have decided that the banks of the Bou Regreg will become the most beautiful spot in the city. You may look from afar and remember the ugliness in which you lived. What I mean by rehabilitating is us finding them a place among us, a place in this beautiful game. As if we were saying thank you to them for implanting so much life in this place, which for years we tried to kill, before suddenly deciding to save.

'I believe that settling them at the heart of this architectural showpiece would not diminish its splendour, but might even add a certain naïve kindness. It won't hurt anybody. We could add to that a giant memorial for the dump, consisting of an artificial hill of various shapes and colours, where children could play without harm. It would be an expression of an emancipated sense of the beautiful, one not controlled by rigid guidelines and hollow considerations. Add to this the pedagogical gain that might result from it, its ability to open people's eyes to the importance of establishing a human relationship with rubbish. I bet people would respect water more as a result of this landmark than for the sake of the beautiful lagoon.'

I listened to Bahia, amazed. When she finished, my first reaction was to ask for her forgiveness, because I had made fun of her idea and attributed it to the depression that she suffered because of the lawsuit.

I told her that it was a truly wonderful idea, but I shared my fears with her, in case her project raised objections for various reasons, which would render its fulfilment impossible. She, on the other hand, demonstrated huge willingness to follow up on the project regardless of the outcome. I felt better about her spirits. Bahia's good mood gave me the opportunity to ask her about the idea, suggested by our son, for an arch spanning the mouth of the river. She repeated that he had told her about it when they went together to see the confiscated land, the day before his departure.

She had wanted to give him a chance to think about a solution for it.

'On our way back,' she said, 'we stopped at the mouth of the river, and there he expressed his lack of interest in the land and the projects surrounding it, but he said that if he could do something, he would install a giant rainbow-like arch that would connect the two banks; a huge, irregular arch, unlike any other. It would be taller than the Qasbah of the Udayas. One foundation would be on the Rabat side, then it would rise to its apex before dropping away towards the second foundation on the opposite bank. A steel arch painted blue to look like a thread of water frolicking over the ocean.'

I asked if Yacine had left anything about the idea in his papers or drawings, but Bahia said no. She thought it was a spur-of-the-moment idea, and he had probably made fun of these projects. He used to say that absurdity was the only thing that could save the city. I did not comment and left the house deflated. I walked for a long time in the alleyways of the old city in the direction of the river, recalling all the simple things I had not achieved. I had wanted to build a small house by the sea, it didn't matter where, but hadn't been able to.

I had wished to visit Havana. Why? I didn't know for certain. Perhaps because of the music and Guillermo Cabrera Infante's novels, or just because an old friend of mine went there on a journalistic assignment and did not return for a year. I always dreamed of getting caught in the net of a city whose embrace would not release me to another city; a city that hugs, breast-feeds, reprimands and licks your wounds, a city where you could live with the impression of building it, one stone at a time, and think of it when getting ready for bed, as if it were a woman awaiting you. Now, however, I had no energy to undertake such a trip. I did not feel like packing my suitcase and going to the airport. The most I could do was stand in the street on the side facing Havana's seafront, awaiting the three tigers to pass, and go with them to the night of the city, opening the box of the language that sprang from the depths of night. How wonderful the city that stripped off the language of day at sunset and donned a different language for night.

I had less glorious wishes as well: losing weight, for example, or mastering the tango, but I had given up everything and was content to keep up an understated elegance that I had learned from my mother.

When I remembered all the things I had failed to achieve, I felt cheated. This often prompted me to compare the effort I exerted when I adopted big causes and the effort I made to fulfil my little wishes. Whenever I made such a comparison, I realised that if I had exerted a small effort to fulfil my modest wishes, compared to the huge effort I devoted to those great causes, I would have been another person today. I admitted to myself, based on this truth, that the fulfilment of all the aims in the world would be meaningless if it resulted, on the personal level, in putting a person's remains in a plastic bag and forgetting it on the side of the road.

I sat down at a café near the river, exhausted from my walk and my black thoughts. I called Fatima and told her I was waiting for her there. At that instant, Yacine appeared.

'Why this serious concern for the arch?' he asked.

'For no reason, I just liked the idea,' I said.

'I don't want you to adopt it. Your projects and mine have nothing to do with each other, do you understand?'

'I do understand, but you're not here any more,' I replied.

'It's you who's not here any more.'

'Listen to me, Yacine. No one needs this arch, not you, me or anyone else. The new project, however, does need it. Among all the material components the new city requires, there isn't a single whimsical element. The arch could be that element, and might be able to break down the meticulous calculations of profit and loss. It might move the city from a path of pure construction to a path of pure imagination. Can you understand that?'

'Yes, I understand,' he replied, 'but your hijacking of the idea upsets me. I don't want another kind of relationship between the two of us. The fact is, I know exactly what will happen: you'll chase after the project to no avail, and then you'll add a new loss to our stock of losses.'

'What if I like the idea and the arch becomes a feature of the city?'

'That'd be horrible too!'

'Why?'

'Because another, more complex relationship will emerge between us, and I don't like that.'

'We have to forget our past disagreements,' I said. 'You know, I don't have the slightest enthusiasm for this or any other project. All I want is to get out of the pits.'

'And the dump?' he asked.

'I don't want to have anything to do with it. Imagine that after all the years I spent fighting imperialism and reactionaries, I end up as an activist for a dump!'

Yacine laughed and asked me, 'And the arch? Do you think it could save the toiling masses?'

'Yes, it would.'

'From what?'

'From getting used to killing imagination.'

He said, 'You're joking. The arch would only redeem a minor thing of concern to you, nothing else.'

Fatima arrived and Yacine withdrew, leaving a cruel sentence hanging in my mouth. She might have noticed its effect on my face, for she asked, 'Are you just emerging from the heat of battle?'

'No, not at all. I was only arguing with myself about a crazy project.'

She asked excitedly, 'Going to Havana?'

'No, Yacine's arch at the mouth of the river.'

Her eyes twinkled, and she said that ever since hearing of the project she had not stopped thinking about it. She also said that building the arch would take our cities in a new direction that might break down the mould of traditions that weighed heavily on our chests.

That was how we began planning the arch. We established a group in charge of the project and identified the doors to knock on and the consultants to use. We said that even if we failed to complete the arch, we would get involved in an unusual cause, one with poetic dimensions that might succeed in moving something that was difficult to move.

A disagreement bloomed in the press between those who considered the arch an aggression against the historical fabric of the city and those who considered it a modern, artistic addition to a view frozen in the past. There were those who saw an arch overlooking the ocean as an invitation to adopt the absolute, and others who saw it as an expression of Moroccans' phobia with any space not controlled by doors and locks. Some considered it a bold proposal to give expression to new needs in the urban environment; others deemed it an expression of the crisis of the traditional left, which did not conceive projects but rather invented the games that messed them up.

The strangest thing we read during this period was an article written by one of the new yes-men, who claimed that the idea was very old and already existed in the development plan for the riverbanks. He added that a naïve campaign based on that idea had been launched to suggest that only one party in the country was capable of visualising splendid things for our urban spaces.

When the Agency invited our association to a meeting on the subject, we understood that the article had been a preamble to the idea's adoption. We were happy. Fatima, as president of the association, presented the elements of the project, its philosophy and its artistic and humanitarian dimensions. She offered a vision backed by a technical report prepared by a firm of consulting engineers and a declaration of support from a group of well-known artists. At the end of her presentation before a number of directors and engineers, there was a slow exchange of hesitant smiles before they all exploded in noisy laughter.

We tried a few times to intervene and resume the conversation. The laughter would subside, but as soon as one of us uttered a word or two, the laughter would resume, louder than before. We had to stop talking entirely and simply watched these eminent people – successful in everything and more refined than the rest of humanity – as they handed paper handkerchiefs to one another, some suppressing their laughter and others in fits. They looked at us every now and then and apologised with partial signs, as if they were blaming us for leading them into this embarrassing situation.

When matters reached a level of awkwardness that made it impossible for them to go on laughing, the director cleared his throat, arranged himself in his chair, and said in a low voice, 'We're sorry! We've been following the arch proposal in the papers, but never, for one moment, did we think that the matter would be so serious.'

'There is nothing serious about it,' I said. 'We only want to make you see that games are also an architectural requirement.'

'Yes, we understand that. While you are no doubt aware that this game would be highly expensive, and with the project in its current state we could not convince anyone to agree to this huge expenditure.'

'We weren't thinking in those terms,' I said. 'It occurred to us that the development project was so bold and so enormous, it might be considered the only project open to such games.'

Confusion pervaded the room, and we instinctively took advantage of it to collect our papers and get ready to leave. The director pushed his chair back and stood up, revealing his great height. 'Anyhow,' he said, 'I hope you did not consider our laughter rude or a way to avoid the issue.'

I said sincerely, 'Laughter was right at the heart of the matter.'

Fatima was affected by the events of the meeting for a number of weeks. She said that what shocked her most was the amount of power those people had, power that gave them the right to turn a public domain like the city into a sphere for their sole, unrivalled intervention. They could decide to set an island in the heart of the river, create a lagoon and put up an amusement park, without seeing their plans as an assault on the space or an attack on the citizen. But they begrudged us for imagining setting an arch over the river, which would not require the confiscation of land or the displacement of inhabitants.

She calmed down after a while and regained her gift for sarcasm. She repeated that we deserved the lack of respect because we had thrown away our revolutionary demands, and our utmost ambition was reduced to acquiring for the Moroccan people a piece of steel to hang over the river.

Bahia, who haughtily watched us abandon her project, never let an opportunity slip without asking, 'Where did the arch go?' I replied most often, 'To the landfill of history.'

Our disinterest did not stop her from revealing the latest news in the rehabilitation of the dump, especially after Ahmad Majd had used his friendship with people in high places and attracted some official sympathy for it. He also introduced many formal and substantive changes that stripped her idea of all its elements of surprise and turned it into a plain melody in the symphony of sustainable development. We did not, therefore, pay any attention to the news or to her arguments that the new design was a victory for the substance, though at the expense of the form. And all as a result of difficult negotiations, where cunning Ahmad Majd played the role of the unstoppable engineer.

It so happened that one evening as we sat discussing the details of our failed projects, the TV news began with two long reports, one dealing with the incorporation of the Akkrach region into a huge project for social housing and the creation of a new city on the ruins of the dump. The second report concerned the beginning of work to build the Gate of the Sea, exactly at the mouth of the river where Yacine, before his death in Afghanistan, had imagined it. It was a steel arch for the river to pass under as if it were flowing through the fingers of the city.

Life's Small Miracles

I

WHEN I RETURNED HOME one evening, I found Bahia lying on the couch facing the TV. She sat up and told me, hesitantly, that we needed to talk. I sat, apprehensive, as she handed me an envelope. I recognised the name of the medical lab located at the entrance of our apartment building. I reluctantly took hold of it, and she asked me to read it carefully, which I did, extremely quickly, expecting one of those catastrophes that only laboratories can cause. I read through it once and then again, but I understood nothing. I looked at her and asked, hardly able to speak, 'What is this?'

'Tests the doctor ordered to check my fertility,' she explained.

'What are the results?'

'Can you believe that I'm as fertile as ever!'

My nerves settled, now that I knew it was not about terminal cancer. 'And?' I asked.

'We can make a new baby!'

I shivered and relived in one second the hell I would have to go through, starting with the maternity ward and ending in the wilds of Kandahar. I got up, nervous, and said decisively and unequivocally, 'That will never happen.'

For almost four weeks we hardly talked to each other, and

then only about simple day-to-day matters. I would spend the whole day out of the house and when I returned in the evening, I went directly to the TV set. I avoided the slightest physical contact with my wife lest she use it as a way to achieve her foolish plan. Fatima visited us every now and then, telling us about her imminent transfer to Madrid, where she had been assigned by her news agency. Her visits lightened the tense atmosphere at home.

One day I told Bahia, for no special reason, that I was grateful to her for having discussed with me the issue of a new baby. She could have obtained what she wanted without my knowledge, though we had not had sex for years. She explained that she had thought about it, but did not consider it an elegant way to resume our relationship, and somewhat demeaning to both of us. I assured her that I understood her longing to have a child, but she had to understand that the matter terrified me. It wasn't a disagreement that could be resolved, but rather something impossible to overcome.

She said very simply, 'If that's the case, we must separate.'

We did. We appeared before a judge and explained our situation to him without embellishment. He first said it was impossible to use my refusal to have a child as a cause for divorce, because having children was the only legal justification for marriage. He said marriage was not like shooting a film on love. He made a feigned effort to convince Bahia to reconcile, and found it appropriate to remind me of the joys of having children, our greatest blessing. He added, 'If God grants you another child, you yourself would be reborn!' When he realised that his words would not change our minds, he completed the procedure in silence, noting down very carefully our monetary agreement without further comment.

I caught up with Bahia after we left the court building as she was getting ready to drive away in her car. I suggested through the car window that we have a cup of coffee somewhere.

We sat down in the garden of the Hassan Hotel and, for the first time in years, talked with pure affection, as if something in the papers we had just signed had helped end our little wars. As if it had placed us on the path of regular people who did not see a mountain of hidden meaning in every word, or get upset when the other splashes water on the newspaper when filling a glass, or chain smoked. We were no longer people who made their lives a succession of nerve-racking moments because, even if they did not say it aloud, they were sick of living together.

Bahia told me that she had thought a lot about the matter, explaining that it was not nostalgia for motherhood. 'You know that I'm not attached to such things, and I wouldn't blame you, on that basis, if you accused me again of being a bad mother. It seemed to me that the best way to avenge this tragedy was to repeat the experience: become pregnant, have cravings, give birth, breastfeed, climb this mountain all over again. You know that pain can sometimes drive you to imagine magic solutions. For many months, every time the telephone rang I expected to be told that the letter was a terrible mistake and that Yacine would be back on the nine o'clock flight! Then the delusion evaporated. So when the lab confirmed that my fertility was still normal despite my age, I took it as a clear sign from fate, and one that I had to seize. When you objected so forcefully, I understood that our remaining together would kill this new baby.'

In turn, I tried to explain to Bahia that the baby would not save me or our relationship. I did not want to chase after something that did not exist. I did not want the child she talked about to see me so exhausted. I did not want to avenge anything. All I wanted was my share of calm, nothing more, nothing less. I wanted to chat in a café on the pavement of life, to comment on the weather, to talk about crimes and football matches. I wanted to go out at night to celebrate something beautiful I had read or seen. I wanted to travel without a reason, aimlessly, to travel for travelling's sake.

Bahia cried in silence and then asked me, 'Can't you do that while being a dad over again?'

'I couldn't do it at all!' I said.

At that moment she stood up and, without looking at me, grabbed her handbag with both hands. She put her sunglasses over her teary eyes, and asked as she was leaving what I would like to keep of Yacine's things.

Distraught, I told her, 'An item of clothing, a T-shirt, for example, or one of his shirts.'

She left, but I did not move.

Yacine appeared, coming to the table and asking if I had just returned from a funeral. I said, 'Something like that.'

'You must feel very light now. Weren't you carrying this relationship like a huge mountain on your shoulders?'

'It's not so simple. What appears like salvation at first sight, once we've done it, makes us feel that we've buried part of ourselves.'

'You always look for the drama in every story,' he replied.

'You're right! Really I should be celebrating the happy event.'

'Or at least you should admit that you're relatively lucky compared to Al-Firsiwi, who is still carrying my grandmother's corpse on his back.'

'We all carry a corpse of sorts on our backs.'

'I hope you're not alluding to me,' objected Yacine.

I was overcome by a sudden fear, so I rushed to explain, 'You're not a corpse, as you well know.'

'What will you do now? Tell me,' he said.

'I'll make space for myself.'

'Before you do, I want to involve you in an important matter,' he said.

'I hope it has nothing to do with preaching and guidance.'

'No, but it's a question of life and death.'

I left the café and Yacine went off without his last sentence provoking me. I was busy digesting my new circumstances, which obliged me to take care of a large number of formalities, not least among them finding an apartment where I could move my occasional dreams. Before doing anything else, however, I had to spend most of that day transferring myself, one piece at a time, from the material and the symbolic spheres, where I had spent a quarter of a century, to a sphere I would have to navigate in an unfamiliar boat. At the end of the day I left my office at the newspaper with the same feeling that I had experienced when I came to Rabat for the first time. I had told myself then that if I could spend a whole night in this city, I could remain here for ever.

I was still walking aimlessly when I called Fatima. I hung on to her voice with all my force. I told her, 'If you can remain on the line until we meet at a restaurant, you'll save me.' But she didn't, and we met half an hour later, during which time I felt I had aged a little.

I told Fatima what Bahia and I had done that day. Her eyes bulged but she did not comment. When I returned to the subject while we were eating, she begged me to talk about something else, because, as she put it, she did not want to say something harsh that evening. She talked at length about her anxieties over moving to Madrid. While I considered this reassignment a way to pull her out of a demoralising situation, she explained to me that it would open the door to numerous fears: fear of the new world, fear of return, fear of separation, fear of adventure, fear of accidents and the fear of dying all alone in her apartment.

I told her that there was no connection between all those risks and where we were. Then she told me that she sometimes wished she had emigrated twenty years ago. 'There are things that we do badly, if we do not do them early in life.'

I asked her to help me with some of the arrangements I needed to make for Bahia, and we agreed to meet the following day in the office of our lawyer friend, Ahmad Majd.

When I arrived for our appointment the next morning, Ahmad was not as cheerful as usual. Fatima sat on the sofa facing his desk, and it looked like she had been crying. As soon as I began talking, Ahmad assailed me with criticism and sanctimony, and ended up telling me that my relationship with Fatima shouldn't have destroyed such a major thing in my life.

'What does Fatima have to do with the situation?' I asked.

'You certainly know that Bahia never considered your relationship with Fatima to be innocent,' he explained.

'And what do you know about all this? What do you know about my private life that gives you the right to make judgments about innocence and guilt?'

I said that in a state of great anger, as I was struck by a pernicious idea regarding Ahmad. When I calmed down I explained to him, while Fatima listened without looking at us, the essence of my relationship with Fatima. I told him, since he wanted to interfere, that our relationship existed in the narrow border between love and other emotions, that neither of us was ever able to cross that line and that we did not regret it. This might have been because at heart we did not need a love affair, but only this liberated bond that allowed us to understand each other in a sea of misunderstanding, where everybody appeared to be right and wrong at the same time.

At that moment Ahmad stood up behind his desk, adopting the stance of an intellectual about to issue a final word of wisdom, and said, 'Do you understand now why I prefer prostitutes?'

I looked at Fatima and saw her mouth wide open, like mine. As our silence persisted, Ahmad added, 'Because they are real beings, not literary creations like you two!'

This joke alleviated, somewhat, the meeting's prevailing tension. We started discussing the separation and the material arrangements and their impact with as little emotion as possible. I gave Ahmad all the documents he needed to deal with the situation and then left to rent an apartment, since I had to leave our shared dwelling. The obvious place for me was the Ibn Sina district, and I went directly there. I found an empty apartment through an estate agent, in the very same building where I had lived years earlier. As soon as I entered one of the rooms and opened the window, I saw the garden fence and the body lit by the streetlamp that had crossed my imagination.

When I told Layla that evening about all these events, she expressed deep concern at what had happened. She was not interested in my return to the neighbourhood; she was concerned about my new life and how I would manage it and whether I would be psychologically affected by the end of my marriage. She was worried whether I would fall into the trap of guilt and self-reproach and would be depressed as a result of the loneliness that would hit me. I assured her that loneliness would not be anything unusual for me, and that I was not heading for a breakdown.

'But you'll have to organise yourself in a different way and take care of things you haven't done before. Listen to me. You must hire a housekeeper to look after the household. I'll look for someone to do that. This new situation shouldn't be a reason for your health, your appearance or your spirits to deteriorate. Do you understand? I won't allow you to turn into a slovenly bachelor, living in a filthy house and wearing creased shirts!'

I tried to point out the romantic aspect of my return to the building. But she did not give up and preferred to list the things the new apartment needed. Half an hour later she gave me another list, and a third one while we ate dinner.

As we were leaving the restaurant, Layla said she wished I could have fulfilled Bahia's wish to give her a new baby.

Upset, I said, 'What the heck? Do you also think I'm just a mechanism for impregnation?'

She rushed to catch a taxi and waved her hand in a cold farewell.

2

M Y ACQUAINTANCE WITH AHMAD Majd dated back to the time I was living in Germany. One of the members of the organisation introduced him to me during an exploratory trip back to Morocco in preparation for my final return. He was a first-year law student then and lived with his Marrakech group in a small apartment in the Qubaybat district. He spent the whole night making fun of my rural German accent, and I was convinced that he had invited me merely for his friends' entertainment. We nevertheless became friends, although politics and life sent us in different directions. Our relationship remained strong, despite being soiled by a single dark spot – the passing and flimsy connection he had with Bahia before our marriage. It bothered me once in a while, but I bore it with a candid patience until I could ignore it completely. I did not think he held a grudge towards me as a result.

He and others were imprisoned at the same time as I. While there, we interacted, dealing with whatever the place imposed upon us in the form of break-ups and contradictory feelings. I was among the first group to leave prison after three years of incarceration. I went back to visit him with our other friends, and we did all the small assignments he entrusted us with.

Ahmad was a conciliatory, balancing element in the group, until he experienced a severe shock: his girlfriend had started dating someone else. The new boyfriend worked on human rights cases and continued to visit him regularly with her. We did our best to get him through the betrayal, but while in prison he was unable to form an emotional relationship that could have helped him get out of that wilderness, despite his meeting many women who visited the prison regularly as members of the organisation, which remained active despite being proscribed and under tabs.

In prison Ahmad completed his graduate studies and built his political life. He had no literary inclinations – though he was mad about opera and classical music – and paid no attention to his comrades' published creative writings, which they considered gems of world literature. So he surprised everybody with a beautiful text he had written. It consisted of sarcastic dialogues between the prisoners and their visitors. It was brought out by a small publishing house and achieved great success under the title *The Visiting Room*. An insensitive filmmaker adapted the book for the cinema and called it *In a Headscarf in the Visiting Room*, a title he considered funny. One critic described it as 'the worst film in the history of Moroccan cinema'. Whenever the subject was mentioned, Ahmad would say, 'Thank God it happened to the film and not the book.'

When he left prison Ahmad spent three years lost, like all prisoners who are stripped of the best years of their life. He opened an office to practise law which was neither a great success nor an abject failure. At the same time he exploited some land he had inherited from his father in Marrakech. He used the plots of land to establish a construction company that expanded amazingly fast. He renovated his father's house in the old city, spending a great deal of money and time to transform it into the house of his dreams, the way he had imagined it since his childhood.

As soon as the house was at its most splendid and had become the weekly meeting place for our group, one of the city's big-shots developed a taste for it and devised a number of reasons why Ahmad should sell it to him, either by force or voluntarily. He put pressure on Ahmad through his business acquaintances and his friends, using incitement and intimidation, as well as suggestions of attractive partnerships. He involved foreigners and people with power in these manoeuvres. Ahmad, who had never been scared of such underhand dealings, held out, sticking to his rights, manoeuvring and delaying, promising and temporising.

One day he went to the powerful man and said to him, 'I won't sell you the house even if you return to your mother's womb.'

'I'm not buying it for myself,' the strong man replied.

'Even if you were buying it for the Prophet Mohammed, peace be upon him, I won't sell it!'

'Do you know that we have porn films that were shot in this house?'

'You have nothing of the sort. No porn film has been shot in my house, as you pretend. As for pornography, say what you want and don't hold back.'

'*We* filmed it!'

'You?' asked Ahmad.

'Yes, us. Through special means,' he confirmed.

'What did you think of our arses while undertaking this noble mission?' asked Ahmad.

'It was a mixed bag,' he said, laughing, and then left.

When Ahmad returned from this strange meeting, he said to us in all seriousness that he would donate the house as an endowment for the Marxist-Leninists of Morocco and their descendants, from one generation to the other until doomsday.

I said, 'The Sharia does not permit endowing a *habous* for the benefit of infidels and heretics. It would be better to assign it to us.'

He replied sarcastically, 'That way we would guarantee its loss, sooner or later!'

'Why would we lose it?' I asked.

'Tell me the case we've won so far.'

I replied, absent-minded, 'We probably saved our souls.'

'Well, say then that we won nothing but the wind!'

We laughed a lot, and Ahmad Majd remembered his father, who had died before seeing his son freed from prison. He said that the house was his way of asking for God's mercy on his father's soul. Then he said, as if continuing a previous conversation, 'All the money in the world cannot bring back the lost years of our lives. Years are not sold in big or small markets. Such deceit! When I think about the years that were robbed from us, simply because one of us had forgotten a stupid book by Lenin in his luggage. Nowadays, terrorists in sleeper cells, with their belts and their explosives, spend only a few months in prison, during which time they enjoy multiple conjugal visits. It's enough to drive one crazy!'

I said in consolation, 'And all for the sake of Marrakechist-Leninism, we can't even say for the sake of God!'

Ever since the old house was renovated, Marrakech became the city of our dreams the way Casablanca had been the city of our awakening. In the former we encountered fleeting pleasures and a cover to hide under. It put miles between us and the facts all around us. In the latter we encountered numerous probabilities and moments of illumination that helped us understand, in the blink of an eye, how things happened, before we lost the thread again and became unable to understand why or how they happened.

I got used to spending weekends in that house, and Ibrahim al-Khayati joined us at times. He did not spend the night there because he felt that old houses resembled tombs and he was afraid to sleep in a tomb.

The upper floor of the house was occupied by Ahmad's sister, who had devoted herself to serving her brother before, during and after his imprisonment. She was a woman whose feelings had been purified by time and who had become a source of serenity. As soon as you met her, her embrace and smile erased any trace of the world's claws, which might have touched you recently or long ago. She spoke laconically, one hand resting on the other, staring at you with two large black eyes, and you immediately felt sorry for those who did not know her. She was fifteen years older than her brother Ahmad, but she addressed him as 'my dear', as if he were older than her. She did it out of affection for him and, as she used to say, in consideration for him, because he was the only brother among seven sisters. Her name was Ghaliya, but among us, for our families, our lawyers and our rights groups, she was known as 'Mother Ghaliya'. She had acquired the name for the many times she had stood at the gates of courthouses and prisons, for all that she endured on the roads and in trains and waiting-rooms, until she became one of those miracle women who, due to arbitrary detentions, were cast into the furnace of a world they never suspected existed. They then domesticated it until it became a fluffy cat playing at their feet. Because this was how she was, Ahmad would say, 'She's *al-ghaliya*, the precious one, neither selling nor buying.' I think she liked the phrase which was taken from Al-Bidaoui's *'aytah*. Whenever anyone joked with her about it, she blushed.

Ghaliya lived peacefully in the house until we arrived. She would then supervise the business of the kitchen, and cook so many dishes it seemed it was the last meal of our lives. Afterwards, she would retreat upstairs or go to visit one of her sisters, depending on the evening's mood. At age sixty-five she did not appear to have totally despaired of trying her luck at building a home of her own. She did not seem to regret anything and lived her life believing that, in any case, only the best would happen to her. If Ahmad married and had children, she would devote her life to raising them, and this would be the best that could happen to her.

Ahmad, though, only ever got as far as the first few pages of his love stories, just like the books he read. We, on the other hand, watched every affair intensely fearful that a woman would appear at the house, thereby causing us to lose it, or even lose Marrakech completely. Whenever we joked with Ahmad about this, he claimed that the house was among the few liberated areas in a city that rich French people had reoccupied without colonisation or a protectorate.

Marrakech had, in fact, literally and figuratively lost its authenticity over the last ten years. Property prices shot sky-high; the old houses, the *riyadhs* and the hotels were lost to their original owners. An earthquake shook the city, wiping away historic lanes, alleyways and neighbourhoods, for palaces, restaurants, residences and guesthouses to sprout in their place. A property war broke out among the new owners, pushing them to compete in building amazing edifices suitable for their exotic dreams. They pulled ceilings, doors and mosaics from here and there, spreading fever in the joints of the old houses, which had to endure the sawing, chopping and extracting of their parts, which were then aggressively transplanted in palaces and *riyadhs* that remained hermetically closed to the city's clandestine nights. The palaces mixed architectural styles that had no connection with Marrakech. These styles and forms were imported by the newcomers, collected during their trips and from films and paintings discovered in India, Turkey, Iran, Mongolia, China, Yemen and Zanzibar. In this jumble, for which they received official permits as a way to restore the memory of the city, that memory was totally and permanently obliterated.

At the heart of this new style, the wealthy piled up the *objets d'art* they had collected all over the world: glassware, mosaics, carvings, vessels, rugs, musical instruments and even columns, marble and pottery from archaeological sites across the globe. Had all this been subjected to an investigation, it would have been the largest collection of stolen memory. The external layout of the city remained the way it had been, consisting of alleys and lanes bearing the names of the city's saints, scholars and tribes. A secret city sprang up in its midst, selling the one thousand and one nights packaged in size and quantity to order. Marrakech disappeared and another Marrakech took its place that hid the loss.

Marrakech lived, grew, built and expanded; it attracted millions of tourists and hundreds of hotels, restaurants and nightclubs. It ate, drank, sold, bought and danced until the dawn call to prayer was heard from the Koutoubia. Everyone found their needs met in the revival; simple people found their subsistence, property tycoons found the fortune they dreamed of and white-slave traders found their clients. We too found our needs in a city years younger than us that accepted us and gave us protection and illusions of safety.

I found in Marrakech the elements that helped me quickly cover the distance between things, a significant achievement for someone like me who needed to exert a superhuman effort, like rowing against the current, to move from one condition to another. In Marrakech, I could put myself at the disposal of the city's whims to do with me whatever it pleased. The city could decide what I did and did not deserve. When I scored an achievement, I told myself that this was what I deserved. At that point I was able to travel vast distances without feeling extreme fatigue, because it was not the distances that exhausted me but rather my burdens. I also found the remains of something alive that moved within me from time to time like a smouldering ember. I experienced that while walking and unexpectedly encountering faces that had not yet lost their primitive quality, faces that came from modest neighbourhoods within the city limits of Marrakech. They crossed the souqs carrying merchandise that would help them survive and keep them at the margins of life and at the margins of people who consume tons of costly things. When I saw the food carts, the spice and perfume shops, the vendors of medicinal herbs, vegetables and fruit, I remembered that all those things had a scent. Places were broken when they had no smell.

Whenever I visited Marrakech, Ghaliya took advantage of my presence alone in the house to talk at length about our childhoods. I never knew why she did it. I talked about my mother and she talked about her mother; we recalled our fear of amulets and saints' tombs. She remembered something akin to a love story that she experienced with a maternal cousin, and I remembered my maternal cousin, an employee at the German embassy, with whom I exchanged passionate kisses on the roof. We remembered dishes we liked and others we hated.

We concluded with the conviction that leaving childhood was the eternal repetition of the exit from paradise.

On one such visit I was getting ready to go out, pleased with this exchange, when Ahmad Majd called, asking to see me immediately. After a nervous discussion we agreed to meet in Ibrahim al-Khayati's house in Casablanca the following evening.

Ibrahim was standing in the living room, which overlooked the garden and the swimming pool. He looked like someone about to announce the results of a TV competition. Ahmad and Bahia, on the other hand, were slumped in armchairs, but as soon as I entered they stood up with unusual enthusiasm and kissed me warmly.

I had only seen Bahia twice since our divorce, once to settle some legal questions and the second time when we visited my father at her request. I had the strange feeling that she had come from a distant past. I told her, sincerely, that I missed her, unaware of the awkwardness of the situation. She was moved and replied in a polite manner that seemed funny to me. Ahmad, on the other hand, appeared restless.

I asked him, 'What's this new catastrophe that you want to see me about so urgently?'

He jumped to his feet trying to control a situation I had not discerned. There was an incomprehensible nervousness in the air, causing Ibrahim to pour tea for ten when there were only four of us. Ahmad was waving his hands and arms with an abruptness that surpassed any verbal construction. He spoke like someone throwing away something he wanted to get rid of.

'Bahia and I have decided to get married.'

The sentence felt cold and heavy when I first heard it, then it became complex as silence surrounded it. I remembered a malicious idea that had crossed my mind when I had been in

Ahmad's office, listening to him trying to dissuade me from destroying something essential in my life. I remembered as well the passing relationship he and Bahia had had before our marriage, one that had bothered me from time to time. At this moment, that insignificant sentence transformed into something hurtful, humiliating and difficult to swallow. I stood up, wishing only to get away from the situation. I had no special feelings towards him, and I was neither angry nor resentful. I was simply disgusted.

So when Ibrahim led me to the garden, looking for words to ease the shock he thought I had experienced, I explained to him that I had no need for consolation and couldn't care less about what had happened. All I wanted to know, if possible, was when it had happened, when had the idea been born – if, that is, the original idea had truly died. When and where had the decision been taken? Was it during those years when we all ate and drank around one table? Was it before Yacine's death or after? Was it when Ahmad was handling the land case or when he was handling our divorce? When and how? Why was it that every time something happened to me, I did not see it coming?

I heard Bahia's voice behind me, saying, 'Please don't bother yourself with useless questions. When Ahmad insisted on knowing the direct reason for our divorce, I had to tell him the story of the baby I wanted and you did not. That is all there is to it. If it will upset you, I won't do it, I swear I won't.'

I told her that it did not matter to me or hurt me. I headed straight out of the garden on to the deserted street on that bizarre Sunday evening. I realised once more that what had happened and the way it had happened, with the words and emotions it had provoked, wouldn't have happened to me had I left at the right time. Why hadn't I left every time it had seemed obvious to leave? Why had I squandered so much existence during a quarter of a century of procrastination and waiting?

I walked for a long time and then got on the seven o'clock train to Rabat. As I arrived in the capital, I imagined Ahmad with his short stature sleeping with Bahia and whispering words of love to her in a Marrakech accent. I imagined telling him angrily that even if he stole every woman in the world, he would never get over the humiliation of the woman who dumped him for his lawyer while he was in prison.

I regretted the cruel thoughts, and thanked God that I had not actually said any of it. I read the day's newspapers before I went up to my apartment, where I slept for a whole day without dreams.

When I woke up I found my voicemail full of anxious messages about my disappearance. I also found text messages from my colleagues at the paper informing me about the recent break up of a sleeper cell. I was reading those messages when another arrived from Fatima asking me to call her. I dialled her number and heard her joyful voice immediately on the line.

'You sound very happy!' I said.

'Not at all. I talked to Ahmad Majd and guess what his comment was on the happy marriage?' she asked.

'You're invited?'

'No, he said to me: what do you expect me to do? I have devoted my life to correcting the mistakes of the left!'

I told her, 'I'm afraid that is going to be the last sarcastic sentence he will utter.'

'Why?' she asked.

'Because he's entering the sea of darkness.'

'Don't be a bird of ill omen. Watch out for yourself. Do you have any new information about the cell?'

'Not yet. I'm meeting my colleagues shortly.'

'It seems it's linked to the Madrid group.'

'We'll see. I'll call you later.'

'Kisses,' she replied.

On my way to meet colleagues at the Beach restaurant, Yacine nudged me and asked, 'What happened to you? Where did you disappear?'

'Do you know that your mother is getting married?'

'Really?' he said. 'Wonders never cease, for the living.'

'Is this your only reaction to the news?' I asked.

'We are not surprised by anything, as you know.'

'I expected you at least to be embarrassed by what happened!'

'Listen, death is no joke. We don't go through all this terror to remain subject to emotions and shyness.'

'Regardless, I must tell you that the main reason for our divorce and the door being flung wide open to this marriage is you.'

'I know, but don't expect me to develop a guilt complex.'

'You also know, don't you, that the idea of the new baby is just compensating for you?'

'No one compensates for anyone. The baby won't replace me; Ahmad Majd won't take your place; and no other woman will replace Bahia. Whenever you get attached to human beings, they become an eternal curse, like the colour of your eyes.'

'I'm surprised to hear you say that,' I said.

'Let it go. Can I ask you to do something for me?'

'Go ahead, ask.'

'Don't be harsh with Bahia. She's a very sad woman.'

3

I SPENT THE EVENING WITH work colleagues at the Beach restaurant, and stayed late talking about terrorism. One of my colleagues remarked that terrorism had truly succeeded when it took up so much of our time. He also said that, in the end, terrorism was one of the dangers of modern life, no less and no more. It claimed far fewer people than traffic accidents, smoking, drugs or illness. Life itself was more fatal than terrorism. We were unnecessarily panicked, he said, and Moroccans in particular were scared of everything.

Some of my other colleagues were convinced that the largest powers would succeed in formulating effective and extremely expensive security policies, leaving only our cities hostage and easy prey for terrorism. Each one of us would then adopt a personal security policy. We would all wear Pakistani clothes and denounce to the sheikhs those who drank alcohol in our buildings and the women who displayed their charms. If one of them wanted to add a young girl from our family to his harem, we would help him fulfil his wish.

'Everything terrorism does has to do with women,' Abbas, a colleague, said. 'Women are terrorism's only concern.'

'Everything we do or don't do is for the sake of women,' another responded. Gradually the conversation became knotty as it touched on political Islam, its ties to terrorist organisations, and who benefited from whom. The disagreements increased and our voices grew strident, until we suddenly became aware of the silence in the restaurant. Someone said as we were leaving, 'It's very late.'

Abbas said loudly as he was opening his car door, 'Who would like to join me at a last stop?'

'Have pity on yourself!' I said.

He replied, with a phrase attributed to Saadi Youssef, 'The nation is perishing, let's perish with it.'

On my way back home I called Layla and talked with her at length about people who entered our lives by coincidence, became predatory beings and devoured our existence one portion at a time, while we were unable to stop them.

'This situation has a clear, precise name. It's called cowardice,' Layla said.

'Not exactly,' I said, 'because the victim might be courageous in other situations.'

'It's still cowardice, because cowardice also means being selective in your courage. There's no greater cowardice than not resisting someone who is eating you up.'

'Well I'm a coward then. That's all there is to it!'

'I don't know why you say that. We're talking in the absolute,' Layla said.

When we ended our telephone conversation, I felt oppressed. I wondered why I asked questions that led me to humiliating diagnoses. Why did I insist on going around in circles on the same spot, raising all the dust of the world around me?

When I arrived home I found a voice message from Ahmad telling me, 'Call me even if you get home at dawn.' There was another message from Bahia inviting me to have lunch with her any day I liked, and a third message from Layla in which she apologised for having been rude. I only returned Layla's call to tell her, 'Yes, very rude.' As soon as I hung up, she called me back and said, 'Why don't you come round?'

I took a quick shower and went to her place.

As I was getting ready to leave her, she said, 'I want to see you sleeping.'

'If I stay another minute, I will fall asleep,' I replied.

She rushed to the alarm clock and set it for five a.m.

'Why the alarm clock?' I asked. 'You'll wake me up when you're tired of watching me sleep.'

'I'll also go to sleep,' she said. 'I want to sense you. I don't mean watching you asleep. I just want to feel that you're here and that you'll fall asleep and wake up like you do normally.'

The alarm clock rang. I got up, dressed and returned home sleepy, half dreaming of Layla standing shivering in front of the lift door, begging me to open my eyes and send her a message as soon as I arrived home.

'I've arrived!'

Ahmad pulled me back out of the clouds of sleep at seven a.m., when he appeared at my door saying, 'Ghaliya packed her bags and left.'

'Why did she do that? What happened?' I asked.

'She's dead set against my marriage. She said, "If Youssef had done the same to you, I would have been equally upset."'

'What did you tell her?'

'I told her that you consented and did not see anything wrong with it.'

'But that's not true.'

'God Almighty, it's true. You consent and deep down you thank God for this divine arrangement that suits you and suits us.'

I begged him to let me sleep, as I needed to be fit to work in the afternoon, but after he left I was unable to go back to sleep. I wrote an article entitled 'Terrorism As I Do Not Understand It' which included some of what my colleagues and I had discussed the previous evening and other ideas that occurred to me as I thought about the explosions of 16 May 2003 in Casablanca. This deadly violence was blamed on social injustice, poverty, inadequate housing, Zionist aggression and the war on Iraq. Some blamed the events on the lack of political solutions. Could we ever comprehend a person's decision to detonate himself in a restaurant, in a mosque, in front of a school or in a funeral procession? How can slitting the throats of children from ear to ear in an Algerian village be a kind of expression? How did we ever give birth to such creatures?

After writing that essay I wrote, without much enthusiasm, another instalment for *Letters to My Beloved*. I discussed how relationships transform us into nourishment to be gulped down. I reflected on the shocks contained in every new relationship, the shocks we feel when we consider objectively what we have become in the eyes of this incredible being. I wrote about how, when we consider the way our emotions are generated, different words fill our mouths, how we walk the city with steps that do not seem to be ours, and how our body awakens near us yet far from us, how we insist it is for us while it insists it is against us.

I then wrote about something I had dreamed, but it was not in a dream: I recognised you from your walk and your hairdo. I was a few steps behind you and I decided to get ahead of you to be sure, but you quickened your pace and I could not catch up with you. Your face appeared and disappeared depending on whether I got closer or farther away from you. I was exhausted and decided to call your name, but I could not remember it or your facial features. I kept following you even when I no longer knew why, or why I wanted to get ahead of you and examine your face. I had the impression that you asked me, 'What?' Exhausted, I replied, 'I do not know.' My mouth was dry, so I entered the first café I found and drank lots of water without quenching my thirst.

When I sat behind the glass wall in the café I felt a heavy weight crumble inside me, but it was not inside me. The front of the café, its glass doors and windows, were reduced to thick debris that separated me from the world, but when it obstructed my view totally, I remembered you once again. I stood ready to catch up with you. 'Listen, I can't get out of the café, it's called the Majes . . . the Majestique, in front of the garden and close to the Grand Hotel. Call the fire brigade and civil defence. Come and save me.'

I WENT to Marrakech for Ghaliya's sake. She received me in floods of tears at her sister's house. I told her the truth: 'I don't like this marriage. There's something ugly about it I can't pinpoint, but my gut feeling is that it will give Ahmad some peace and save Bahia.' She kept raising and lowering her hands, opening and closing them, as if she wanted her hands to say what her tongue could not express. Then she told me that she was concerned about our friendship, but I reassured her that nothing would ruin it. She smiled and said everything around us had changed and we couldn't understand anything any more. I was about to tell her that the only thing that had changed was our tolerance, but I refrained, lest I add to her confusion.

We returned together to the old house. Ahmad had opened it up for the evening gathering and had filled a large straw basket at the entrance of the main hall with fragrant rose petals.

As soon as Ghaliya crossed the threshold, he filled his hands with petals and threw them wherever she went, in front of her, behind her, and over her head, while she tried to stop him, embarrassed and tearful. But he continued to shower her, mumbling mysterious supplications. I thought that it would be difficult to erase from our life someone capable of dousing Ghaliya's anger with rose petals. Ahmad could transition smoothly between sitting on a moped flitting through rain, and the position of a holy man comfortable in his eternal pose. He went effortlessly from praying at Sidi Bel-Abbas Mausoleum to an evening at the Pasha Club, without incurring any split in his personality. He was permanently in control and forever brittle.

The following day Ahmad and I were returning to the house from a long dinner, when suddenly, a few steps from the house, our heads and bodies were assailed by a barrage of sticks and chains. As I fell to the ground, holding my hand to a bleeding wound on my forehead, I heard Ahmad call Ghaliya and all his neighbours by their full names and at the top of his voice. Then I heard him collapse amidst the sound of escaping foot-steps while windows and doors were being opened as people woke up and rushed us to the emergency room.

I ended up with ten stitches in my head while Ahmad suffered a broken left hand, along with many other minor wounds of various hues. I was lying on my hospital bed when Ahmad was brought in – his moans preceding him – and laid in the bed opposite, his broken arm resting on his chest in a sling around his neck.

As soon as he was leaning comfortably on a large pillow, he turned to me and lamented, 'They slaughtered us.'

'If you don't sell them the house, they'll kill you!' I said.

He replied angrily, 'By God, never, even if they stick the Koutoubia minaret up my arse!'

I burst out laughing just as Ghaliya entered the room. At first and because of our laughter she thought she had entered the wrong room. Once she had made sure, she rushed in, exclaiming, 'Is this a time for laughter?'

Ahmad joked with her to help her get over her fright. Once she had calmed down and was responding to his words with broken laughter, I beckoned her over, and when she came close I whispered in her ear, 'The bride brought him good luck and happiness!'

All her resistance melted away and she gave in to laughter that made her whole body shake.

The police visited us at the hospital. Ahmad assured them that he was not aware of anyone who had a score to settle with him that would have led to such an assault. When the detective inspector turned to me, I lowered my gaze and assured him that Ahmad knew a specific party and person who had previously threatened him for refusing to sell him his house. I assured the officer that although I had nothing to do with the matter, I declared, on my own responsibility, that the only party that would benefit from this attack was the one I had mentioned. Ahmad shouted and swore at me, but I maintained my accusation each time he calmed down.

The detective inspector asked me later if I had a legal connection to the house, and if I did, had I received a threat from anyone. I told him I did not. He gave a broad grin and then left with his team.

The following day, almost all the national press – the independents, the party newspapers and, according to Ahmad, those backed by powerful personalities – carried photographs of us lying side by side in hospital. Our faces revealed the traces of late-night partying more than they did the effects of the attack. There were various accounts of our ordeal: some concerned the familiar property dispute, others gave the attack a mysterious political dimension and others made crude allusions to immoral ventures.

Since we left hospital on the day these stories appeared, the old house started to heave with visitors from midday. By evening – and typically for Ahmad – the whole of Morocco was having its picture taken with his broken hand. There were journalists, politicians, artists, writers and celebrities from the left, the right, the centre and the margins; people from the political administration, royal circles and civil society. Ahmad was in full splendour as he held court, welcoming, bidding farewells and dispensing biting remarks. When the president of the Council of Ulema noticed that the break was, by God's grace, to his left hand and would not interfere with his ability to write, Ahmad shouted at the top of his voice, 'Eminent Faqih, once again the Left is broken!'

I wrote two articles about the incident focusing on the role of the real-estate mafia in Marrakech. These were followed by a rebuttal from the person accused of being behind the attack. This took the form of a verbatim copy of Ahmad's statement to the police and a complete denial of the existence of a score to settle. The rebuttal concluded with the following sentence: 'No one sells and no one buys in this story!' All that had been concocted in the matter, he implied, was simply the product of the imagination of a journalist in search of fame.

Ahmad was ecstatic at this denial. He did not give a damn that I had been insulted, but kept repeating that what mattered most was the official, public and clear denial.

Ahmad and Bahia got married on a weekday without any celebration. The following week, however, they sent a card to all their friends and acquaintances informing them of the marriage. Before they left for Italy on their honeymoon, Bahia invited me to lunch at a restaurant overlooking the Bou Regreg. While we were sipping our coffee, she asked if I still suffered from those strange symptoms I'd had. I tried to explain to her that despite losing my sense of smell and the ability to respond to any concrete or abstract sensation, I believed I understood life better and did not experience any handicap as a result of what I endured.

Then we recalled our crazy plans, the rubbish dump monument and the arch at the mouth of the river, and we laughed until Bahia observed sadly that we now laughed at our projects no matter how important they were in our lives, whereas we used to cry for the smallest failure in Nicaragua. I said that the saddest thing was having cried in the past.

As she was getting ready to leave I secretly thanked her because she had not mentioned Ahmad. She handed me a carefully packed parcel and said, sobbing, 'These are some of Yacine's clothes.'

I walked her to her car and felt downhearted. As soon as she disappeared from view behind the restaurant's fence, I was overcome with profound anxiety. If Yacine had not appeared right then, I would have thrown the parcel in the river because it resembled something bleeding.

He said, 'You seem to be making the front page nowadays.'

'Not to my credit though.'

'You're too modest. Your article on the real-estate mafia caused a big stir.'

'I hope it won't cause the sticks and chains to stir again.'

'It might stir something more dangerous.'

'Are you warning me?'

'I'm not qualified to answer. Listen, I have information unrelated to that subject which I must reveal to you.'

'What kind of information?' I asked.

'Something horrific is being cooked up in Marrakech.'

'Like what?'

'A terrible explosion!'

'When?' I asked.

'No one knows.'

'When you say information, do you mean specific information about the group, the people and the whole scenario, or is it only a prediction?'

'A bit of both. If you take the fact that I am talking to you from the afterlife into account, it's a prediction. But if you get rid of these imaginary boundaries, it is factual information with only the date and time missing.'

'We must organise ourselves to face it then.'

'Exactly. But take care, you absolutely cannot tell anyone about this,' he insisted.

When I stepped out of the taxi, my hand was hurting. I realised that I was gripping the bundle of clothes tightly, and I was sweating heavily. I sat at my desk, opened one of the drawers, put the bundle in and then locked it shut, as if I would never open it again. For some obvious reasons, this simple and very quick ceremony led me to another ceremony, where I was surrounded by the voices of Qur'an reciters and a great deal of earth and stones poured over the drawer. Someone had placed a tombstone without a name or date on my desk near a photo of Yacine at age twenty.

I talked with Layla and she asked me out of the blue, 'Do you think we might live under the same roof one day?'

'I can imagine it, but I don't believe it,' I replied.

She then talked at length about her daughter, who was over-awed by her stepmother. 'Can you imagine that whenever she spends the weekend with her, she returns obsessed by everything to do with her. The way she laughs, her clothes, the way she eats. I listen to all this quietly and would put up with all the suffering in the world to keep her with me. Then I lock myself in the bathroom and cry.'

'It's a passing phase. Don't worry about it,' I said.

'*Passing*. You call it passing? I wish! Regardless, I'm very scared. Scared of losing her. That would be the end of my life.'

'She won't leave you. No one leaves their mother!'

'Two days ago she asked me if children should necessarily accept their biological parents!'

'That's a normal question for children.'

'But she also asked if a daughter could replace her mother.'

'Don't worry too much about it. Remember that you hassle her every day with homework, washing up, her clothes, exercise and the like, while she lives with her father and his wife at the weekend, hassle free. But it will all come to an end.'

'And you, why don't you believe we will live together?' she asked.

'No particular reason.'

'Spit it out! Otherwise you won't be able to put up with me!'

'How could you live with someone who'd never know if you'd changed your perfume?'

'I won't change it.'

I wanted to end the phone call, but she asked me, 'Are you all right?'

'Nearly.'

'Take care of yourself. I don't want anything to hurt you. Please stop playing the role of the fighter for justice. Do you promise?'

'Yes, I promise, because I'm not fit for that role or any other.'

4

I SPENT THE REST OF the day in a state of anxiety. In the evening I went into work and found two e-mail messages, one from the director of the paper asking me to follow up on the Marrakech story and the other from Fatima telling me she was in a serious relationship with a man from Kosovo. She asked me to visit her in Madrid to give her my impressions of the man. This news cheered me up, and on my way back home I mentally planned another visit to Marrakech and a possible trip to Madrid.

In Marrakech I resumed my investigations into public land, foreign investments in tourism, the lobbies for property development and the power bases. One evening Ahmad contacted me from Rome. Extremely upset, he asked me to abandon the subject. I asked him how he knew what I was working on.

He told me nervously, 'All of Marrakech knows. And everyone also knows that it will cost you your skin.'

I tried to convince Ahmad that my work had nothing to do with ideals in defence of justice and truth. 'It's just a game,' I told him. 'Do you understand? The whole country is full of games, and I'd also like to play. You're saying it's a risky business, but all games are risky. Life itself is a dangerous game!'

He did not sound convinced when the call ended. I told myself I would call him back later. At a minimum, I needed to know who was trying to bury the story. The city was abuzz with talk of property scandals. At parties, in cafés and on the street, there was nonstop discussion of deals and bribes and fortunes made in the blink of an eye. Yet there were no signs of anger or any sense of shame in those conversations, and the word on the street never reached the corridors of justice or even aroused the curiosity of the investigative bodies.

To a great extent the situation resembled a staged spectacle that amazed and amused people as they watched the scenes, not suspecting that the show might one day turn tragic. This was also the predominant attitude towards the endless stories about sex, crime and the so-called secrets of the old regime. Peeking through keyholes seemed to have become a way to manage public affairs. Because I liked this observation, I hastened to use it as a caption for the investigation I had completed. In so doing I gave the impression that I was not at all suggesting that the information I was providing would amount to anything, but would merely add another brick to the edifice of the nation's snooping.

In my investigation I listed all the areas that had been incorporated within the urban zone. I provided the names of their owners, the dates of purchase, and the way they had been incorporated. I identified the plots where construction was allowed and who benefited from the process. I listed dangerous violations regarding the legally permitted number of storeys and the construction and design plans that related to them. I wrote how Marrakech's palm trees had been killed, its public parks uprooted, and its oases springs dried up for the city to be secretly divided into parcels and plots that benefited the big fish. I listed the networks of middlemen in the medina, those with the demolition and construction permits and the dealers in organised ruins. I provided the names of the nouveaux riches who had sniffed out where the action and the permits were and took control of them directly or indirectly. I mentioned prominent personalities who provided protection and the authorities who eased the way, as well as the new faces who with one hand pulled the strings of the land, the nightclubs and prostitution. I wrote about the speculative practices and the networks of foreigners selling Marrakech beyond its borders. I revealed the rings of smuggling, money laundering, child prostitution, hashish, paste and powder, and everything else related to the miraculous flourishing of an insomniac, fearless, unabashed city.

When the investigation was published, Layla called me very early in the morning to tell me that I had lost my mind and that she hated me because I wanted to play the role of fighter for justice. Then Fatima called to say that the Spanish press was interested in the subject and wanted to carry the investigation. Ahmad called to tell me that a very important person who liked what I had written wanted to contact me.

'I won't lose my skin because of the story then?' I asked.

'If it were up to me I'd take your skin and your bones. But who understands better than the palace?' he replied.

After this intriguing conversation, the trail went cold. Days passed without any trace of the investigation appearing in another newspaper. The street was not in uproar and no legal procedure was set in motion. A total and oppressive silence prevailed over the issue. The only comment was two sentences published in a semi-official newspaper, which read: *'This happens only in our country. No sooner do we succeed in achieving something, as we did in Marrakech, than a raven hastens to drop a fly in the milk!'*

142

Though I received timid and secretive encouragement from some of Marrakech's marginal figures – old freedom fighters, forgotten writers and *malhoun* singers – it became impossible for me to spend evenings in some of the restaurants and night-clubs mentioned in my investigation. I was subjected to vicious attacks and puerile aggravations in those places; once, in a nightclub, a person went so far as to pee in my drink. I would have drunk fluids meant for the sewers if not for the warning I received from a woman I knew.

As for the important personality, I was indeed contacted by him and invited for a memorable cup of coffee at his lovely home. While there I listened to his analysis of the situation and received a fresh piece of news, one that I kept to myself, as befitting a civilised human being. A few days following that astounding meeting, the authorities demolished two floors that had been added to a building without, as it was rumoured, a permit. The demolition was surrounded by huge security measures and received wide press coverage and shook public opinion. A few minor scandals surfaced in connection to the exceptional permits that had allowed some restaurants in the old city to raise their roofs to rival the Koutoubia. But the whole matter did not last more than a few hours in a press that knew how to turn the page extremely quickly, even when it gave the strong impression that nothing, no matter how big or small, was beyond its control.

While property remained the focus of money and business in the city, many were convinced that Marrakech's huge success in the field of tourism was the beginning and end of wealth. Ahmad, on the other hand, developed the theory that the North laundered drug money in real estate, the South laundered bribes in real estate, and real estate laundered itself with time.

I said to Ahmad one day, 'You are a man of the law. Tell us what can we do with that knowledge.'

He replied quite seriously, 'Write about it in the papers!'

'And leave all those unpunished?' I said.

'Defamation is the only possible punishment these days,' he replied.

LAISSEZ FAIRE, LAISSEZ PASSER! I left Marrakech determined to remove myself completely from the issues of the moment and return to those of my childhood. I wanted to go where my father was living the last chapter of his life, a prisoner of his blindness and the tourist circuit of the city of Walili. Every day he constructed an opulent palace out of Roman stones, the stones of the Rif and Bu Mandara, and through the fabric of his narration to foreign visitors took revenge on centuries of absolute truth. I would revisit the theft of Bacchus after a quarter of a century, just to revive that story in a country where stories do not last long. We could compare today's thefts and see that in the past we had nothing like the impudence of today's thieves, preening peacocks who showed off their cars, their djellabas and their yearly umra.

I imagined a child who grew up at the statue's feet and filled his eyes with Bacchus's stony complexion. While the statue remained an adolescent, the way it had come out from under the chisel centuries ago, the boy became a man eking out a living in a bleak windblown expanse. I too wanted to step down from the pedestal to which I had been pinned for years. I wanted to walk and get away, as befitted a stolen statue.

After I returned from Marrakech I suffered more severe anxiety attacks and had to go to hospital and submit to a series of frightening tests. During this, Fatima contacted me a few times from Madrid and said she would not allow me to die.

Once I was able to joke, I told her that I had not died out of respect for her wishes. She then filled me in on the latest developments in her relationship with the Kosovar.

'I've moved in with him, but haven't given up my apartment. I don't want to take uncalculated risks.'

I told her that she had made a wise decision, because there was nothing better for our spirits than having a place to ourselves.

When I left hospital I knew that I was quite healthy in body – as shown by the medical equipment – but I also knew that I was not all right. My body carried me with difficulty, while I carried it with difficulty too. Layla visited me a few times in the hospital, and when I left it I tried hard to feel her presence. In the taxi we looked at each other and I knew from her expression that she was worried about me, but I could not make that connection internally and did not *feel* that she was doing it for my sake. I was not afraid that she might suddenly get out of the taxi and disappear for good. Had she done so, I am not sure I would have been saddened by it. I lived as if walking were my only activity, in the expectation of arriving at a specific place, or of not arriving. I simply did not care what would happen, except that in order to walk I had to remain standing and actually walk.

When we arrived at my apartment I was flabbergasted to find an entirely different space. Layla had transformed a colourless, almost dead apartment into a spacious, light-filled, dynamic place. As soon as I entered I felt something both dense and delicate within me, something I had not experienced for years. I realised, at that moment, that people who were able to tame places and give them new life were endowed with a special magic that gave them keys to the human soul and made them capable of growing spacious gardens within it. I extended my arm towards Layla and I walked, mesmerised, until I reached her body. I felt as if I understood something very deep, connected somehow to the transformation she had wrought upon the apartment. It was as if by choosing colours and pieces of furniture, by filling some spots and leaving others empty, she had drawn a map of her own body. This map had no connection whatsoever with the trajectory of a thinker or a visionary, but was the result of an instinctive interaction between bodies and places.

It was a momentous week. Layla told me that she loved me, even if she could not live with me under the same roof, and even if we had to organise our lives in an unusual manner without room for the day-to-day. I was unable to say anything in response. She was hurt and did not contact me or answer my phone calls for three straight days.

That same week the Ministry of Justice announced that a number of prominent people had been arrested for corruption involving property deals in Marrakech. While my investigation had not mentioned any of the implicated persons or projects, people believed I had played a small role in this heroic action.

Back from Rome, Ahmad called me from the airport to announce, without introduction or show of emotion, that Bahia was pregnant. I said half joking, 'One more Muslim!'

He replied haltingly, 'Another of our generation's miracles!'

In the midst of all these events, I thought seriously about my relationship with Layla. When I thought of her like a distant gleam from a vague past, I was overcome with confused emotions and was on the verge of declaring my love for her. But as soon as she stormed the present with her youthful body, her language and her delicate presence, everything went dark and I was left only with her critical importance for survival on this planet. But that was not enough to declare my love. We do not declare our love for water, the blue of the sky or the rays of the sun. When I understood the situation in this way, I decided to share it with her, to let her know the difficult position I was in and to let her know that the problem, in the long run, would be our ability to set the clock of our relationship to the right time.

She listened to me until the end, and I had the fleeting impression that she understood the situation more clearly than I had explained it and was happy with it. When she said that only I needed to reset the hands of my clock, we laughed and indulged in what she used to call a reconciliation with the world, which was nothing but an unruly hour or so during which we pretended to quarrel violently before enjoying each other with passion.

The arrest of the big-shots gave the press free rein to take a substantial bite at the subject of real-estate corruption and chew it gluttonously. Newspapers went so far as to issue condemnations even before the trial started, and when it did begin in the midst of endless procedural battles, people had already spent their anger by talking about the issue. The case was buried under a thick layer of dust within days. For a while, the inhabitants of Marrakech joked about the demolished storeys, the unfinished buildings and the plots of land abandoned until forgetfulness allowed new projects to begin on them. Conversations would stop completely when people saw a driver hastily open the door of a luxury car and one of the major figures of the lawsuit step out.

I thought it only decent to call Bahia and be among the first to congratulate her. I did this with an honest sympathy that surprised and pleased me. We talked about the expected baby with a certain complicity that prompted me to say that, after all, I agreed with its arrival. She was quick to say that in any case she was going to consider it *our* baby. Those words put an end to any hope that this innocent affection might continue. I ended the phone conversation, struck by the complexity and fragility of the human soul.

This period was filled with expectation and apprehension. Bahia spent the pregnancy lying on her back following doctor's orders, while in Madrid Fatima had one miscarriage and one abortion before she gave up, once and for all, the idea of having children. All of us were concerned about news of failed explosions in Casablanca, the death of an engineer in a bomb blast in Meknes and ambiguous threats that no one could confirm as either real or imaginary.

At the same time, and for unknown reasons, issues of morality dominated the media. These were not related to politics, management of public funds, bribery, random favours and the nouveaux riches, but were limited to sex scandals. There was the case of sex tourism, where indecent pictures appeared on porn sites advocating gay and lesbian orgies and child prostitution, particularly in Marrakech and Agadir. There were reports on gay marriage in Sidi Ali Benhamdoush, a fancy-dress party for gays in Ksar al-Kebir, transsexual nights in Tetouan, and cases of incest and rape of minors. Not a week went by without these charged subjects appearing on the front page of a national paper. Ahmad Majd claimed Moroccans had become so disturbed that they had begun exposing their genitals, the way women in low-class neighbourhoods did after a serious altercation.

We followed the news closely because our friend Ibrahim al-Khayati acted as defence lawyer in many of these cases – not because, as malicious tongues put it, he was homosexual like his clients, but because he was a true fighter for justice, defending the need to respect the law, to ensure a fair trial without discrimination on grounds of race, religion or sexuality, and to protect the legal system from the pressures of public opinion. The cases dominated discussion at our evening gatherings in Marrakech, Casablanca and Rabat. We agreed or disagreed only about what was fabricated about the stories that caused ink to flow and spawned editorials and comments both at home and overseas. It was as if Moroccans' only preoccupation was their desire to know who was banging whom.

There was no convincing answer to why the subject dominated our lives. Some people attributed it to confusion over values, due to easily acquired wealth and excessive emphasis on material success. Others attributed it to the atmosphere of freedom, which encouraged involvement in all topics. Others blamed it on a sort of tourist morality, since some of the practices were not furtive and covert any more, but open and visible like the billboards promoting visits to 'the most beautiful country in the world'.

Alongside this was an overarching and inexplicable anxiety, despite the economic boom in some sectors and flourishing tourism. Although the country was emerging from years of stagnation, it was as if people had become more fearful of losing everything and more wary of the misery lurking behind surface success. We were trying to understand why we were anxious and calm at the same time. Ibrahim al-Khayati was the most anxious among us, and went so far as to say that the overall atmosphere was charged with something menacing, as if we were heading for a rupture or a storm that lay behind the calm.

Bahia gave birth to a baby girl. Ghaliya was the first to tell me. I did not feel anything special. I shut myself off from the news and tried to imagine what would happen to us with the arrival of this new being. As I tried to overcome my state of emptiness, I found nothing better to do than call Al-Firsiwi, who was very nice to me at the beginning until he exploded in rage.

'The curse has struck!' he shouted. 'The Al-Firsiwi family line has been severed by our own doing. I knew that introducing new blood into the family would pollute it. It has fallen down a well, and we have buried it for good.'

'Is that why you killed my mother then?' I asked him. 'To restore the line's purity? You are nothing but a stupid, racist murderer!'

His voice reached me, hoarse with emotion. 'You are talking to your father. Have you forgotten that you are talking to your father!'

He yelled like a deranged man, which forced me to end the call, leaving his gruff voice echoing in my ear.

When I put the phone down, I was trembling all over. I thought of one thing only, to call Layla and ask her to come round immediately, because something was about to happen to me. The more I thought about it, the weaker and more depressed I felt. My mobile phone was close to me, but I did not have the strength to pick it up. I felt a sudden regret for having failed to tell Layla that I loved her too and that it did not matter whether we lived under the same roof, since we did not need roofs and columns in order to live safe from the threat of collapse.

At that moment the scent reached me. I thought I was only remembering it, but it lingered in a distant and hidden way, before advancing as if someone were bearing it towards me. I felt something disperse before my whole being, and my pores opened to absorb the fragrance emanating from everything known or unknown to my life. As the scent invaded my body, it acquired an identity that I remembered and knew: it brought Yacine to his feet and pushed him towards me, as it had whenever he came through the door or walked down the hallway or jumped down the stairs. Here was the scent of his comings and goings, his presence and his absence, rising suddenly from everything that surrounded me.

I opened my desk drawer and pulled out the package Bahia had given me several months earlier. Trembling, I opened it, and the scent of his lost body reached me. I had found him or finished mourning him. I had mysteriously recovered my sense of smell. I placed his clothes over my face, inhaled deeply and wept.

We're Pieces of an Eternal Mosaic

I

'I'M MOHAMMED AL-FIRSIWI, your guide for this visit to the greatest Roman city of the Mediterranean basin. I speak German because I spent twenty years in Germany. I worked there and attended night school at its universities for more than ten years. I built there and destroyed, the way it befits a man who loves Germany. I earned a great deal of money there and lost it in this land where nothing flourishes except olives, carob and riddles.

'Like most of you, I too would like to see Germany remain forever a glorious country, facing everything with unmatched power, succeeding at everything it does and maintaining, despite its apparent toughness, a tenderness known only to poets and philosophers. If you have noticed an accent in my speech, this is not due to the countryside, because, whether you know it or not, the rural language is a branch of Germanic. Yes sir, yes, you are right. It is a local Amazight dialect, but believe me, it has a direct connection to the language of Goethe.

'Like most of you, I married a German woman who was most devoted to her conjugal duties. Perhaps she believed that taking this attachment to its extreme required that she commit suicide in this happy land. That is why she did it gladly, not far from this site, on the hill located behind you, immediately after the asphalt road. You will discover later that the place was very suitable. Of course, all places are suitable for suicide! What am I saying? I mean that this land is, in a certain way, the land of her ancestors. It was only fitting for her to relay her message to them near the ground they had trampled with their feet.

'Some of you may wonder how a blind guide can lead you through the tortuous alleys of this great city! I must remind you that it is a city from the past; the ruins of a city from time immemorial. In other words, it is nothing but darkness and only the blind know how to walk through it well. By the way, I would like to draw your attention to the fact that the period from 285 AD until the coming of Idriss I was known as the Dark Ages because we know nothing about it. But now that we know, I am happy to inaugurate another Dark Age that extends between Idriss I and me.

'We will be going down the incline that stretches before us. Please take your hats and all the water you can carry. There is no shade on the site and not a single cloud at this time of year, and I have no desire to bury another German in this land. Before we walk down, look around the small square where we're standing. Do you see the stone plinth to your right that still retains part of a small black foot? There stood Bacchus carrying on his shoulders bunches of grapes from my country, from the vineyards of Bab al-Rumailah, before the statue was stolen in mysterious circumstances. Some believe that an important government official took it to please his Italian mistress, and there are those who believe that the antiques mafia smuggled it abroad. Some even think that I personally stole it and sent it to a German antiquarian. Evil tongues say that Bacchus got drunk in Al-Firsiwi's bar and lost his way back to his plinth, or fled in boredom from this tedious land. Personally, I will admit to you, and I hope you won't report me to the police, that I stole it and buried it in the courtyard of a village mosque located on the foothills of the mountain behind you, as my contribution to bewildering archaeologists in the middle of the third millennium when they find him drunk in the ruins of an old Islamic building.

'We will proceed very carefully down this slope, from where we will cross the River Fertassa, whose springs are located in Ain Fertassa. I fought a legal battle worthy of the war of Basus for that place. Nowadays it's merely a tragic sliver of water, whereas in the past, the Romans used to catch fish there as big as the donkeys of this good earth!

'Now that we have crossed the bridge, I want you to catch your breath, and then move to your right and proceed on the path parallel to the river. Don't forget to drink even if you don't feel thirsty. There is nothing more dangerous for the human body than dehydration. And I am talking from experience, as I forgot to drink for many years and my existence dried up completely.

'Look towards the mountain from the path. There is a series of beautiful plateaus abutting the mountain that overlooks the city. At a certain time of the year, the sun rises through a gap between the blue plateaus and the white mountain, providing an extraordinary display of nature's wonder. In any case, as these uplands greet the rising sun every day, they always have a light that cannot be extinguished. See how the forests at the top have shrunk like thick hair that has not been combed for centuries? Next, look at the gardens that stretch down all the way to the valley. The city eats its most delicious fruits from there, but I don't know whether the Romans ate them before us. You can see that even if they did, this did not prevent their civilisation from vanishing.

'Everything is fleeting. At this time of day, shortly before noon, the colour of the hills changes to navy blue. You will notice upon our return that it has changed to light green. The hills tend to adopt the colours of the time, and when night surrounds them, they stand out no matter the weather. Even in the darkest of nights, their soil glows.

'No soil glows? No sir, indeed some does, and there are glowing trees and glowing forests! Please don't argue! If you have not noticed that the Black Forest at Baden-Baden glows, it means you are blind like me!

'We will begin our actual visit with the cemetery, as everything begins and ends with cemeteries. One can only properly understand a city through its graves. From there you can clearly make out the scheme of excavations. The war – your war, as you well know – was the key to this historical discovery. War is the other key to understanding cities and geography. For this city we are indebted to World War I, which razed many of your cities. Consider the creative fertilisation between intersecting ruins.

'German prisoners of war, among them Hans Roeder, my wife Diotima's grandfather, excavated Walili from the bowels of the earth with the help of the local inhabitants of this mountain, descendants, most certainly, of extinct Roman lines. All that matters is genealogy. All the destruction and the extinction that befall civilisations do not matter, as long as there are descendants to one day remove the stones and soil from whatever is left. Every being God has created on the face of this earth is searching ruins for something that has been or will be lost. It was Lyautey who brought the German prisoners here for this mission.

'He was a sly fox and a clever manipulator of memory. But believe me, it was the children, especially Fertassa's children, who dug up the first features of this city while at play. One of them might have even pulled out a stone with inscriptions on it or a piece of mosaic while looking for something to burn. Who knows!

'One day in the 1920s, Zarhoun opened its eyes and saw General Lyautey observing the whiteness of the city from the Cave of the Pigeons high up there, while down below on the plain that stretched to the banks of Wadi Khaman, his military regiment, his scholars and the broken-down prisoners were busy opening up this space before you. It is primarily important for the north-eastern region and the areas surrounding the Triumphal Arch and the Forum. From there the famous bronze and white marble statues and dozens of artefacts were dug up, some of which were destroyed while others are still there. When you go to the capital, ask about a forsaken museum located in Barihi Alley. There you will be able to see the collection of bronzes which includes Juba II, Cato, the handsome youth, the old fisherman and the horseman, Bacchus and the horse, the attacking dog, the bull, the head of Eros sleeping, and many others which escaped with their skins from this land. You will also see a marble statue of King Ptolemy that was not found here, but you will understand from his white gaze that he would not have survived long. All those works were taken to the capital to be close to Lyautey's residence. Had they remained here, they would, today, be no more than detailed descriptions in a police report, as happened with Brother Bacchus.

'Will the excavations continue? Of course they will, especially at the hands of the Dumyati scholars, those experts in magic, in order to extract the forgotten treasures with the help of the blood of the rosy hand – the hand of luck – and the magic word. Let's forget about it. You'll never understand it, so concentrate with me on the site!

'I'm saying confusing and mysterious things? Yes, madam, when I open the tap, I can't control the gush. The waters of the sea would not suffice to tell you all that this head has been through.

'Over there are the recently discovered Idrissi baths. You can have a look inside. It is all that archaeology has found to date from the Islamic period. Idriss I was more interested in building a bath to perform the major ablutions than in establishing a dynasty. This is a state that has been performing its ablutions since the dawn of creation without ever achieving the purity it aspired to.

'Three centuries before Christ, Walili appeared in its Punic guise, and in 25 BC the Emperor Augustus appointed my dear brother Juba II head of this kingdom. He was an Amazight freeman who had been brought up in Rome and married Cleopatra's daughter, according to the norms of that time, before ascending the throne. That is exactly what I did, being raised in Germany and marrying the daughter of a German Kaiser before ending up in this hole!

'Here the Amazight dynasty might have flourished and filled the world, and we wouldn't have had an Idriss I and an Idriss II, but the Amazigh have no luck. As soon as Ptolemy ascended the throne following the death of his father, Juba II, the Romans fomented strife in Walili, and Caligula ordered Ptolemy's assassination. He then put an end to Aedemon's rebellion with the help of the Roman army, backed by local alliances and betrayals. The only thing that has destroyed us Amazigh has been betrayal, from Ptolemy to Abd al-Karim al-Khattabi.

'Now look towards the ruins of the eternal triangle: the governor's residence, the Tribunal and the Triumphal Arch. Consider this severe grandeur, which witnessed a succession of kings, governors, merchants and wise men. There is nothing left of this teeming life, yet this magnificence still shines through the cracks in the ruins, a testimony to the everlasting, a reflection of that dormant force that life leaves behind even after it ends.

'Here you will meet a certain piercing look that has been directed at us since time immemorial, and directed at this moment as we proceed along the trace, or the trace of a trace. We come after archaeologists, prisoners of war and anonymous workers who all raised fresh soil for this day, to provide us with an eternal moment on the soil of yesteryear. We follow them as they raise the columns of the palace or the curvature of the arch, as if they were pulling them from the belly of the war they left behind. Among them was my wife's grandfather, who, according to what Diotima read in his little notebook, buried in an accessible location his hat and a book of poetry he had written during the war and during the excavations of Juba II's realm. That place was supposedly a low-ceilinged room not too distant from the arch, where there is the wonderfully carved statue of a supine male with an eternal, stony erection.

'You will soon realise that the penis as a fertility symbol is carved in many places, which means finding the notebook would require the mobilisation of other prisoners of war, all for a work of dubious value.

'Forgive me, but I nevertheless advise the women, in case they find a carving of this kind, to place their hands on it and wish for something related to the subject. My wife used to do so, and she attributed many of our delicious adventures to that practice. I personally cannot believe that I made love in this low-ceilinged room, given that I am not such a bohemian. It was most probably because Diotima made such a wish while holding the carving. How else could we find her grandfather's book other than looking for it in places that turned us upside down? Who knows? Her grandfather might not have buried anything in these spots. He might have made such a declaration only to add a mysterious touch to his ordeal and minimise the humiliation of imprisonment.

'Diotima learned this path by heart, its names, its role, its doves, its olive presses and its mosaics, before she even stepped on this land, using Roeder's notebook that the family had kept after his death. The first time we met I talked to her about Walili. As soon as I spoke that name, she took it as a blinding sign from fate that made her agree to marry me without hesitation. She thus fell into the snares of the house of Firsiwi. Only that decisive shot set her free.

'We are now in the north-eastern quarter where the nobles' homes are found. We will head eastwards, close to the home of the procession of Venus. Let's go in, if you don't mind, and consider this wonderful mosaic. One section shows Hylas, Hercules's companion, by a spring where he has come to drink. But he is being abducted by two water nymphs who are overcome by his beauty. One of them grips his chin and the other his wrist. The artist added two scenes, one representing a hunter who has shot a bird with an arrow. This led to his arrest and his being tied down and flogged. The second scene shows the same person being tried and condemned to be thrown to wild beasts.

'In another part of this mosaic we see Diana, the goddess of the hunt and twin sister of Apollo, accompanied by two nymphs and bathing in the middle of the forest. As you can see, Diana is naked. Her right foot is inside the bath and her left hand is catching the water flowing from the mouth of a winged horse. At the bottom of the picture appears the hunter Actaeon who dared look upon the naked Diana. She punished him by throwing some of the water on to his face, changing him into a stag that was devoured by his hunting dogs.

'These are really wonderful scenes, and I am sure their makers charged the merchants of Walili a high price for them. I doubt, however, that the wealthy inhabitants of Walili, busy with their presses and their oils, really loved those myths. That they had them painted in their houses, in bright colours, no doubt delighted them and provided them with the feeling of superiority needed to maintain their influence in the city.

'Now, please gather round. We are now in the middle of the Decumanus Maximus, the main street, four hundred metres long and twelve metres wide. At the northern end of this street is the Tangier Gate, directly above is the Zaytoun Hotel, the last achievement of your humble servant. Then there is the village of Fertassa, and farther away the Cave of the Pigeons. If you cross this mountain you will find yourselves in a village called Lkouar. Beyond it you will find Dakkaora and then Dhar El Khoulf. Then all you have to do is cross the valley and you will find yourselves face to face with the hamlet of Bu Mandara, where Juba III, known as Al-Firsiwi, was born and grew up. He is the man now guiding you in this total darkness.

'If we go down the main street, to the south, we will reach, as we are now doing, the Triumphal Arch that bears the name of the Emperor Caracalla. No one was victorious over anyone. The arch was simply an acknowledgement of his favours on the part of those who received Roman citizenship during his rule and those who benefited from a total and comprehensive tax exemption. This is to let you know that the desire to triumph over taxation is deeply rooted in our history, from Roman times to the present.

'During the times of Severus, the district of the public buildings and the temple, in other words the Capitol, dedicated to

163

the divine trinity of Jupiter, Juno and Minerva, was added to the city, as were the courthouse and the public plaza.

'Watch your step. I apologise for drawing your attention to things I do not seem qualified to help you with, but the warning is mentioned in the guidebook. In other words, it is part of my responsibility.

'We have arrived at the Orpheus house which contains the mosaic that bears his name. In the public wing of this house, between the reception hall and the courtyard water basin, there is a rectangular tableau in black and white, representing Neptune riding a chariot pulled by a hippocamp and surrounded by a group of sea creatures. Within another frame bordered by geometrical designs are nine double-headed dolphins with crescent shaped tails playing in the waves. I should point out that dolphins are believed to provide protection against the evil eye and are also charged with transporting the souls of the dead to the farthest location in the sea.

'The mosaic of Orpheus's house is the largest circular mosaic in Walili. It incorporates, as you can see, perfectly executed scenes of various animals and birds. In the middle is an octagonal tableau representing Orpheus playing the lyre. Were it not for his fine clothes, I would have mistaken him for a shepherd from Moussaoua. This large mosaic was discovered in the years 1926–28, and it is the only one in the southern quarter. According to the legend, Orpheus descended into the underworld to rescue his beloved Eurydice. He was able to enchant the gods with his beautiful playing and they allowed him to restore his beloved to the living, on the condition that he did not look at her until he had left the underworld. But Orpheus either forgot the condition or could not wait. Or he did it deliberately, preferring to discover the enormity of the consequences of his action rather than following the rules. It is also possible that he wanted to see his beloved as she returned to life, with a beauty that would never be hers, preferring this tragic end to her gradual aging into an ugly woman in another life. Anyway, as soon as Orpheus looked at his beloved, she melted away and was swallowed by the shadows. The gods did not permit him another descent to the underworld, forcing him thus to withdraw from the world and spend all his time crying or playing music, enchanting birds, lizards and wild beasts with his sad melodies. In submission and obedience they would crouch at his feet, passively placing their ferocity in his hands.

'That's according to the myth, but in the mosaic there is nothing but vivid colour and form, for the wealthy to receive their guests in sumptuous surroundings that would give them a sense of inferiority to the end of their days.

'What's that, madam? You've found a magnificent male? Congratulations. It won't be the first or the last one during our trip. Every house has a sculpted fertility symbol with a permanent erection. Hans Roeder said that he buried his poems near a carving of this kind. Consider these people's stupidity. When we began excavating, I asked Diotima, "In which house exactly?" She replied, "Beside a white stone male." Tell me, in God's name, is that a suitable address for a place to visit?

'Ever since then we have dug whenever we came across a male in white stone. We dug openly and in secret, by night and by day, until we acquired a bad reputation as antiquities thieves and treasure hunters.

'One morning I shouted in a state of despair, "Under which male did you bury your poetry, you son of a bitch?"

'I was arrested and subjected to a long interrogation concerning Diotima and the poetry book. When Bacchus was stolen, I could find no one better qualified than myself to have committed the crime!

'In the small notebook that my wife's grandfather left behind, there was a poem entitled "Diotima" that my wife always carried with her as a talisman. It read as follows:

> You endure in silence but they do not understand you
> Oh sacred life, and you quietly wilt away
> Because you search among the barbarians
> For your people in bright sunlight,
> Those great, compassionate, departing souls.
> But time passes quickly
> And my mortal hymn will see anew
> On that day someone like you
> who will name you, Oh Diotima
> Close to the gods,
> And among the heroes.*

'Thank you, thank you. I am delighted you like the poem. Let's say that it is a mysterious hymn about tragedy and love, the subjects that people never tire of. If you've had enough of all this talk about mythology, we can visit the nobles' houses in silence, although the nobles love chatter.

'As you can see in this mosaic, tragedy is after all nothing but a decorative element. The depictions in the houses and the baths consist of exuberant scenes, despite the violence of some of their myths. Mournful themes are completely absent in these works of art, and even tragic spirit seems like distant wisdom or poetic amusement. Hylas is torn to pieces by nymphs, Actaeon is torn to pieces by his dogs and Cato the Younger commits suicide in Utica. The endless blood and tears recall an Egyptian or Mexican soap opera, and have nothing to

---

* Part of a poem by Hölderlin.

do with the way life was lived in Walili, which consisted of people spending long hours in hot baths, rubbing their bodies with olive oil and enjoying the company of women and young boys to die for.

'Since we've mentioned Cato's suicide, let me explain that on this mountain and its environs, suicide is considered an eternal tragedy. I personally know more than one person who committed suicide by jumping from the Cave of the Pigeons, as if responding to a call emanating from the belly of these ruins. Even my wife Diotima committed suicide with a gunshot on the hill overlooking this site. The last thing she talked about was the sunset. Just imagine, the woman never paid any attention, in thought or word, to the sunset, even though it is an eternal phenomenon, except once the few minutes before her suicide. For all those reasons I gave up my sight, since there was nothing more left for me on to which to cast my mind's net.

'Now I see everything with my hands! Lady, please do not laugh. I can see the colour of your eyes with my hand. Let me try. Ha, ha, ha, beautiful too. The fairness of your skin is amazing, especially with your dark eyes! I am right, aren't I? I saw clearly, as it is said. I would cut these fingers off were it not for their seeing this beautiful face! No, no, please, madam. I am the one who thanks God for the pleasure of touching your face.

'We will now enter the house of the acrobat. Here there is a playful mosaic, a parody of the horserace, showing an acrobat riding a donkey backwards, and carrying a jug and a sash in his right hand, which together symbolise victory. A scene which for us makes a representation of war into a fantasy, as if the warriors, when they concede or are defeated, have nothing other than this ironic imitation to tame their craving for war.

'This is the house of the handsome youth. The mosaic that decorates the dining hall consists of four circular medallions in

167

the corners, intertwined with four other oval medallions. The centre of the tableau is decorated with a mermaid riding a hippocamp, while two dolphins swim between its legs in the opposite direction.

'Once again the dolphin acts to ward off the evil eye. This does not mean that dolphin and fish lived in this river, just that mosaic makers had pattern books that they showed to their wealthy customers, some of whom suggested elements of their own. We all add something of our own.

'The handsome youth is one of the site's most beautiful bronze statues. Discovered in 1932 under a metre and a half of stones and soil, it represents a naked adolescent of exceptional beauty. If I had to steal something from Walili, I would have stolen the handsome youth and placed it next to me on this dark path, between the mosaic and the ghosts, instead of leaving him to kill his endless days in a forgotten museum, where he hears the voices of the drunks from the nearby bar and the news bulletins from the radio studios. While crossing this place, I would like you to pay attention to the mosaic, which represents an extremely fine-looking crab. I consider it the loveliest scene among these ruins.

'Here is Bacchus, the god of wine, once again. This time he is riding a chariot pulled by tigers only whose claws remain to be seen. Bacchus is wearing sumptuous clothes and a laurel of vine leaves; he might be holding vine branches. Whenever I find Bacchus painted, carved, or even alive, my inner sense of battling comes to life. I have fought many wars for his sake! When I built the hotel and after I obtained a licence to sell alcohol; when the Cantina became a meeting place for the poxed and the drunk, and when it was stolen. In the mosaic in front of you, we see Bacchus in one of his encounters with Ariadne, daughter of King Minos. Legend tells us that Ariadne helped Theseus defeat the Minotaur after she helped him get out of the labyrinth. But he abandoned her alone on the shore of the island of Naxos, where the god Bacchus found her.

'Notice the extreme multiplicity of Bacchus, to an extent that surpasses the needs of the legend. Time left him behind and he became a stone that Al-Firsiwi carried on his back, crossing the rugged roads with him, in search of the courtyard of an abandoned mosque where he could bury him.

'Had the mosaic artists continued to innovate their colourful stories, they would have made Bacchus meet Moulay Idriss and placed in his hands a bunch of the Bu Amr grapes renowned in the region.

'Let's move a little further down. This is the house of Hercules with a mosaic representing the labours of Hercules. As you can see, the tableau represents three different subjects. In the middle we see Ganymede kidnapped by Zeus in the form of an eagle and taken to Mount Olympus. Inside the squares we find the seasons in the shape of the upper part of a woman, and finally we see the labours of Hercules: Hercules strangling serpents as a child, Hercules taming the Cretan bull, Hercules hunting the Stymphalian birds with arrows, fighting the nine-headed hydra, defeating the queen of the Amazons, battling the Nemean lion, and Hercules picking golden apples from the garden of the Hesperides. There might be other labours in the mosaic that I have forgotten.

'Look at the details carefully. You will see extraordinary feats and other extremely simple ones. I personally consider every human being a greater or lesser Hercules. Had I enjoyed a similar reputation, I would have appeared on a huge mosaic: Al-Firsiwi strangling the scaly forest serpents of Zarhoun, Al-Firsiwi bringing Diotima back from the underworld, Al-Firsiwi committing to memory a poem by Hölderlin at the night university in

Frankfurt, Al-Firsiwi concluding a winning deal to rent the Hall of Oil at the Zawiya, Al-Firsiwi building the Zaytoun Hotel, Al-Firsiwi burying Bacchus, Al-Firsiwi changing into Antaeus and twisting Hercules's arm before exiling him to Bu Mandara.

'You laugh because you are drawing sharp boundaries between reality and legend. A mistake, a grievous mistake. Are you sure, sir, that you never did something miraculous? You don't remember. Just like that, you don't remember. As if it were possible to forget a heroic act you performed! You want us to joke? Let's joke, sir. I can assure you, that sometimes shit itself is a miracle!

'In the good old days, I made something akin to a contemporary mosaic with a Roman spirit. If you ever visit the ruins of the Zaytoun Hotel, you can see it in the lobby. There you will still find the scene of Abd al-Karim al-Khattabi on his white horse submitting to the French. Orpheus is with him, playing his lyre while the beasts of colonialism crouch at his feet. Then there is a scene of Al-Firsiwi senior carrying a gazelle from Mount Salfat on his shoulders and your humble servant fighting a snake from Ain Jaafar.

'I am the only nation whose founder saw it as workshops and ruins during the same era.

'In all the mosaics of the hotel, there are Roman tesserae that I took from bags in the storerooms, where they were piled up for decades without anyone aware of the scenes that were destroyed in the haphazard gathering at the hands of your blessed ancestors. No one is able to recognise them nowadays. In return, you will easily recognise the new style, characterised by a mocking cubism that cost me next to nothing. The work was done by a painter from Asila, called Abd al-Wahhab al-Andalusi. He used to drink in the hotel lobby and tessellated me and my great ancestors while he talked at length about his aversion to Andalusian mosaics, which were imprisoned by blind geometric squares and devoid of features and movement.

'To return to our subject, the labours of Hercules are simply a metaphor for the unattainable that clings to the human. Since, as a professional guide, I am required to present you the information in complete neutrality, I will spare you my opinion about the possible and the impossible. We had a teacher at the night university who used to say, "The most widespread possibility in our lives is the impossible!" This is, however, just German philosophising that neither suits us nor for which are we suitable!

'After the public fountain on your left, you will find the northern baths which I will let you visit on your own, the bath being the only place I can't enter dead or alive!

'What a bore having to repeat the same thing every day while trying to make it exciting and enjoyable, as though it were being said for the first time. If Bacchus, Orpheus and Hercules knew how much I talked about them and celebrated their life histories, they would make me king of their stupid tales.

'Let them all go to hell, them and their northern baths, and all Romans as well. I will wait for my Myrmidons in this wasteland whose only shade is my own. I am the tree and the man resting in its shade. There is no hope of a breeze and no need for one. No one has died of the heat in these places. If they take too long visiting the baths, I will have to occupy myself by thinking about my tragedies. Then they might find me crying like a child whose mother has forgotten him in these ruins.

'Come along. Didn't you like the baths? You say you did? You must admit, however, that the tour of the mosaics that I have devised is the most beautiful tour of all.

'Good, I am flattered by your admiration. It is rare for anyone to win the approval of the German people! I have to tell you a secret, though. I conceived the tour of the mosaics for myself, because in this darkness that surrounds me, the mosaics are like an inner vision bursting with colour and movement. Blindness has helped me become part of a magnificent mosaic for all time. Whenever I think about that I feel better and sense that I am close to the logic of life.

'During this tour we have to visit the house of the knight, where the bronze of the horseman was found – one of the most beautiful pieces in the collection of bronzes. It also houses the mosaic I told you about where Bacchus finds Ariadne.

'If you insist on learning about Roman daily life, on your way back you may visit some shops, oil presses, houses and the modest districts. My advice to you, however, is to leave all that to the experts who see the wonder of the age in every stone, and only take away with you the myths of the big houses.

'Now, we are descending once again towards the small bridge on the River Fertassa. I would like you to take one last look at the chain of green hills, which at this time of the afternoon will have a light-green hue under the glossy veil of a blue sky. Does anyone remember the sea-blue colour of the mountain at nine in the morning? Of course no one does. We all see the wonders of nature once or twice and then forget them. In spite of the eternal inherent in these wonders, the most awesome thing we remember is the forgotten and the fleeting. The mountain does not care about us. It does not see that we see it and love it passionately, it neither expects nor wishes that, and it does not worry about that never happening. It is like a rose described by an ancient poet in these words:

The rose does not ask why
It blooms because it blooms
Not caring about itself
Not anxious to be seen.

'Yes, yes, it is the teacher I told you about who recited those verses, expecting us to be transported in rapture, the way you were now. But instead, we roared with laughter, and he was upset with us and declared that the older humanity gets, the more it loses its poetic inclination.

'I do not know what devil made me say to him, "It is people who age. Humanity is ageless."

'He asked me, "Where are you from?"

'"From Greco-Roman civilisation," I replied.

'"I am not surprised," he said.

'I do not know how to recover the sense of humour I appreciated at once in those verses. Do you think they are funny?

'No, you do not find them amusing. Good, let's drop the subject.

'I have a last comment to make before we bid the mountain goodbye. I always found the streams of water rushing out of your German mountains amazing. Do you see any water connected to this mountain? Do you see waterfalls, the expanse of a lake, or flowing springs? Nothing at all? Yet right at the foot of this mountain, cold springs flow, some profuse, others scarce. No one hears them, and their charm is only visible in the gardens and through the birds living in the valley. These mountains cry or laugh in silence. Who knows what goes on in the mind of a mountain!

'The tour ends here! Sorry, but before we close the book of mosaics for good – with you at least – allow me to draw your attention to this tableau that represents Medusa's head. It is the

173

only mosaic at this site used like a painting. According to mythology, Medusa defied the goddess Minerva with her beauty. Minerva punished her by changing her beautiful hair into terrifying serpents and gave her eyes that could turn everything she looked at into stone. You can examine Medusa's face at length; her gaze will not turn you to stone. I tell you that from experience, as I have often sat before her hoping it would happen to me. How many stones have I piled up inside me while staring into her eyes. It looks like I will go on wandering for a long time, a living body among the stones of this city.

'Thank you. Go back to your homes with Bacchus's blessings and my own. As for me, I will drink my afternoon tea here under the fig tree, whose shade covers the whole café.'

2

'Yes, tea, as usual.'

What a difficult day it has been, selling people laughable legends, as well as your own ones, while you have nothing to do with it. You search the tones of their voices for a comforting yearning, but nothing, nothing at all of their own lives filters into you, and nothing of your life penetrates them. It is as if they, these stones, you and everything else in these sites had been thrown up by a hasty archaeological dig to deny a time outside of time, and a place outside of place. And then there is this heat, this heavy dumb heat. Why do trees not grow in ruins? Why does no one dare plant an olive tree in this wasteland?

Then you start your day with a pointless discussion about the end of your lineage. What if they come to an end and vanish for ever? What would humanity lose by shutting up the wombs of the Al-Firsiwi family and throwing the keys into the sea?

Lineage. What a heavy word. As if we are able to give birth again to Mohammed ben Abd al-Karim al-Khattabi and those who were with him. The springs of the fighters have dried up, and all we produce nowadays are merchants, smugglers, middlemen and estate agents, plus a few acrobats gifted in the parody of war and joyfully riding donkeys backwards. The only fighter that the lineage gave birth to was Yacine, but he was lost without a legend and without glory.

Youssef must understand that he was talking to his father. He's unconcerned with what will happen in the centuries to come because he lives in the present, in restaurants, bars and airports and sleeps with an assortment of women. But this furious blind man spends his days chasing Hercules, Antaeus, Bacchus, Orpheus, Hylas, Venus, Medusa, Ariadne, Juba and Ptolemy. He drives this mythic flock from century to century, all the way to the banks of the Khumman, leaving it there to ruminate in the shade of the laurels. Youssef works on fleeting stories and novels that wilt as soon as they are picked up. I, on the other hand, work for eternity. What interests me professionally is knowing where such pimping will have led after five hundred years.

I know that he will never accept his mother's suicide, but what can I do to convince him that I did not kill her? Regardless, we killed each other. Over time, everything we do to the other half of our relationship becomes a grave mistake. Who can pretend they have never deliberately and repeatedly murdered someone they no longer love?

I did not kill Diotima with a bullet, but I might have killed her with twelve years of live ammunition, if only for not doing anything extraordinary for her. I did not tame the country of the barbarians for her sake, I did not find her grandfather's poetry book and I did seek her after I came out of the labyrinth.

I must admit, though, that Youssef's suffering is unlike any mortal suffering. Between his mother's suicide and his son's death, his life resembles an unfair slap in the face. But why do I have to pay the price? To hell with Youssef's minor pain! It cannot compare to Medusa's agony when she saw her hair change into terrifying serpents, or when she met an enchanting man she thought would be the love of her life but who turned to stone as soon as she looked at him.

What can we call Orpheus's suffering as he turned to look at his beloved, knowing very well that he would lose her because of that hasty look? Now that's suffering, not the shedding of an orphan tear after drinking a glass of fine wine!

He shouts at me as if I were a servant who had renounced his allegiance. What a disgrace! It would have been better for him to come to my aid and save me during the ordeal with the hotel, instead of following the news from afar and dumping his miserable advice on me. No one will decide for me. Let him wait until I'm dead and gone and then he can do whatever he wants. As long as I'm alive, no one decides behind my back.

I said I would not sell the hotel, and I meant it. I sold everything to pay the debts. Now I have nothing but ruins. But I am happy with that, happy to rival the ruins of Walili. I am happy to stop by the Cantina on my way back from the site and listen to the babbling of drunk customers, the way it happened a long time ago. With my exhausted vision I see Diotima sitting on the throne in the lobby, protected by my eternal mosaic, in my house, the house of the handsome young man.

This is the only war that resembles the Rif's war of liberation, because it is fraught with pride, malice, stubbornness and resistance. The 'genius', that government official, says that patriotism nowadays is having a development project! God Almighty, what's the connection between this philosophy and your insistence on sequestering the hotel and offering it as a gift to your wife and your brother-in-law? Do you mean to say that the bankrupt are the traitors of the age? Fine. Why don't you erect a gallows to speed up growth then?

Youssef and his lawyer friend insist that I end the story in an elegant way. What does elegance have to do with it? Are we doing business with Yves Saint Laurent? If the issue is basically dirty, why do we insist on making it look good with ridiculous reasoning?

I had planned to put the hotel in my wife's name, which would only have been fair. This is where we wove the fabric of our relationship, in one of its rooms we found our path, and through its complex lawsuits over debt, water and the bar we built our life. But I had an intuition that it would fall into their hands, and a mysterious presentiment made me change my mind at the last minute. She was neither angry nor sad, as if she expected it and secretly wished for it. She told me in a moment of harmony that the genius's wife visited her and engaged her in a discussion about the brilliant future of the hotel, casting allusions that would have made an ascetic's mouth water. Well, well, the story is suspicious. Otherwise, why this insistence from my son, my own blood!

He shouts in my face without shame, but forgets that I am right. Having children is not a secondary issue, otherwise God would have ended it with Adam and Eve. Life gives birth to life and death gives birth to death, in perpetuity. I can imagine his anger when he learns that it was my idea. Yes, I was the one who told Bahia, 'Why don't you try for another child? If you want to stay alive despite Yacine's death, you must listen to the laws of nature. Otherwise death will swallow you, because death gives birth to death and life begets eternal life!'

He wanted to die in a state of sadness, that's his problem. Why does he shout in my face? OK, let's drop the subject. He'll soon return to his senses and understand that lineage is not an insignificant matter. Just think about the number of wars we averted, the plagues, the famines and the accidents we were spared, from the Rif to Bu Mandara, from Bu Mandara to Germany, and from Germany to Zarhoun. We faced the year of the war, the year of famine, the year of typhus, the year of perdition and the year of pox. There was also the war with Spain, the war with France, the war with thieves and bandits, the war with Oufkir, with Dulaymi and with Al-Basri. We even fought wars against windmills, against the years of immigration, the 'Years of Lead' and the years of Al-Bu Kalib. We crossed all those deserts without ever giving up the perpetuation of the descendants. This weak being was born half dead and endured smallpox at the age of five. He fell in a well when he was hardly six, and aged seven Bu Habbah's gun exploded in his hands. He memorised the Qur'an at nine and his mother, may her soul rest in peace, slaughtered a rooster at the tomb of Sidi Abdallah on the last Friday of every month. She did not do it for him to succeed and to win the endless battles and wars he fought, but for his mere survival. After all that, we want to wipe out this nation! What for? Because Sidi Moulay Youssef can't stand the sight of a pregnant woman? By God, if the situation were only a matter of exceptional energy and strength, I would have married a beautiful and fertile woman and would have given birth to a new generation. I would have filled this lazy country with descendants from the geniuses of the Rif!

Oh, I feel so sorry for Youssef! It would have been more honourable for him to back me verbally, to say out loud that no one had the right to take the hotel by force from its owner. It was my right to decide against reopening the bar. God's land is wide and vast. Whoever has a development project in mind, let him move far from these mountains where the wind whistles. Whoever wants to lodge foreigners in charming rooms overlooking the souls of the Romans, let him build a place for them over the Cave of the Pigeons. Why this insistence? I am certain that it is not a matter of profit and loss, but what counts is that it came from his mouth. The genius said he wanted the hotel and therefore the universe had to comply, even if it meant bombing Zarhoun with napalm.

What do you want from this city sleeping so peacefully near its mausoleum? Look in the mines of the cities where, most certainly, your companions play with gold. Do you think they would have handed you these rusty keys, had they seen the glint of the dinars behind their doors? You can dig tooth and nail from the Spring of the Skull to the Valley of the Dead, but you won't find anything to put between your teeth! Pay attention to names, my son. A city that is located between a skull and the dead, what do you expect from it?

I have memorised all the battles of this country. If I were to put them in a mosaic, it would be the most wonderful mosaic in the world, and the largest and the most stupid! There is the battle of Bu Hmara against the country of Awlad Youssef, the battle of the commander Qatirah against the country of Bab al-Rumaila, the battle of chief Al-Ghali against the country of Al-Mars, the battle of the Khalifa al-Haymar against the country of Al-Hamri, the battle of Bsilty against the country of Bu Riah. What has become of all this territory that everyone fights over? Lives were lost, acts of vengeance have been postponed, and there are courts, judges and bribes, battles to enforce the law and physical coercion. Yet poverty remains king here, reigning over the throne of that Zawiya. It is said that it was a curse from Moulay Idriss against the inhabitants, who gave him away to his enemies, the Abbasids, who poisoned him. It is also said that it is the blessing of Moulay Idriss. It guaranteed people subsistence and their abstinence and did not allow the accumulation of wealth.

This was your old man Al-Firsiwi's mistake. He thought in a moment of wild elation that he could overstep the authority of the holy Wali and build an empire drowning in wealth. The truth is that nothing grows in this luxuriant shade, where height and wingspan are made to measure. It was obvious that somewhere there was a terrible mistake, you in your Mercedes with the German woman next to you in full regalia, numbers spinning in your head and deals you could sniff out from afar. It was obvious that somewhere there was a terrible mistake. The land, the olive trees, the carob trees and the Cantina!

Before all that, there was this damned arrogance that, more than anything, pushed you to humiliate decent people. It is true that some of them were no more than miserable, effaced individuals, their teeth and their looks destroyed by smoking *keef*, their skin yellowed like those who spend most of their time inside tombs. Why did you put them on display, to mark an occasion or otherwise, before the masses, to cheer you and honour you, rolling up their trousers to work for you, and begging, yes, stretching their arms to beg? You thought it was a wonderful spectacle, a splendid scene that you eternalised in the mosaic of the swimming pool. It represents a row of stunned individuals with their emaciated arms stretched towards Bacchus, who showers them with gold pieces of different shapes!

You should have thought a little about it, discredited the devil and felt ashamed for humiliating this holy flesh. Don't you know that there is no relation between their appearance and their origin? What you saw drowning in the putrid smell of wine or hash was nothing but a *jubba*, and only God knew what was inside that *jubba*. You knew that. You knew it very well, and you knew that your grandfather was in the habit of organising a monthly reading of the entire Qur'an for Moulay Idriss. But it was haughtiness, God damn haughtiness, and God damn this faith in money and worldly matters.

Let's forget that. Here you are paying in this world and reaping what your hands have sown. Your son shouts in your face and almost insults you. You are becoming aware, a little late, that this earth loves only the oppressed. It is a world that loves poverty and considers it an irreplaceable, divine companion. The people eat only barley bread and water. They never think about inaccessible, delicious foods. Instead they manage with what is given to them on earth and in heaven, repeating, 'God, you did not create this in vain. May You be praised.' When their minds stray from this comforting feeling, they are tossed by the wind and wander, as you did, until they plummet into a bottomless darkness.

Look in other mines, smart one. I can sell the hotel to your friends, renew my wealth, and return to my German den. Nothing can prevent me from doing that. God only knows that the idea keeps running through my head, and the appeal of starting a new life is quite strong. But I learned by listening to the ruins, I learned to let things come to me. Why would I bother to go to them? When they are meant to come, they will come!

Youssef is fed up with headaches. He does not want to engage in any fight, no matter how insignificant, even against himself. I told him that there is no retirement in war. Among God's creatures are those created to fight and those created to make truces and lick boots, and also those who are here to get bored and die as a result. Youssef cannot end like this, however. He is a peaceful man who chats in cafés and dreams in trains! I do not understand what happened to them all. After all they endured, they changed into ashes blown away by the wind. I hear some of those who were with him in prison embellish their words, as if they were jars of balsam, to provide a philosophical interpretation of appeasement. I do not know what happened to them and I do not understand this fever that they have raised to the level of Sufi chanting, calling for reconciliation, reconciliation, reconciliation with the past and with the present, with the self and with the other, with reconciliation itself. As if a great war had ended. How stupid!

Youssef asked me, 'Why do you want me to fight for the hotel? The hotel is not a cause and even if it were, it's your cause!'

One day I will have to tell you that I am proud the hotel is my problem. I know that you consider only those grand illusions, on whose ruins you now lie, a problem. As for me, I managed to introduce a German woman with painted lips into the sacred precinct of the Zawiya. I built a three-star hotel which hosted tourists and served alcohol to the customers. I built the empire of the carob; I introduced a modern electric press that was the first step in breaking with Roman-era traditions. Not to mention the sanitary towels, the condoms, the cheese making, the modern method for preserving olives and modern sewing techniques that Diotima introduced to the remotest corner of those forgotten mountains. Ultimately, only French colonialism and your humble servant have changed this country. If you want me to tell you what I think of your revolutionary projects, I will tell you that they were nothing more than a misleading fart. There is no better proof than the fact that today's authorities – after the reconciliation of course – placed you all naturally side by side with the 1970s paintings in their modern reception halls.

Ah, I really regretted my pigheadedness with Diotima. She used to say, 'Just like you know how to come, you must know how and when to go. If you are one hour late, you will remain here for good. Your inability to go will collar you and your feet will sink into the quagmire because you waited and hesitated.

The longer you delay, the more your veins will die and change into ropes that tie you down.' She also said, 'If a building starts to collapse, you must get out immediately. Otherwise it will fall on you and on your dreams and it will change you into its image, in other words, into ruins.'

Whenever I saw the structure about to fall, I would quickly patch up and paper over the cracks and claim that every building was liable to crack. The thought of leaving weighed heavily on me until it became a gravestone I carried on my back. I experienced mixed feelings: fear, refusal to admit defeat, repulsion at gloating and hope in an imminent victory that would renew the glories of the Amazight kingdom in the Walili region. But the cracks that seemed small and manageable grew bigger, and so did my stubbornness and Diotima's despair.

The war took a new turn when one of its savage phases flared up over the abandoned ruined houses in this graveyard city. As is well known, there is no room in this tortuous mountain for new construction. If you want to build, you have to find an abandoned plot and look for its owners or its heirs in the back of beyond, and buy it from them, according to procedures more complex than those for the self-determination of the Western Sahara. When, out of numerous parties, you win possession of the ruined site in a fierce struggle incorporating advanced investigative, espionage and pursuit techniques, and even magic spells, you can begin building one more tomb on top of the rest to sell, pawn or swap.

I entered this war in total ignorance. I lined up allies, prying eyes, brokers and investigators. Luck was on my side and I made more out of the ruins than anyone before me or after me. Ruins in Tazka, Lamrih, Sidi Abd al-Aziz, Lalla Yattu, Sidi Amuhammad Ben-Qasem, Likhtatba, al-Qli'a, Bab al-Qasbah, Li'wena, and Ain al-Rjal. Big and small ruins, and medium sized, that covered the whole twentieth century and parts of the eighteenth and nineteenth centuries. I even managed to buy ruins from the Saadi period. It would even have been possible to reconstruct the whole history of places, genealogies and wars and the doings of ancient and not-so-ancient Zarhoun families thanks to the decrees and deeds found in those forgotten ruins. This funerary trade gave me the opportunity to establish a web of connections with Rabat, Casablanca, Tangier and Marrakech, which consisted of the heirs of the abandoned houses or the dealers gifted in counterfeiting documents and title-deeds – those able to assail families busy with their present-day lives and surprise them as messengers from years past, overcoming their bewilderment with a ceremony of cash payments in the presence of a notary public.

Diotima was not interested in this activity and did not feel comfortable or optimistic about it. She accompanied me only once to check the ruins of the Saadi period, a source of pride for me. Among the stones and dust she saw a giant snake that looked at her with tearful eyes. She fainted many times that day and begged me to explain the rationale behind the madness in running after ruined houses. I could find nothing more convincing to say other than, 'It's business, Diotima, simply business! In this graveyard city, what other trade can we engage in, to win and lose? Wall Street here consists of someone's ruins up for sale, so-and-so's ruins snatched up by Al-Firsiwi and so-and-so's ruins missed by Al-Firsiwi. Can you understand that and stop turning it into the tragedy of the century?' Fine, now all of that has turned into ruins of another kind.

Let's leave this pestilent place. Everything is behind me as if it had happened to another person. The ruins I sold for peanuts to pay the hotel's debts are now being sold for millions right in front of me. I hear the news and assuage my pain in silence.

Then, hurt, I take the mosaic tour. I begin with the tableau of Medusa and tell her, 'Look at this hard stone. What are you waiting for here, beautiful woman who angered Minerva? All those who contemplate your face are nothing but old stones. There is no hope. Believe me, there is no hope!'

Let's move. Where is the stupid taxi, let's move! No heat is worse heat than Walili's heat, as if it were the accumulation of centuries of blazing heat. At midday a hellish white veil covers the fields that stretch behind Wadi Khamman. Go to hell, there is nothing I can do for you, this land. It is time for my sacred siesta. I will go all the way to the last stone that still belongs to me in this city, and before that I will wend my way to the hotel. I will walk through the ruined lobby and the garden and then leave, followed by women's perfumes and the voices of vociferous drunken men struggling to find the right word to say. Are there truly any right words? When Youssef shouted in my face, 'You are nothing but a stupid, racist murderer,' I was angry and, for the first time in many years, I felt the words hurt me. You can't imagine how happy I felt after that. I thought I had lost the ability to experience such feelings, as a result of the state of total atrophy that only made it possible for me to raise minor storms of anger that dissipated in their early stages. Were those exactly the right words to restore my humanity and my desire to go on living?

They really were the right words! To be accused by my only son of killing his mother and to be considered, on top of that, no more than a stupid and racist murderer! Language is so easy. You can make it destroy a whole country without blinking. I understand what it means to be a racist murderer, but a stupid one? Murder is always stupid: there is no clever murderer. It doesn't matter. One day, I'll tell him that his insistence that I killed Diotima means only that he always wished it! Hah! A man who writes about love and who is branded a leftist hopes that his mother is murdered by his father! We want to procreate, but we give birth to a monstrosity. So be it. The monster is among us.

I will dig in vain around this rotten seedling. I will not achieve much and I will not succeed in developing antagonistic feelings for Youssef. I just can't stand the idea of quarrelling with him, that's all. I'd like there to be a certain complicity between us, something that would help me find my bearings on this parched island.

When Diotima was busy with this mountain and seduced by the possibility of finding her grandfather's poetry book, everything seemed settled and clear, heralding remarkable futures. I felt that I had done something great for this place, that I had come to a kingdom about to fall, infused it with my soul, and placed it on the road to an exciting adventure. The possibility of finding German poetry under Roman ruins filled me with a dazzling conviction that I was embarking on a universal mission. But Diotima with her piercing vision saw that we were heading towards utter darkness. When she got that idea, I don't know, but I remember her sitting on one of the hotel balconies and me not noticing her until I was going up the hill on my way back from the dig site. I had enough time to invent a story to dissipate her doubts, but I did not do it. When I reached the lobby I found her standing there, ready with her question.

'Where were you?'

'I was wandering around Walili,' I replied.

'Were you looking?' she asked.

'Why would I look by myself like a madman?'

'Haven't we agreed that you would only look for it when I'm there?'

I said sharply, 'I was not looking and I couldn't care less about finding this loon's hat or his poetry!'

But the seed of doubt was planted in Diotima. She thought I had found the book of poetry and buried it again to keep it for myself. That was because a few days before I had unintentionally left on the breakfast table a piece of paper where I had written:

Come on, it suits me to be silent, do not let me see again
See what is being killed and let me at least
Go in peace to my solitude
Let this be our true goodbye.
Drink, then pass me this holy poison,
Let me drink with you from the Lethe – saving river of oblivion –
A brim-full cup to help us forget
All the hatred and the love that was.
I am leaving,
But the time to see you
Might return, Diotima,
Here, anew.
Her blood has been totally shed by desire,
While aimlessly, we proceed.*

When I realised that I had forgotten the piece of paper, I looked for it anxiously. I came across Diotima sitting in the lobby with frozen features. When I stood before her, she rose and said in a metallic voice, 'When did you start writing poetry?'

I adopted a blasé, semi-sarcastic attitude and replied, 'From the moment we began looking for it under the rubble.'

---

*   Verses from a poem by Hölderlin.

'I didn't know you had a drop of tenderness in you to make you write poetry!'

'There is no relation between poetry and tenderness, please. It is only a question of daring,' I explained.

'And where do you want to go and which holy poison do you want to take?'

'Those are just poetic meditations,' I said.

She watched my face for a long time as if she were looking for a trace of poetry hidden under my skin. Then she took the piece of paper out of her pocket and handed it to me.

I was folding the paper nervously and getting ready to leave, when she asked me, 'Have you found the book?'

I shook my head, in sincere and honest denial, and left.

That incident, if we can describe it as such, was responsible for turning my relationship with the poetry book upside down. Something happened that day that made me consider the book as a last testament addressed to me and not as Diotima's inheritance based on family ties. I was responsible for saving the poetry with all this meant in terms of violence, exile and eternal fire. If I had not yet become aware of the value of poetry in my life, it was because my fate was preparing me for this striking encounter, which made me consider poetry a fluke of nature. It was like walking carefree, totally absorbed by one's musings, and then suddenly finding oneself face to face with a waterfall cascading down from high above. Thus was born my relationship with poetry. I would even come across it while changing the wheel of my Mercedes under the blazing sun. This was also how the lost book of poetry came back into my life, as an adventure that concerned me alone, without anyone else being involved, whether related to Hans Roeder or not.

We shall see, Youssef, which of us is better able to domesticate ruins. Your father has not spent a day without seeing a building collapse and people around him remove stones and earth and pull out wounded souls. We used to begin the day in Bu Mandara by lifting tons of earth from the Rif to restore the image carved in our memory in exile. In Germany we started our day thinking about a lost paradise of unknown location. Here I identified with the ruins until I became an abandoned house myself. Even the beach house you encouraged me to build in the country was destroyed by the Al Hoceima earthquake. Sometimes I tell myself that if I had not built that house, the earthquake would not have happened. I then curse Satan and say to myself, everything comes from God.

Driver, slow down a little. Wouldn't you like to have a drink at the Cantina? Why do you always refuse this offer? Every day I say, let's go and have a drink at the hotel bar and take a look at the mosaic before going home, and you tell me to go on my own and drink the wind! Fine, I will go and I will drink the wind. There is no place like the Zaytoun Hotel to drink a good wind!

Let's begin then with a visit to that hotel, or to its immortal remains. You may now put aside your hats and your heavy bottles of mineral water. Diotima used to sit here surrounded by nymphs and dolphins. Here sat the poxed, scratching and getting drunk. In this mosaic, Bacchus lavishes his munificence on the worthy, and in this one he finds Ariadne wandering lost on the shores of Naxos. He looks at her and sees that she is more beautiful, more dangerous, more delicate and more prone to despair than the labyrinth itself. Here is the mosaic that depicts the fall of Ptolemy drenched in blood, trying to behave like a king or die for the sake of a noble cause and be pardoned.

Here is Bacchus again meeting Medusa by chance, and she changes him into stone with her enchanting gaze. He was condemned to remain at the entrance to the site, a statue of black granite posing as an eternal adolescent, carrying bunches of grapes from Bab al-Rumaila over his shoulders, until a stupid thief toppled him from his glorious throne!

No need to hurry, you stupid taxi. Your old man Al-Firsiwi is ready for the glorious return. Drive slowly. Why are you looking at the city as if seeing it for the first time? Don't worry about me tomorrow. I will sleep in the lap of the nymphs and swim with the dolphins in the opposite direction, as befits a respectable mosaic like myself. What are the dolphins? Drive, my son, drive. You have nothing to do with this world! None of us have anything to do with this world.

The Book of Elegies

I

I STOPPED WRITING *Letters to My Beloved.*
One morning I sat at my desk and became aware, even
before thinking about the matter, that I wouldn't be able to
write another letter to the woman I had loved and forgotten,
even though I hadn't forgotten I was still in love with her.
Nearly every love story encompasses an expansion in time, for
many are the lovers who tell each other: 'I loved you before I
loved you' or 'I loved you ever since I was no more than an idea
in the universe' or 'I love you outside the time that brings us
together' or 'I love you at a time that does not belong to us any
more' or 'I will love you for ever'. And many other words that
lovers use to give their overflowing love an impossible infinity.

The story of the lover who loses his memory and is unable
to find his beloved in a defined form is, to some extent, the
story of our relationship with everything we build in our lives
and one that we confuse with our delusions and doubts. Over
time we are unable to confirm which are the material and
concrete aspects of this construction and which are nothing
but defeated dreams. We wonder what is truly fulfilled in this
blend. What is it that we call our life? Is it the things that were
or those that could have been?

As I asked those questions, some confusion developed between me and the personality I had invented. I had the impression that what I had endured for years while writing those letters was a loss of memory. I had considered the letters emotional compensation or a presentiment of the memory loss that I would later succumb to. Perhaps in some fashion I projected on to Layla when I met her and found in my relationship with her a sort of substitution between what was and what never existed. But in my relationship with her, paradoxically, it was she who anchored me forcefully in the present. She surrounded me with a wall of reality that made me recover all at once important details in my relationship with people and places, not as a form of recollection, but as multiple and real possibilities.

Fatima was the first person to celebrate the end of my letter writing. She told me it was grounds for optimism and considered it an announcement that a new life would begin. She asked about Layla, and I told her that we lived totally connected but at a distance. Layla herself showed no interest in my stopping, just as she had shown no interest in the writing. She had her own theory about the matter, as she believed I was wasting real talent in writing unreal texts. She would tell me that if she had a similar talent, she would write immortal literary texts rather than wasting it writing essays that died the moment they were born.

While I gradually restored some of my forgotten desires and got used to a simple life, without giving in to the bitterness all around, Ibrahim al-Khayati was fighting heated battles in the jungle that was Casablanca. He was drowning us with him in cases that did not impinge on us, and Ahmad Majd found in them fertile material for his mockery. He called this period the time of biological struggle, because of its close connection with most people's sexual lives.

I used to spend some of my weekends in Marrakech with Layla, until she told me during one of our return trips that she would never go back with me to that city. I tried to convince her that the big house, Ghaliya, Ahmad Majd, and even Bahia and her daughter, were all a major part of my life and people I relied on as a harbour where I could find peace from life's storms. But she said that she hated the city precisely because of its role as a harbour, and that she would end up hating me if the disgusting place continued to control my life. She explained that she hadn't severed her ties with many things in life in order to throw herself into a combination of the remnants of a remote past and a present detached from its surroundings. I told her Marrakech was only a city, not a legend or a lie, just a place that made it possible to choose various paths that no one controlled. She said that she did not want a city that required all those linguistic tricks to define it.

She then settled the problem by saying, 'Do you know what it means to impose on me a city I hate? You're inviting me to hate you!'

As she was talking I saw her face ablaze, not in anger or out of stubbornness, but simply in mortal perplexity, akin to the expression of a person lost in a maze. I hugged her with all my force and said, 'To hell with Marrakech and pleasure. I'll go there by myself every now and then just to watch its hidden disintegration. You're right, it's a city unfit for our story. It's nothing but heavy ornamentation and accumulated layers of paint. As for us, we are living a white story, like a Japanese garden devoid of plants and colours, studded only with bits of rock, and millions of pure pulses dancing in its darkness.'

I knew she was the woman of my life. When a woman can make a city drop from your life like a dead leaf, it means that she has built countless cities inside you. I almost told her that, but the emptiness haunting me returned and nipped the blossom in the bud.

I accompanied Ibrahim al-Khayati to Zarhoun to help him gather information for the gay marriage case he was handling in the village of Sidi Ali. On the way I rang my father and apologised to him for what I had said in my previous phone call. He was calm at first and then burst into tears. I was annoyed that he was so upset by our disagreement. I repeated my apologies and told him I regretted every word I had said. But he went on crying, and I thought he had been hit by a new bout of depression, one of those that had become part of his life ever since he lost his eyesight. I began joking with him, putting on a show of meaningless levity, until he stopped me with a bald statement: 'The hotel mosaics have been stolen.'

I told him I would come immediately and ended the conversation.

Al-Firsiwi was standing in the hotel lobby, in the middle of the ruin left behind by time and thieves. For the first time in years I was moved, and I felt injustice, anger, bitterness and love, all at once, for this blind man struggling alone against a tragic stubbornness that was intent on breaking him every time he raised his head. Al-Firsiwi told me that he knew the thief, it could not be anyone else. Ever since the man had come to the area, he had wanted nothing more than to acquire what was left of the Roman heritage.

Ibrahim al-Khayati said, 'But this is not Roman heritage, it's private property!'

My father took me by the arm and led me to the old lobby, where he asked, 'Who is this man?'

'An old friend. Ibrahim, you know him.'

'I don't want to talk to someone of Ahmad Majd's sort, or others like him,' he said.

'He's not like him.'

'All right. He must understand that the thief knows that the hotel mosaics contain Roman pieces. Even the most novice expert would know how to pick them out of a pile of new tesserae!'

'But why do you insist on saying that this man is the thief?' I asked.

'I know because he would benefit from the destruction of the hotel and putting pressure on me to sell. He was the one who stole the lanterns from the site storehouse two years ago. He also stole the gold ring the British found a year ago.'

'Forget about those things,' I said. 'You must calm down and think what should be done about it. Plus, there are very few stolen pieces compared to what's left.'

We talked with Ibrahim, who advised us to report the crime without saying who we thought had done it, rather than accusing a man in authority without any damning evidence. He advised against saying that the mosaics contained authentic Roman pieces, because that would mean that the only recognised and self-confessed thief would be Al-Firsiwi. We all agreed on the matter and went to the city centre to eat grilled *kofta*, for which the city was renowned in the East and the West, although Al-Firsiwi insisted that its only distinguishing features were the dirt and the flies.

Ibrahim and I then left for the village of Sidi Ali. Ibrahim was representing several men who had been arrested during the town's annual festival held around the tomb of Sidi Ali, a grandson of Al-Hadi Benissa, one of Morocco's famous Sufis. According to legend, a woman named Aisha was brought from the East by Sidi Ahmad al-Daghughi, a pupil and a disciple of Sidi Ali, for his sheikh to marry and thereby to put an end to his prolonged celibacy. But the marriage did not happen.

I wondered about the mysterious chemistry that made contradictory things arise from the same source. The Sidi Ali festivities drew large numbers of homosexuals, fortune-tellers and worshippers. In the same location and out of the same spiritual feelings, the supplications of the worshippers encountered the throng of agitated bodies. Why did Sidi Ali never marry and why did queers gather around his tomb? No one knew.

The alleged gay marriages and arrests had made a scandal in the press. But when we arrived at the village, we could not find anyone who had attended any of the weddings. We could not even get an exact description of events organised for the festival. Visitors behaved according to their own norms, people said. Some of them adhered to the order of the Hamadchas and shared their famous mystical possession. Others watched the blood ritual, when some of the possessed broke clay water jugs over their shaved heads, or beat sharp hammers on their heads as they swayed to the Hamdouchi beat. Some cared for their deep wounds by passing a piece of bread over them, while others slaughtered a goat in the throng around Aisha's grave, or hung a piece of clothing on her holy tree, believing she could help them find a spouse. Some people spent long hours waiting in front of the booths of the fortune-tellers.

The inhabitants of the village gave thanks to God and called for God's mercy on the holy Wali, grateful for all the additional income they got from the slaughtered animals, the stall and room rentals during the festival and other business. No one asked questions in this mountainous village that stood peacefully under the shade of olive and carob trees. No one interfered in what did not concern him and no one could tell exactly what would happen behind closed doors at nightfall, when the Hamdouchi whirling settled into its entrancing monotony. No one knew who would marry whom and who would sleep with whom. No one knew and no one wanted to know. If such things happened, they happened with the knowledge of authorities. If homosexuals attended the festival, no one knew them or disavowed them: they melted into the hubbub of the festivities. Perhaps only the secret police knew, and maybe some of the phoney therapists who confused Freud with the miracles of Sidi Ahmad al-Daghughi, or journalists whose imaginations were fired by lurid stories.

The people said forgetfulness had enfolded them for centuries. They had endured wars and famines, given birth to scholars, leaders and walis, but no one had been interested in them, published their news, or made a comment. Anyway, who were these gays? Was even one of them from Sidi Ali or nearby villages? Of course not! They did not know the face or name of anyone like that. If there really were any, they must have come on the heels of sustainable development. They came to make the region prosper and encourage cultural tourism. Had they come that year for the first time? Was it conceivable that such a defined ritual could spring up overnight? In that case, Aisha's site with its almost dried-up spring, its mud, its tree and its slaughtered animals would all have been improvised that year as well. That also went for the male and female fortune-tellers who were visited by the wealthy grandees of Casablanca, Rabat, Fes, Meknes, Marrakech, Tangier and the Gulf countries. The residents told Youssef and Ibrahim that they were being lied to and that everything that went on in the village, especially during its festival, was with the knowledge of the authorities.

When we left the village on our way to Meknes, Ibrahim al-Khayati wondered whether the commotion hadn't been created by a specific group to serve a specific purpose.

'What should I say to defend the young men who have appointed me?' he asked.

'Say what some newspapers have said: it's their sex lives and they're free to do as they please!' I said.

He did not reply.

I was saddened by what had happened to my father at the hotel and by his condition in general. I remembered his rigour, his sharpness and his bright mind too. I compared all that to his present frailty and his bewilderment as he felt his personal world crumbling under his feet. I said to myself that I might be able to forgive him one day, and if that happened I did not want it to be due to his physical collapse and the end of his power, as demonstrated in his lost eyesight. We are all defeated by death, but nothing is worse than to be defeated by life.

My mother struggled with my father and loved him at the same time. It seemed she wanted to put a raging camel inside a bottle. I never saw her cry; silence was the expression she excelled in. She was a genius in devising horrible forms of silence that drove my father mad. He would fume and froth with rage and threaten to cut out her tongue, saying she was not using it to talk as God had intended when he elevated human beings above beasts.

Neither of them helped me understand the other. Diotima did not explain my father to me and Al-Firsiwi did not reveal who Diotima was. Each one painted the other as a dark abyss that totally engulfed them. Whenever I saw my father now, lost in the ruins of Walili and his memory, I visualised a poet who sprang from the belly of the earth to decorate a forgotten city with his inner mosaics, always trying to point out the tragic fate of every poetic experience in this world.

I talked with Ibrahim al-Khayati about Al-Firsiwi on our way back, and I said that I would return to help him look for

Bacchus. He told me that investigating an antiquity theft would not interest anyone. People had got so used to stories of theft that they had become part of protected heritage. Try to announce, for example, that Morocco had not seen a single theft for three months, and you would see people demonstrating in the streets, denouncing this obvious failure in public life.

A few weeks earlier the French police had found seventeen thousand discarded archaeological and geological pieces that had been smuggled from Mali, Mauritania and Morocco. The news only preoccupied an ordinary civil servant close to retirement, who wrote a letter to a local paper wondering where those thousands of pieces could have been, since there wasn't such a number in all of Africa.

'Suppose you follow Bacchus's trail till you find him in the collection of a rich local or foreigner,' Ibrahim said. 'What would happen then?'

'Nothing would happen, but I might be able to draw attention to the fact that if we continue on this path, we will soon find our whole country in other countries!'

We also talked about his twins, as he referred to them. Both loved pop music, rap, hip-hop and heavy metal. One of them had spent a few weeks in prison, in a case involving alleged devil worship. I said I admired the two young men, who were completing their foundation courses very successfully and had a band known throughout Casablanca. As we approached the last toll in Casablanca, Ibrahim al-Khayati's face darkened suddenly, and he told me with great emotion that the two young men might be aware of the true nature of his relationship with their father. They might have a permanent aversion to him.

'Can't you discuss the matter openly with them?' I asked.

'Impossible. Do you think they would show any understanding of the matter?'

'Why not? Wouldn't they understand that you are what you are, and that everything you've done, you did for them? Do they understand that the luxury they're living in and that all they've accomplished is thanks to you? Yet they don't understand that you are what you are before they were born and had an opinion?'

I was angry because I had suddenly become aware of the injustice that underlined our hypocritical social relations. None of us had any scruples about wolfing down everything in sight, without pausing to criticise the way the dishes had reached our mouths. In our heads, we all lived in a system of forced labour that made others – all others – servants at our disposal.

As a result of my anger, I said to Ibrahim, 'Listen, you must tell them the truth, and tell them also that if they don't want to be your children because of that old story, all they have to do is leave your house and disappear from your life. Then you will see what direction their aversion takes!'

'But if they choose to stay with me only because I'm providing for them, it would be a real tragedy!' he said.

'In that case you must make them say they're proud of you and, if they want to continue living with you, ask them to love you openly and fully.'

We both laughed to break this sudden tension, and then talked about the new restaurants in Casablanca. Ibrahim told me that the 'aytah was losing its place in the city. I told him that I would not have gone with him to those places even if they were still there. 'Frankly,' I said, 'I don't know what you like about all that ugly shouting.'

Ibrahim would not shut up, and we spent hours arguing back and forth about the subject, until we finally sat facing a tired waiter and ordered two cold drinks.

I said to him, 'Forget the subject completely. The 'aytah is the most sublime art this people has produced. Can we talk about something else now?'

Ibrahim smiled and said, 'We are an incomparably fanatical country. Consider the way they deal with music, dance and song. There is no such art form that has not suffered condemnation and discrimination, from 'aytah to hip-hop!'

'You're exaggerating. All artistic expressions were natural and spontaneous until the plague of darkness arrived. It forbade and allowed whatever it liked. It was unable to defeat dancing and singing, but managed to impose the hijab and the umra on the libertines of our women's bands!'

2

LAYLA RETURNED FROM A quick trip to Madrid and I went to meet her at Casablanca airport. I suggested we celebrate her return at Ibrahim's house. She seemed happy at the idea, saying, 'I like that man.'

'You either like him or we go to Marrakech,' I said. She made a face of teasing indignation and said that she loved me, and that, for the first time, this was happening in a completely different way, a calm, relaxed and cheerful way, like slow, effortless breathing. I held her small hand in mine, took a deep breath, and said to her, 'Me too.'

'You too, what?' she asked.

'It's also happening to me in a completely different way!' I explained.

We had a lovely time with Ibrahim and his twins. Layla was excited and talked about everything with great enthusiasm. But when the conversation turned to the songs of new bands, there was a serious disagreement between Layla, Essam and Mahdi. Layla thought the songs, aside from their occasional sarcastic and rebellious spirit, were abominable. Their lyrics were vulgar and devoid of imagination, their music was primitive and incomplete. Essam, who had spent time in prison in the case of the devil worshippers, considered this music and rap, hip-hop and hard rock an expression of a new identity, that of the modern cities sinking under the weight of contradictions and living with the threat of terrorism – yet still staging astonishing popular festivals.

'Despite all that,' said Mahdi, 'we love our country, but your generation doesn't understand us and doesn't understand this love. Then again, we don't want to be philosophers or politicians. All we want to do is sing and dance and love this country in our own way.'

When we went to our room I teased Layla with an H Kayne rap tune based on the melody of 'So What, We Are Moroccans'. I told her, 'This is an explosive Aissawi rhythm: "It's going boom, it's going boom, so let's go boom too."'

She laughed wholeheartedly and said, 'This is not an Aissawi song but a Buddhist prayer. Move a little, like this, with your shoulders and your feet. Don't move your arms. Jump up with your body, not your feet. No, no, without bending your knees and without moving your head. Leave your head pointing at the sky and follow it with your body as if you are about to spring out of a cloud. God is Magnificent! God is Magnificent! Yes, yes, like this. Why are you looking at me like that? As if you wanted to jump into an abyss, or have already jumped?'

'Yacine says something scary is being organised in Marrakech.'

'Who's Yacine?'

'My son. Have you forgotten?'

'Youssef, please leave your hand where it is. I don't want to know. Don't say anything.'

'Do you think he's still in touch with them?'

'I don't know how you can want to do that.'

'It seems that he meets with them and supervises their projects.'

'Look at your feet. I've never seen a man with more beautiful feet. I want you to tease me with your toes. Let me show you how to do it. Like this. Do you like that?'

'Yes, and I love the idea of you finding pleasure in my feet. In all honesty, I've never done this before. It's great when a woman likes your feet. Truly amazing.'

'What?'

'I feel as if it's me doing it.'

'Yes, yes, it's really like that, not as if. Please don't stop.'

'Do you think Yacine is deceiving me?'

'I want you to ask me to do something you like.' Layla said.

'I will, and I know you will do it without me even asking,' I said.

'I know that this arouses you a great deal.'

'It does. I love it when you're like this, when you're looking at me as if you were about to jump out of the window. Do you want me to turn around? I want to hear your voice and imagine your look while you're falling from the window.'

'I love you. I love you,' she said.

'Layla.'

'Mmm!'

'Layla!'

'Yes.'

'Do you think Yacine would dare involve me in something bad?'

'Are you serious?' asked Layla.

'Of course I am. Do you think this is a joking matter?'

Layla jumped up and said, 'I thought you had invented a crazy story to increase the thrill.'

I pulled her towards me and said, laughing, 'I thought you didn't understand the ploy.'

At breakfast, before the others woke up, Layla told me that even though we didn't live under the same roof, we had to make vows, even if only between the two of us, to announce to ourselves that we were bound to each other for eternity.

I agreed and started organising a ceremony in my mind.

Mahdi and Essam appeared. They obviously liked Layla, enjoyed her company and did not hesitate to shower her with special attention. Layla had a magical influence on them that gave them a certain precocious maturity. Mahdi asked us both to attend a performance organised by their band, Arthritis. I smiled as I always did when I heard the name. Essam got upset once again and asked me if I wanted them to call it Blossom or Harmony, for example. I told him Arthritis was an appropriate name, particularly since the whole country was lame because of arthritis.

'Of course we'll come,' I said. 'I don't like the music, let's be clear about that, but I like the spirit in these concerts. I especially like the total conviction visible on the faces of the musicians, the singers and the dancers. It's an almost ideological belief stating that they have found their way.'

I took the train from Casablanca to Rabat. During the trip I felt semiconscious, repeating to myself Layla's name with the strong feeling that I was calling her, that she had just left the carriage and would return at any moment to bring me back from this state of unconsciousness. But she did not return and I kept calling her, mumbling every now and then, 'Call me please. Do not stop talking to me.' I had the express feeling that her words, even meaningless words, would keep me connected to life, and if she stopped, she would interrupt the electric current feeding my existence and I would inevitably descend into darkness. I felt her hand stroking my cheek, but the voice I heard was not hers. I heard her say, 'I am here.' Then I heard a stranger's voice say, 'He's coming to' and then a sharp voice say, 'No use, he's dead.'

As if challenged by this ridiculous statement, I suddenly shook myself and sat up. Before me were an astounded woman and a man who greeted me warmly and said, 'I've had a similar reaction on the fast train many times. Don't worry. There might be a magnetic field that causes certain people to have these fits. Who knows what will happen when fast trains start running everywhere in the country. Half of Morocco might faint!'

But the man's words did not help me, and I found myself once again the victim of a post-seizure depression.

Lately I had been able to overcome this depression by returning to the box, as Layla called it. The box was the store of feelings, images and words where we spontaneously put all that happened to us in moments of intense love. In the box I would meet a person who was almost the me I longed for: outgoing, authentic, relishing life and, even better than that, capable of making someone else happy. There I would meet a body that I did not control, one that lay in the shadow of its desires. I would meet a woman with the extraordinary ability to make words and things equal in density, fragility and temporality. I would meet her in her overwhelming desire and its precise gratification, in the rapidity of her arousal and its subsidence, in her ability to pre-empt everything and capture all that crossed the vital space of our anxiety: visions, dreams, repressed fantasies, smells, colours, crazy words and signals. I would meet her in the stories, since the box was in essence a box of stories, a pile of unlimited possibilities for what happened and did not happen. This multiplicity might be a way for me to get over my depressions. What I needed was a first breach; in other words, a thread of light that made it suddenly possible to break through a wall.

I called Layla as I left the train and told her that I was going back to look for Bacchus. She asked me if this would help me find some peace, and I told her that it would and I would at least be close to Al-Firsiwi. I didn't like to see him forgotten and ostracised. She liked the idea, and then said unexpectedly, 'Why not write a story about Ibrahim al-Khayati?' I told her we would have to discuss that some other time.

In the days that followed I thought of preparing an outline for a possible novel about Ibrahim. In the end I found myself reviewing the landmarks of his life: his idealism, his professional success, his lover's suicide, his marriage to his lover's widow, his relationship with his mother and with the twins Essam and Mahdi, his involvement in thorny cases such as the young musicians and gay marriage, the attempt on his life and his overall emergence from the rubble of the 1970s without convictions or bitterness. Finally, his appearance at the end of the century as an eloquent expression of a struggle that defied definition. When I finished writing this preliminary outline, I realised it was not a novel. It was simply Ibrahim's life, the story etched on his face, and did not require someone to write it anew. If I wanted to write a novel about Ibrahim, I would have to invent another life for him, a life closer to the realistic scenario of a man without miracles. This would be a huge endeavour and would require energy that I did not have. It would also be a venture without guaranteed success.

I asked Al-Firsiwi to tell me, frankly, who stole Bacchus.

He settled himself comfortably in his seat and said, 'Listen, Youssef, son of Diotima, this weak man was strung up by his feet and flogged night and day for two months. Do you think that if I knew, I would have gone on enjoying the beatings, for the love of God?'

'But you have been saying many things ever since,' I replied.

'I say what I like!'

'Among the things you say is that you buried Bacchus in the courtyard of a mosque in one of the mountain villages.'

'Very likely! One possibility among many others.'

'I know you have many accounts you'd like to settle. You probably want to punish this region by destroying one of its timeless antiquities.'

'It's not worth so much fuss. It's an ordinary statue of the god of wine posing as a dusky adolescent. Even from an artistic perspective, it's not a masterpiece. The Prado in Madrid and a museum in Florence have wonderful white marble statues of Bacchus. One of them, I can't remember which, has the shadow cast by the bunch of grapes sculpted on Bacchus's shoulder. How can one compare this with the dull appearance of the granite adolescent? Please! Spare me! He's standing as if he had just come out of Jupiter's thigh. Every land inherits what God granted it in intelligence and kindness. All this commotion, including some stupid people crying over a stolen memory. Let it go. What nonsense!'

'All right, all right. No need to get all worked up about it. I said maybe. It might be one possibility among others, regardless of the value of Walili's Bacchus. He disappeared in mysterious circum-stances. Can you help me find an avenue to search for him?'

'I haven't the slightest idea,' he replied.

I opened my briefcase and took out a book of poetry published a few weeks earlier in Frankfurt and titled *Elegies*. I said to Al-Firsiwi, 'You know, an interesting book of poetry titled *Elegies* written by an obscure poet called Hans Roeder has been published in Frankfurt.'

He turned his face as he did when he wanted to listen care-fully. I waited for him to say something, but he did not open his mouth. His features remained stiff as he sat listening in agitated silence before he asked me, 'Can I touch it?'

I handed him the book. He spent a long time feeling it with his slender dirty fingers, then he opened it and buried his face between the pages, breathing in the smell of the paper, the letters and the printing press. Then he said, 'I have no doubt it is a good book!'

'It is the literary event of the season in Germany,' I said.

'Germany is a great poetic nation.'

'That's not what it's best known for,' I said.

'It doesn't matter. It knows itself and so does poetry.'

'People say you have something to do with this book,' I told him.

Al-Firsiwi laughed nervously. 'Is there anything in this world I'm not connected with?'

'People say this is the poetry book that Hans, Diotima's grandfather, buried in the ruins of Walili.'

'It's possible,' he said. 'Why not? Though it's a matter that would make Diotima turn in her grave!'

'The introduction states that the publisher received the book from an anonymous sender, and that the poems are those of a German soldier who was held prisoner in Africa and partici-pated in excavating a Roman site. Don't you think that is more than enough proof that you found and sent the book?'

'Does the book include two elegies, one addressed to Juba II and the other to Diotima?'

'Yes, yes it does,' I said enthusiastically. 'And the introduction says that they are the best poems in the collection!'

'Then I've screwed Hans Roeder with those two poems!'

'But why didn't you publish them under your own name?'

'I'm not interested in that. He buried his poems in Walili and I buried my poems between his poems. No one will ever know what lies under the rubble and what comes to the surface. Plus, I did it for Diotima's sake, as a final salute to her restless soul.'

I opened the book to the page where Diotima's elegy began. I read two lines, but Al-Firsiwi stopped me with a sign of the hand as he stood up. His face had bloomed as a result of this story; he was proud of himself and looked somewhat happy. He went to his safe at the far end of the room and took out a big envelope.

He handed it to me, saying, 'Here's the manuscript of your great-grandfather's poetry. I only found it after losing my eyesight. One evening I became very depressed, and the hopelessness of being blind pushed me to wander among the ruins, where I found a pile of dusty papers and a worn-out hat. They were in a room in a ruin, not far from the house of the handsome youth and close to the statue of a prone male, a symbol of fertility that did not last long in these halls. I slipped into the manuscript two poems that were not part of the savage intensity of Hans Roeder's poems. I had written them as elegies for two important people in my life who did not live at the same time, but they both lived long in my heart, and at the same time.'

'What about Bacchus?' I asked.

'Listen, when you begin digging, there's only one chance in a million that you'll find what you're looking for and countless chances that you'll find things you haven't even dreamed of. You've found the manuscript, now forget about the worthless adolescent.'

3

Fatima sent me a text message saying that she had travelled to Havana with her partner. She said she was doing it for both our sakes. The following day I felt a mysterious apprehension that something might happen to Fatima and was haunted by the idea that I should travel to Havana. Before dawn the next morning I awoke sad and exhausted, and called her, unaware of the time difference. Her voice came from deep sleep as she tried to calm me, while I was delirious, repeating that Havana was not suitable to be a dream. It was nothing but a prison that looked like Al-Firsiwi's bar, where illusions from different time periods stood side by side.

'What's happened to you?' asked Fatima. 'Havana is a real city. There are dreamers and malingerers, drunks and people who struggle to feed themselves, and once in a while, they dance. Listen to me, this city has a night, it only has night, a quick, thick and amazing night.'

I told her about the poetry book, and she said that I was lucky to have such an intense father. I was saying that I felt a dense fog was covering me, when she yawned and begged me to tell her what to do with the man sleeping in her bed. I told her, half-joking, 'Smother him with a big pillow.' I sent her a kiss, hung up and turned off the light to go back to sleep.

I went back to sleep, and dreamed that I was in Havana and the world of Cabrera Infante. I was walking down Calle O, leaving the Hotel Nacional, then crossing Avenida 23, passing in front of the Maraka, and returning quickly to the Nacional, where I had recently left Fatima. I told myself that if Arsenio Cué arrived before me, he would undoubtedly sleep with her. That explained my unexpected aggressive attitude with her when I saw her in the lobby reading the schedule of night parties. I dragged her violently to a corner in the garden where it was extremely hot and humid, and began to devour her. She put up languid resistance, interspersed occasionally with fast, savage parries. I had the feeling I would ejaculate before she reached her climax and decided to slow down, but when I needed to get it back to the same level, it escaped me. I would get close to ejaculating but fail to reach my aim, despite trying a few times. I was swimming in sweat and woke up startled, surrounded by unbearable heat. Then I dreamed that I was with Fatima, Silvestre and Cué, spending the evening in the Sky Club listening to Estrella Rodriguez. I sneaked out of that place and stood at the end of the street under a foggy lamp, listening to Bustrofedon talking about Cuban women and singing an old song, that went something like, 'Girls without charm, without a proud stroll, without the queens' lure, cannot be Cubans.'

As my dream continued I found myself in a noisy street following a fast-walking man who I would soon discover to be Yacine. What are you doing here, Taliban? Are you, like me, looking for Guevara's face to stuff it in an old suitcase? I ran behind Yacine with a great effort that made me hear my quickened breathing. Then I noticed Guevara pushing a vegetable cart in the middle of the street. I stopped to tell him that it might be dangerous to drive his cart between the crazy cars. Never mind. Yacine too thought that Fatima was in danger. For some reason, she would find herself in hospital or in a morgue and not at the bar of the Nacional.

I was awakened by Layla's phone call, her voice asking, 'Where are you?'

'I'm in Havana.'

'Are you all right?'

'Almost, but why don't we run away to Cuba?'

'Have you gone mad? Even our favourite Cuban writer is in London!'

'True! Let's run away to London then!'

I was unable to leave my bed. I was thinking about Layla, Havana, Yacine, Marrakech and Ibrahim al-Khayati. I was thinking about the suffering of Al-Firsiwi and Bahia and about Ahmad Majd and his big house. I was thinking about obscure sexual adventures and a large swimming pool where I could dive in and breathe deeply under the water. I was thinking about all that at once and could not concentrate on one specific detail. When I tried, I was assailed by various details from contradictory topics. When I finally pulled myself out of this swamp, I had no strength left and found nothing better to do than lie on the couch and fall again into a troubled sleep.

Over the weekend Layla and I went to Casablanca. We attended Essam and Mahdi's performance; we drowned in the racket of Arthritis and laughed at the innocent words the boys in the group uttered to express an anger lacking any serious- ness. Layla noticed that most of the songs had a religious flavour as a result of the traditional expressions found in the lyrics of the Gnawa, the Aissawa and the Rawayes orders. I told her that most of them had been tried in the devil worship case because of the T-shirts they wore and not because of the songs they sang. When the noise reached its peak, we left. We lingered a little in the Casablanca night before meeting Ibrahim al-Khayati and some of his friends at a restaurant. Ahmad Majd was there and he teased Layla for boycotting Marrakech.

Layla and Ahmad Majd got into an argument about the city, which ended with Layla shouting, 'Do you want the truth? I hate Marrakech and I hate that stupid house of yours that you call Al-Andalous. I shit on all those tacky ornaments you boast about to foreigners. And I hate you, you more than everything else I've mentioned.'

Ahmad responded with some allusion to his years in prison.

Layla exploded. 'No one has the right to feel superior to us because of his years in prison, especially if he was rewarded for them. Didn't you all say that you were reconciled? But I don't know with whom. Whoever's been getting drunk tonight with the reconciliation money should keep his tongue under wraps. I don't owe any madman anything! If you can't be proud of the price you paid, it means that you loaned the system a few years of your life and got them back later with hefty interest!'

I pulled Layla back by her waist and told her, 'We must leave immediately.'

She did not object, and on the way home I told her I did not understand her antagonism towards Ahmad. She said that she could not fathom why I had such horrible friends and that she hated them all.

'Didn't you say you liked Ibrahim al-Khayati?'

'I take it back,' she said. 'I hate you all.'

When I held her hand she did not pull away, and after a period of silence she said, crying, 'I was horrible to Ahmad Majd. I must apologise to him.'

I tried to undo some of the damage by inviting everyone back to Ibrahim's house. Layla apologised, and Ahmad somehow transformed her apology into a collective, public admission of his countless virtues. As the evening progressed I enjoyed listening, for the first time, to the chattering of the men and women Ibrahim had invited. They did not seem to have any of the pretensions or overblown professionalism we normally encountered in Casablanca. They were a new generation of officials, contractors and liberal professionals who led a very pleasant life. They talked about big business deals and stock exchange listings, about foreign investment and the property market. They discussed Casablanca's new hotels, restaurants and dance clubs. They talked about all that without any bitterness, disapproval or affected regrets, and were pleased with the city's new entertainment options. It seemed to me then that success and wealth had become agreeable beings, as if a sweet breeze had pushed the ogre that they once symbolised into a far corner.

Slowly the atmosphere cleared and everybody lightened up, and people began telling risqué jokes and recounting the scandalous sex stories swelling the city. At this point Layla got upset and asked to leave the vulgar atmosphere. I walked her to our room in Ibrahim's house, and there she wondered how I could have such crude friends. I told her that they were Ibrahim's friends, but she objected, saying, 'You too were laughing at their jokes.' I tried to tease her but she recoiled. So I kissed her and returned to the vulgar soirée.

The evening came to a dreadful end when someone called Ibrahim and told him that there had been a huge explosion at a nightclub called Horses and Gunpowder, and that police cars and ambulances had been running nonstop for more than an hour, which meant there were a lot of victims.

We went to the beach area, but before we arrived at the nightclub we found security checkpoints that prevented us going any further. Ibrahim tried in vain to convince the security men of the need to let us pass, so we stood there amid a nervous and noisy crowd. We kept calling Mahdi and Essam, but all we got was their voicemails. I told Ibrahim nothing indicated that they had been at the nightclub, but he said nothing indicated that they had not. The voices of young men and women trying to get through the security cordon rose hysterically. One after another, ambulances passed by, the crowd wailing and crying at each one. Someone came from the other side and flung himself on to the barrier. He said that there were hundreds of victims and that their remains were spread over the area as far as the sea. The wailing got louder once more, until a security policeman informed us that the explosion had been caused by gas canisters and had only caused a few injuries. Through her wailing, a woman said to him, 'May God send you good news.' But another person came up to the security barrier and said two men had blown themselves up in the middle of the nightclub. Someone asked if there were dead people, and the man replied, 'Ask if there are people still alive.'

I told Ibrahim it might be better to go back home, where we would hear less random news. But he thought we should go by the hospital to make sure Essam and Mahdi were not among the victims. The hospital had no news of any explosion, and had not received any warning that a large number of victims would be arriving at the emergency room. We went home broken. As we crossed the garden we heard the jittery sounds of a guitar, and as soon as we opened the door there were the voices of Essam, Mahdi and the members of their band. They were in the living room, which still showed traces of the earlier soirée.

Ibrahim shouted at them, 'Stop this bloody mess!'

The room fell silent and Ibrahim collapsed on the closest sofa, shaking all over. I told everyone about the explosion at the Horses and Gunpowder. Mahdi said they had been there at the time and were told that a truck transporting gas had exploded in a parking lot near the beach.

'What about the nightclub?' I asked.

Essam said it had been evacuated, in case another explosion was part of the programme.

'Then there were no victims?' I asked.

'We don't know. There might have been. We'll find out from the news bulletins.'

I said, 'You don't seem bothered by what's happened, or by the fact that there might be dead and injured or terrorised people, Ibrahim among them, who almost lost his mind over worry for you. All that is mere detail?'

'They are details, not mere detail,' Mahdi said.

The others laughed, and one of them said with feigned seriousness, 'The fact is that the explosion present in your head did not happen.'

I was gripped by a desire to slap the young man and controlled myself with difficulty. Then I walked over to Ibrahim, pulled him off the sofa, and led him to his room, shouting at them without looking back, 'We don't want to hear a sound from you.'

I heard Essam say in affected Arabic, 'May you have a good night.'

The group responded with noisy laughter.

The next morning was the kind of morning I hated: Layla was in a rotten mood, the young men were asleep on the living room sofas, Ibrahim had gone to his office, the maid had yet to arrive, the kitchen was a mess and coffee was not at hand. The only thing I could do was put on my shoes and go back to Rabat. Just then Ahmad Majd called and asked about the previous night's explosion.

When I told him it was just a gas explosion, he said, somewhat surprised, 'Then nothing happened to Essam and Mahdi?'

'No, nothing happened. If it had, we would now be in the funeral procession, while you are lying in bed waiting for detailed news about the incident.'

Layla and I went out, a sea breeze, moist and fresh, erasing the rotting smell of the closed house. I would need an entire day to get over this morning.

Layla was walking fast and crying. She said she was scared and wanted to see her daughter immediately. We went to the railway station, and since we had to wait for half an hour, I suggested drinking a cup of coffee.

Layla replied, upset, 'I don't want coffee or anything else. I want to see my daughter. I'm ashamed of myself. What would I tell her if I had been killed in the explosion? What would she have done? She has no one but me.'

I said, 'But you were sleeping in a bed where nothing exploded.'

'No,' she said. 'I was sitting in a restaurant, then I was in the street and then at a silly party!'

I drank my coffee quickly, reading the newspapers' banner headlines about the arrest of Al-Qaeda sleeper cells. This was for the second time in six months. I scrutinised the names carefully as if trying to see their faces; I had a vague feeling I would recognise one of them. I always had a premonition that I would recognise someone on the list, one of those confused people we never expected to find in a terrorist organisation, the kind of person who would eat and drink and laugh with us and visualise us as flying remains while staring at our faces.

We got on the train and sat silently side by side. When we reached Rabat, Layla took my hand and asked while squeezing it, 'Do you hate me?'

'Not yet!'

I did not see Layla for a week after that. We talked for hours on the phone about everything – her daughter, her little quarrels, domestic matters, funny incidents about her ex-husband and our own limited concerns, which we could cover in one minute. But whenever the conversation touched on the possibility of our seeing each other, she quickly changed the subject. It was as if the explosion had cast a dark shadow across our relationship.

Fatima returned from Havana and gave me a call. She was clearly quite anxious, so I assumed she was not on good terms with her Kosovar live-in boyfriend, but I did not ask. We talked about Ahmad Majd, Bahia and their daughter and about Ibrahim al-Khayati. She asked strange questions about everyone and wanted to know to what degree each one of us was in harmony with himself.

I said to her, joking, 'The only person I know who has a good relationship with himself is you.'

'I wish!' she said firmly.

The following week she surprised me one morning, standing at my office door at the paper, greeting my colleagues, who welcomed her warmly. We went to the Beach restaurant, where I ordered a meal of crab and slices of salmon in cucumber sauce.

She said, laughing, 'I know that you'll smell nothing of this massacre!'

'On the contrary, I'll smell the most specific scents and the very weakest ones.'

She looked at me in surprise, and I explained that a miracle had restored my sense of smell.

She smiled affectionately at me and asked, after a moment of silence, 'What was the first meal whose aroma surprised you?'

I said, defeated, 'Yacine's shirts, years after his death.'

I observed her face with its fine features, typical of the women of the Atlas. Her eyes had become a little larger, and their blackness was a transparent shade surrounding her whole face. Her lips jutted out as if they had grown fuller in reaction to the prominence of her cheekbones. I told her that her slimness was very becoming. She smiled without interrupting her fierce struggle with her crab. When she dipped her fingers into the bowl of lemon water, all the sadness in the world overwhelmed me, and all I wanted was to put an end to the meal as soon as possible.

We were leaving Al-Jazaïr Street, having first passed through the Udaya and talked about its planned tunnel, and proceeded along the wall of the Mellah and the bank of the Abou Regreg. We went by the grain market, which had been transformed into ateliers and was decorated with huge façades advertising the Emirati enterprise in charge of the building. There were beautiful drawings revealing blue water and happy children with rosy cheeks. Fatima asked me about the lofty building crowned with solid domes and facing the Sunni mosque on one side and the news agency where she worked on the other side. I told her it was the museum of contemporary art. She was amazed by the sudden changes in Rabat, but I suggested she hold her comments until she visited the Villa des Arts that faced the mosque on the other side, and awaited the transformations planned for the Lyautey residence to become another altar to art in the capital. She would then see how the 'forbidden city' had come out of its lair.

She asked me, joking, 'Why do they surround this poor mosque with all these satanic spaces?'

I said, 'Don't exaggerate. There's not a single devil in the capital.'

Fatima left me in front of the parliament building. I continued on my way behind the colonial building and wondered about the vulgar and provocative parallel building enlarging the parliament, using the same architecture as the old courthouse. I asked myself about this insistence on an imaginary harmony, when contrast was the best approach to obtaining sudden beauty. When I reached my apartment I was exhausted. I took a pain reliever and slept soundly.

Fatima told me that after spending time abroad, she found Moroccans optimistic and lovers of life. I asked her, 'By God, where did you meet this wonderful species?'

She said everyone she met at parties and family gatherings, and even some people she encountered on the street and on the train, was like this.

Whenever I had this sort of discussion, I felt depressed. I sensed a huge gap separated me from the reality that surrounded me, and I wouldn't ever truly understand what was happening. I saw from my vantage point that people appeared amazed by the new things that occurred around them and were eager to get involved in this fast-paced life. I saw them as having lost any possibility of escape from the trap, and I couldn't predict what would happen to them when they awakened. I saw in the image projected by other sources of observation a country forging ahead heedless, even of those who fall off its open carts.

I talked with Layla about the subject and she said in a decisive manner, 'You're right, you have no reason to be optimistic. Don't pay attention to the gold-plated superficialities. If you scratch below the surface, you will find layers of rust and emptiness.'

I said, 'Fatima is back from Madrid.'

She was not happy with the news. 'I don't want to have anything at all to do with that woman!'

'But we have to go with her to Marrakech,' I explained.

'You must definitely forget that,' Layla said.

When my silence lasted too long, she added, 'If this annoys you, you can just cancel the idea of going to Marrakech.'

'It's impossible.'

'Of course it's impossible. I know that you would prefer to get rid of me rather than give up Marrakech.'

Later, I repeatedly tried to convince her that my interest in Fatima and joining her on her Marrakech trip was an essential matter, and had nothing to do with a possible physical relationship. For me Fatima was not a woman in a sexual or amorous way. She was more than that. She was a geographical phenomenon in my life.

I tried to pull Layla out of an ingrained cycle of enmity towards Fatima, but I failed. She was overcome by jealousy and decided, with no possibility for retraction, that I had to choose between travelling with Fatima and our relationship.

This upset me very much and made me tell her angrily, 'I choose to go with Fatima!'

In the train that took us to Marrakech, Fatima talked in a terse manner about her Kosovar lover. He had suddenly revealed a mean streak in Havana, something that made her realise, with great concern, that he did not have an iota of dignity.

'And then what happened?' I asked.

'When we returned to Madrid, we arrived at six in the morning. I put my suitcase on the luggage cart and went to the exit without waiting for him. An hour later I was in my apartment, getting ready to go to bed alone, as I have always been.'

I asked her if she regretted anything. She said she was upset for not having understood at the right time, and then she asked me about Layla. I told her that I could unmistakably say that she was the best thing that had happened to me in the last few years, but I did not know how to organise my life with her.

'It's a true love story,' Fatima said. 'That's why you can't organise anything. All you have to do is let your imagination run freely and write an unprecedented love story.'

Her reply annoyed me. I heard in it an allusion to the fact that I wouldn't live with Layla in a true love story, but would rather experience a kind of literary fantasy. I replied somewhat harshly, 'But Layla is real. She is not the product of my imagination.'

'What happened to you in reality was that you occasionally went to bed with a woman who was able to reconcile you with pleasure. But look at the story you wove around the subject!'

I felt suddenly blocked and remained silent. I watched the red fields devoid of vegetation, except for clumps of dispersed cactus trees. There on the nearby horizon was the road leading to Marrakech, which would soon expand to Agadir. In a few years the country would be connected by those empty roads, praised in anthems for uniting people and putting an end to isolation. Fatima loved roads, arched bridges and major highway projects. She said that they suited Hercules's soul very well. They complied with the idea of the bare land from which adventurers extract new features.

We arrived at the big house and found Ghaliya busy preparing dinner, and Bahia overwhelmed by the commotion of baby Ghaliya, while Ahmad Majd was talking on the phone with the calm of someone who has awakened on a deserted island. I left Fatima to reconnect with this lively ambiance and went straight to my room, intent on napping until night-time.

4

YACINE PLACED HIS HAND on my cheek as he used to do when he was a baby. I opened my eyes, inhaling the scent of a distant childhood. I smiled at him. He told me that this was his last appearance in my life. He would then disappear for good.

'Listen to me,' he said. 'I don't want you to misunderstand me. I'm not anybody's messenger. I have no connection with anyone, and there is no connection between what happened to me and what is happening to you. There is no connection between what I was and what I am able to read in tomorrow's paper. You will be obsessed for a long time trying to understand how this happened. There is no "how" in the matter. An idea does not survive long as an idea. Try to jump one metre. Then try to think about it for more than one second, and you will be unable to jump for good. All there is in the matter is the fact that a spark passes through your brain and says to you, "Why not?" and then you jump. This is how I found myself over there. I did not know whether it was a beginning or an end. I only knew that if I did not do it I would remain suspended, all the way to eternity, at that point on the pavement where I allowed the idea to survive more than necessary.

I say this to put an end to the matter. I mean, in order for me to put an end to it. As far as you are concerned, you won't stop digging in this grave. You will follow in the footsteps of your ancestors, the diggers. Will you find anything? I don't know. You might be able to extract a city from inside you, a combination of Zarhoun, Düsseldorf, Rabat, Bu Mandara, Frankfurt, Bu Dayrab and Marrakech. You might find poetry in the prosaic ruins that surround you. None of that concerns me! You must know that I will always manage to escape the control of the descendants. I will soar alone and fall alone as I always did.

'Listen carefully. Jamaa al-Fna, the Mediterranean Press Club, the medina entrance from the side of the seller of smoked heads, near the olive and falafel shop. Free yourself from the balcony of the café. Nothing deserves all this attention on your part. Listen to the call of someone looking from the narrow window of an old house. He is talking to another person on the roof of a nearby house, and asking, "Has the person concerned arrived?" The other replies at the top of his voice that he does not know. You, however, must stand exactly under the spot where the call originates or under the window. Look closely in the direction of those who leave the alley and melt into the throng of the square. You should not concern yourself with those entering the medina. You should know that in this narrow place it is difficult to distinguish between those entering and those leaving, but everything depends on this distinction. You will see a billboard that shades the alleyway with its dull glimmer. You will incidentally read on it that Marrakech welcomes cinema lovers. You will then see a large poster that covers a large area of the wall, and if you read it you will know the whole programme of the film festival. I beg you, do not read it. If you busy yourself reading it – and I know that an overwhelming temptation will push you to do so – you will miss the critical moment.

'Why am I telling you all this? Why do I run to you specifically? It is either your fate or mine, we can't escape it. The face is that of a child who grew up very quickly. His cheeks are those of a healthy baby and his eyes are the eyes of a tired man. It is a face that looks like many others, like the face of the greengrocer located near the fuel station in Al-Zizafon Street, the face of the teacher at the private school located behind the general's house, or the face of your brother-in-law who lives in Germany, whom you haven't seen in years. Look at his hands next. Why is there a blackness creeping up all his nails? Why does the silver wedding ring sit so lightly on his thick little finger, making the hand look dead? Where has the man sprung from? From Sidi Youssef Ben Ali? From Daoudiate? From a vault in the old medina? From the enclosure of Marrakech or from the night of Casablanca? Or from the nameless margins?

'You told me once that you recognised people's origins from their walk. Pay careful attention then to this unhurried gait, slightly off-centre as if the person were trying to avoid an unexpected obstacle. Can you tell where people are heading from the way they walk? No. No, you can't know. No one can tell whether a person is going towards the centre of the square or to the Conference Hall, or the Hotel La Mamounia. His body stretches towards all those places without taking the direction it points to. It is the camouflage of a person who knows what he wants.

'The sleek buses are lined up in the square, unloading hundreds of weary tourists. The sun covers this city like a *tanjiya* dish cooked over high heat. This is the end of the tour, after the tombs of the Saadis, Badie palace, Bahia palace, the Koutoubia, the house of Si Said, the Pasha's house, the lighthouse, and the Almoravid Dome. Here, the scalded faces take a break before they are split among the hotels of the city. Do you think he is here, hiding in an obscure corner, waiting for the gathering of foreigners near the buses? Do you think he is observing the situation carefully from behind the cart of an itinerant vendor? Scrutinise his features closely, if you can get near him. If the designated moment has arrived, a vivid yellow colour will cover his face. In that case do not leave him at all. But if the time is still far off, the burning sun will turn his face bluish. So stay close to him but only look at his face occasionally. It would be better to look at his feet, the feet of a duck in a hurry wearing impromptu socks and knock-off trainers.

'If he is not there? You will ask yourself if he wasn't just an apparition that sprang from the fear present in each one of us. If, despite his socks, his Pakistani shirt and his uneasy look, he wasn't just a simple construction worker on his day off, or a cleaner in foreigners' houses who has just taken a quick shower before noon, for fear of being surprised in a state of impurity? At the exact moment when you ask that kind of question, a person's colour might change from blue to yellow, the colour of death. Beware of falling victim to this suspicion when you can't see him. If he is not where we left him a short while before, he is now at the entrance to the Mamounia, which is packed with cars, buses and taxis, and where the smoke of Cuban cigars extends from the restaurants to the Churchill Suite or Orson Welles Rooms. Do not take the risk of leaving this golden square. There, in the same square metre, huge fortunes compete and our friend can raise the pillars of paradise.

'Why are you looking at me like that? You have not been assigned a mission and you are not anybody's messenger. You just gave birth to a naïve angel who flew from the Trocadero to Kandahar, certain of his return.

231

'Tell me, you who understand everything, what are twenty years? Almost nothing! Why don't we start from zero?'

I wanted to touch his cheeks, but I only caught the smile that accompanied the movement of my hands. I opened my eyes to the darkness of the room and distant voices coming from the ground floor. I forced myself to get up and go downstairs, but I was not able to answer my mobile phone, which had been ringing for more than an hour.

I drank a lot of water, then I asked Fatima and Ahmad if they had been talking from the moment we arrived. They said they had been.

Layla called at the same moment.

'What's the matter?' I asked tersely.

She replied meekly, 'I'm just seeing how you are. Does that annoy you so much?'

I told her that I was very anxious because of the strange things happening to me with Yacine. She returned to the subject of Fatima and said she would like us all to meet in Rabat. I agreed and told her that I would have loved to be with her at that exact moment. I told her I missed her and I asked if she looked beautiful that day; she said she had done everything she could to look lovely. Then we said superficial things to each other that are usually said by teenagers. Before we even ended the call, I felt a heavy weight on my chest, as if I had failed to say or do something I should have. I found myself going towards the door, opening it and looking at the alleyway, which was filling up with new voices speaking various languages.

I looked at the wall opposite the big house and saw that the pigeon that had been agonising when we arrived had died. There was a green patch around its head from the fluid still oozing from its beak. I closed the door, and when I went through the kitchen I said to Ghaliya, 'The pigeon has died!' She told me that it had been folded in upon itself since the day before. I shook my shoulders and said, 'At least it didn't die by having its throat cut!'

She thought I was making a joke and replied, joking herself, 'Unlike the pigeons I'm preparing for dinner. Sidi Ahmad spent the whole morning cutting their throats. They were flapping their wings and squawking, thinking he was about to feed them. Poor birds. Nothing frees them from the human except death.'

I collapsed on the sofa. I was about to ask Ahmad about his new property development projects when my phone rang again. It was Ibrahim al-Khayati, who told me in a shaky voice with a weepy tone that Essam had been missing for two days. I asked some questions and then shut up. Ibrahim said Mahdi was almost deranged and that he did not know what to do. I was upset by the news and told him that I would come either that same day or early the next.

Dinner was chilly. We talked in subdued voices as if we were afraid of waking someone up. After dinner we split into two groups: Ahmad Majd's guests, who loudly discussed the fate of the land in the city centre that had been bought by the Jawhara Group, and a small group consisting of Fatima, Ahmad Majd and me, who briefly discussed various scenarios for Essam's disappearance, including the more tragic ones. But Ahmad scolded us, saying we were the kind of people who would bury a person before he was dead. We did not disagree.

On her way to her room, Fatima said, 'There's no need to panic. Bad news always travels fast.'

We took the six a.m. train to Casablanca, and when it started off Fatima said she had not slept a wink the previous night. I told her, 'Try to sleep. We have a long day ahead of us.'

233

I picked up the newspapers and saw Essam's picture on the front page of the paper I worked for. I raced through the article and learned some details about the various possibilities the police were considering. Among them were kidnapping by a fundamentalist Islamic group, a settling of scores among alleged devil worshippers, or an escape abroad following a period of psychological instability. Then I read Ibrahim al-Khayati's appeal to Essam, asking him to think about his mother, who had lost her ability to speak since hearing the news of his disappearance. I shared all this with Fatima, whose eyes were closed, but she did not react.

I was engrossed in reading an article about a property developer's denial of reports he had bought state-owned land for a nominal price, when Fatima said, 'I find Ibrahim's appeal in the paper strange.'

I waited for her to elaborate but she did not. I said, 'If Essam learns that his mother is in a critical condition because of him, he will return quickly.'

'And if he doesn't know?'

'It would mean that something has happened to him.'

'Or that he didn't read the papers,' she added.

'Do you think Ibrahim concocted this on his own?'

'I don't think anything. It's as if I were in a movie!'

'But you're right about there being something strange in Ibrahim's appeal. Why does he say Haniya lost the ability to speak after her son's disappearance? Have you ever heard her talk to anyone?'

'Of course she spoke, gossiped, joked and laughed. She just didn't do it with everybody or in a group.'

I wondered if the allusion to Essam's psychological instability was not in fact a reference to the uneasy relationship between Ibrahim and the children of his former lover.

Fatima said that people's gossip would tear everything to pieces.

She then sat up, refusing to sleep, and said, 'My problems seem so trivial compared to what happens to others!'

I smiled in an effort to encourage her to speak, but she digressed. She explained that her separation from her Kosovar lover was unbearably painful, even though she was determined and convinced, and her decision was final. 'I don't think I'll ever get over this hurt,' she said. 'It's a feeling of profound loss that will mark all my life. Imagine, I got pregnant twice in succession. The first time I lost the baby ten weeks before the due date. There was no sign of anything unusual until I woke up one night, swimming in my waters. I visited the doctor ten times a month and everything was as it should be. There were no signs of anything being wrong, and the baby was fine. Then I suddenly went into labour and the baby was born alive and died before my very eyes. It was stretched out to its full length in that illuminated unit, awash with all the tears in my body.

'You know what? My body rejected that baby of its own accord, without any interference from me, as if it knew the violence of this stupid impregnation.

'Then one day I knew I had been wrong from the outset. It was as if I had gone down, very fast, from the seventh floor to meet a man I was waiting for. I went with him. I ate and drank with him and made love with him. Then I became pregnant and I had an abortion. I read, stayed out late, danced, travelled and then I suddenly discovered that he wasn't the one!'

'But where's the man you have been waiting for?' I asked her.

She looked long into my eyes and smiled. 'You . . . One day I will kill you!' she said. We laughed for the first time in a day.

We entered Ibrahim al-Khayati's house hoping that Essam had returned, ending the ordeal. But when we walked into the living room, we were overwhelmed by the gloomy atmosphere and abandoned our hopes. Layla was the first to greet us; her eyes were red and swollen. Ibrahim on the other hand remained in his seat, absent-minded, staring at the empty space of the room. When we greeted him, he did not seem to recognise us.

We spent the rest of the morning in anxious conversations with Mahdi and Ibrahim and some of the young men of the band who had not stopped visiting the family. As for Haniya, she remained in bed as if in a coma. The only time she lost her temper was when Ibrahim touched her cheek in an attempt to rouse her from her despondency.

At two in the afternoon I took Fatima and Layla out to lunch. As we walked through the garden, we crossed paths with the police team investigating the disappearance. They engaged us in a casual conversation that ended with them checking our identities. They pointed out that the investigation would benefit from every piece of information, big or small, we could provide.

Once out in the street, Layla abandoned her unnatural calm and began discussing the disappearance, unconcerned by our search for a nearby restaurant. Her verbosity seemed to be her way of dealing with Fatima's presence and controlling it. I took her by the arm and told her that I felt like I had not seen her for months. She said that there was no need for me to imagine as it had been ages since I'd last seen her. We entered an Italian restaurant hungry and agitated.

The investigation was going in various directions. Essam and his band were in an ambiguous position. On the one hand, there was their entrenched conflict with various Islamist movements, because their songs poked fun at religious dress, beards and language. The matter had gone all the way to parliament, where the government was asked what it intended to do to put an end to this trivialisation of expressions like 'in the name of God', 'there is no power but in God' and 'God suffices' and their being used as terms of scorn and sarcasm.

There was also pathological hostility between Arthritis and other bands associated with devil worship, not only because Essam and the others had denied the existence of any connection between them and the Satanist trend, but because they had gone so far as to dub themselves an Islamic singing group. This had led a local Muslim leader to invite Arthritis to perform in the city whose municipal council he headed. But the concert turned into a chair-throwing fight when the band gave in to the audience's demands and sang provocative songs such as 'Islam isn't in beards and rags'. Despite all that, the Muslim leader had issued a statement condemning infiltrators at the concert who had provoked the fight and praising Arthritis for respecting the spirit of religion and rejecting its false façades. At the time, Essam thought of changing the name of the group from Arthritis to Lantern, but Mahdi and the rest of the group refused categorically, thus increasing the tensions among them.

Essam had been profoundly shocked by his arrest in the devil worship affair. He and other band members had been accused of belonging to a worldwide Satanist movement, and the prosecutor had read passages from various publications and slogans. Essam was not religious, but he would never have joined a movement that promoted such ideas and spread them recklessly. When the judge asked him whether he was convinced that Satan was a friend of humanity who connived with them and shared their desires, he nearly answered: 'Who is this new Satan?' But seeing the stern look in his lawyer's eyes he had replied very calmly, 'I believe in God and His Prophet.' From that moment on Ahmad Majd had turned his defence of Essam and the others into a torrent of sarcastic remarks that shook the court. He had talked about Satan's relationship with music, young people's relationship to Satanism, and the phobia of conservatives regarding anything beyond their own tastes. He had referred to the state that feared its own shadow, and about the rap songs that began with praise of the Prophet. People in the know had understood that the presence of Ahmad Majd – a friend of those in high places – in court to defend such a case constituted official support for the young musicians. Ahmad attributed the flyers and posters distributed by the young men to the foolishness and irresponsibility of youth and as a way to undermine the overzealousness of the security agencies. Essam's acquittal confirmed the intuition of the 'smart' ones, whether they were right or wrong.

Nobody knew for sure, but Essam's extended period of isolation and his inclination for mixed-up, dervish-like practices that combined Sunni Sufi traditions and popular rituals, together with various other religions and spiritual movements, probably went back to the impact of that trial. Among the immediate results of this sudden change in him was the increasing sharpness in the discussions he had with Ibrahim al-Khayati, discussions that were more like severe judgements. He frequently confronted Ibrahim over his relationship with his biological father. According to Mahdi, Essam never missed an opportunity to bring it up. Essam also attacked his mother with a barrage of double entendres that revealed scorn and disdain for her relationship with Ibrahim. This dramatic development appeared to have ended Haniya's reserved and timid comportment in public, and she unsheathed an unequalled ferocity that she first directed at Essam and Mahdi, and then forcefully at Ibrahim.

During those difficult months following the devil worship trial, things had kept happening, one stranger than the other.

Essam had become openly religious, while remaining the main lyricist for Arthritis, which in turn went from success to success. Essam's newfound religiosity had forced Ibrahim to submit, with a great deal of disguised depression, to a change in his private life, which until then had included enjoying festive dinners and Casablanca's nightlife. He then crowned this house arrest with a quick *umra*. Upon his return, I had asked him if he had felt anything special while performing his *umra*. He had confessed the pilgrimage had not moved him in any way. On the contrary, whenever he tried to concentrate on the experience, it escaped him hopelessly. Haniya found strength in standing up to Essam's attacks and decided to extend her control over the home. She was pitiful, though, despite her attempts to shout orders at everyone. She who had long lived submissively in the shadow of a tree called Ibrahim al-Khayati now appeared to be breaking the branches, picking the leaves and destroying the buds for no real reason.

Mahdi, on the other hand, had watched his world collapse with a great deal of patience and wisdom. At the time, he wrote his famous song, 'Enter the Valley'.

> If you are caught
> And go to and fro
> Without finding a way out
> Enter the valley
> Stay in the middle
> And wreck their plan.

After Essam's trial and new religious fervour, the media had portrayed him as a shining example of repentance. There had been further arrests of young musicians, amid persistent – though false – rumours that Essam had revealed the identity of one of the devil worshippers to the police. All of this had lit the fuse of hostility between Arthritis and most other Casablanca bands. As a result, the investigation into his disappearance veered in that direction, and we endured a whole week of contradictory reports about the arrest of a devil worship group that had kidnapped Essam, followed by the arrest of a terrorist cell that claimed to have abducted and murdered him. Ibrahim al-Khayati meanwhile received a phone call saying Essam was fine and needed some cash and medicine, but since the call was not repeated, all hope of finding a related lead evaporated.

Mahdi, meanwhile, was preparing to travel to Paris to begin his studies. We all thought, without knowing why, that he might find his twin brother there, in the city of miracles. We repeated this possibility so frequently that it almost became a certainty which eased the pain caused by the disappearance. We even began to find remnants of the old ambiance in Ibrahim al-Khayati's house, a mixture of levity, joy and consolation.

One evening Layla began remembering how much Essam loved her and lamenting bitterly that the investigation had not achieved anything and that oblivion had gradually permeated the case. When I reminded her of the complexity of cases of kidnap, abduction or murder, she grew even more fearful, and admitted that she manically envisioned frightening possibilities.

'Such as?' I asked her.

'I'm reluctant to say. I'm afraid a malignant worm has settled inside me and makes me smell foul things from a distance.'

We sat on the edge of her bed trying to organise our thoughts. Essam hated Ibrahim. He hated the idea of interacting with him as a father, and of Ibrahim interacting with Essam's mother as a husband. He knew about Ibrahim's homosexuality and about his relationship with his father, and this was unbearably embarrassing to him. His only outlet was showering Ibrahim with insults, curses and contempt. Layla said Essam had even slapped Ibrahim one day while they were in the swimming pool, and told him never to go in the pool while he was there. 'I don't want your body ever to get close to mine,' Layla quoted Essam as telling Ibrahim. 'You're not a body but a moving brothel.'

'Did he really say that? Did he actually slap him?' I asked, stunned.

'He did even more than that,' Layla said. 'Mahdi said one evening they were sitting in the garden with the rest of the band, practising a new song, when Ibrahim returned from an evening out. A bit tipsy, Ibrahim greeted the young men from behind the glass door of the living room before going to his room. At that moment Essam got up and walked towards him. Mahdi asked him what he was doing. He said casually, "I'm going to kill the bastard."'

'So much hatred. As if Ibrahim had bred poisonous snakes in his bed and not innocent offspring,' I said.

With frightening calm, Layla said, 'That's why I believe Ibrahim killed Essam in the swimming pool and buried him in the garden.'

I shivered with horror. What Layla was saying was consistent with the vague misgivings I had had for days that posed a possibility as horrific as it was unexpected. Ibrahim had enjoyed a calm life, removed from our anxious worlds, busy with the details of the life he loved, unassuming and without exhausting assumptions. I found myself visualising him burying his victim, then glumly sitting with us and deploring this disappearance. I imagined all the minor agonies that must have assailed him as he watched Essam grow hostile and Haniya come out of her shell. We used to meet and talk, and he may have mentioned once or twice issues with the twins, but we never had any idea of the fire that must have been consuming them. It seemed so easy for the beast to be born, and so simple to cross to the shores of hell.

I was overcome with a feeling of despair at how life found satisfaction only in destroying us, and had an overwhelming fear of being alone. I shared my thoughts with Layla, and she tried to console me by caressing my face and head, but I felt nothing.

She said without much enthusiasm, 'You can stay here if you're willing to get out of bed before six in the morning.'

I quickly undressed and lay down on her bed, certain she had saved me from unbearable suffering.

At work the following morning, I was busy writing a short article on how property and tourism funds were recovering debts owed by the property mafia, and was looking into the secret behind the ability of three big-shots to avoid repayment. Banks appeared to be negotiating easy terms for the debts of some of their clients, thanks to the sky-rocketing prices of the land mortgaged by the banks. I was embroiled in a heated discussion with the editor-in-chief, trying to convince him to publish the names of the three big-shots who refused to pay their debts in good times and bad, when I received a call from Ahmad Majd. Like a bucket of cold water being poured over my head, he told me that Ibrahim al-Khayati had been arrested and charged with killing Essam. I asked him, spontaneously, if the police had found the body in the garden.

'There's no corpse in this story,' Ahmad Majd answered.

The Ravens

I

AL-FIRSIWI SANK INTO A state of despair. When my half-sister and her husband returned from overseas, he quickly sold them the hotel. His only condition was that he be allowed to recover the blue Roman pieces of mosaic remaining in the halls and on the walls. To that end, he spent almost six months sitting in the lobby of the hotel passing the pieces of mosaic between his fingers. He would place the pieces he believed to be of genuine Roman origin in a bag beside him. His actions provoked the pity and scorn of the employees and the new owners. During that time he overheard all the plans for repairs, extensions, additions and alterations around the hotel. He wished he had the right and the energy to come up with different ideas; he could have made a thousand suggestions for changes and replacements. His son-in-law had entered into a partnership with the wife of a well-known government official. He heard the wife's voice one day as she talked to the contractor about using the mosaic. He did not say a thing, but sang for more than one hour and in all dialects and keys, 'Read the contract, my cousin.'

When he had finished collecting the tiles from the Roman mosaic, he put the bag on the back of a donkey and descended from the top of the hill in a noisy procession with villagers he had brought along. The procession entered Walili from the side of the Tangier Gate, then continued down the main street in the direction of Caracalla's Arch, as if it were in a victory parade, returning from war. As he went, Al-Firsiwi reminded people of every twist and turn of his personal epic, from the day he took over the market with his German wife on his arm to the moment he returned the mosaic to the state, the very entity that had abandoned Juba's kingdom. However the state did not stop at neglect and turning a blind eye to thieves, Al-Firsiwi said, but gave the governor free rein to plough corruption and reap the fruits. The wife of the genius wanted to decorate her swimming pool with the Roman mosaics, but Al-Firsiwi swore to God that she would never do it.

'It is not enough to be a thief, my dears,' he said. 'You must have brains enough to differentiate between Roman mosaic and the tesserae of Bab Bardayin. Old man Firsiwi can do it by touch. When you tried to rob me last year, I made a point of crying over what I had lost in front of rich and poor. In reality, as soon as I touched the empty spots you left after the theft, my gloating heart danced with joy. You had taken nothing but the mud of the region covered with Fes blue.

'How stupid that was. They are not coins that you would recognise easily, though your honourable husband has often mistaken a glob of spit for a silver coin from the Saadi period. It is mosaic, in other words, the splinters of the human soul scattered in God's earth. It is the meeting point between water, clay and fire. It is the creative power of the imagination that transforms inert matter into the light that glows in the faces of water nymphs. You don't get it? I will pay you a day's wages simply for making up this parade and testifying that I turned over to the Moroccan state a part of the great heritage it has neglected.

'This bag is full of broken faces, those of warriors, heroes, gods, women and beasts. It will soon be added to other bags and boxes also filled with faces and fragmentary bodies, abandoned in storage rooms where rats and grasshoppers play. See how great civilisations with their brilliant shapes, colours and beauty end up in the dark corners of those sons of bitches. So will be Al-Firsiwi's civilisation, my brother, "yamis oma", in the Berber tongue of eloquent ignorance. Behold the State of Al-Firsiwi, the state that gave this land the electric olive press and petrol pump, sulphur to treat the pox, the carob trade, the Zaytoun Hotel, the Cantina of the esteemed Bacchanalians, the war on plastic, the treatment of solid waste, beekeeping and the condom. This will all end up in fathomless darkness. The state that made you, riff-raff of forgotten tribes, a people to be reckoned with, the great State of Al-Firsiwi is today undertaking its last official act in this region. It is preceded by a magnificent donkey with a bag of another civilisation and another state on its back. To hell, O defeated state. Diotima's smile in her final resting place bids you farewell.'

People listened and exchanged complicit smiles, and they proceeded scared and surprised. All the while Al-Firsiwi was immersed in his hallucination, holding the tightly closed bag with care. He headed in the direction of the blue mountain until he reached the governorate building, where the informal handing over of the bag took place, as if it were a passing joke. The joke did not stop the governor handing Al-Firsiwi the receipt he requested, one that included the number of pieces after they had been counted. The governor asked Al-Firsiwi to specify the number of pieces, and he said 13,624. The governor wrote the number down on the receipt and loudly stamped it, and Al-Firsiwi left totally satisfied with the procedure.

After Al-Firsiwi surrendered and placed his treasure of Roman mosaics in the hands of the governor, things began to happen quickly. Authorities ordered Al-Firsiwi's arrest. But Al-Firsiwi had left the city – people saw him though he did not see them – after eating breakfast at the marketplace café. The man seemed to melt into the blue mountain, as he used to call it. He left unconcerned by anything, while the police were quick to announce their failure to find him, as if the inability to find a blind man were a remarkable success. All the TV news bulletins showed the face of an officer announcing with a smile that his forces had looked for the fugitive from justice in every fold of the mountain without finding a trace of him.

When matters had gone that far, I decided to get involved in the search for my father, fearful that his disappearance was due to a fatal accident rather than exceptional cunning. The day I arrived in Bu Mandara, expecting to hear news about his disappearance, Al-Firsiwi contacted me from a mobile phone number I did not recognise. He told me that he did not want me to look for him or rescue him from oblivion. He said that the warrant for his arrest had no foundation because the pieces of mosaic were nothing but soil, and he was the only one who had declared that they were Roman. Think about this great country, he said. A blind man sitting in the lobby of a ruined hotel, passing the pieces of mosaic between his fingers and then declaring that this one was a pre-Christian Roman piece, and that one was the work of potters from the dawn of the third millennium, while those were from the ovens of Tajmouati in Fes and dated back to the beginning of the twenty-first century. Those imbeciles believed that and issued arrest warrants, he said. Confession was the best evidence, and as long as Al-Firsiwi himself believed that, he had no fear that the most modern labs would prove he was making fun of all of them.

'Why wage these fake wars then?' I asked.

He replied angrily, 'Give me an honest war to end my life with. Do you want me to die in peace like any other dog?'

I talked with Al-Firsiwi for more than an hour, as if I were meeting him in a dream. Every now and then he pointed out events that linked me to him, as if everything had ended a long time ago, as if he had really disappeared for good. I was listening to a voice talking to me about the Firsiwi who did not kill Diotima, the Firsiwi who had mysterious love affairs and wrote poems about the death of love, the Firsiwi who buried Bacchus in the courtyard of an obscure mosque in the blueness of the mountain. He talked about the Firsiwi who did not like his life at all.

'It's true,' he said. 'I don't like the name or the family it connects me to or the village where you're looking for me. I don't like the Rif, which is supposed to be a lost Eden but is nothing more than a passage for wind. I don't love Diotima who stole her means of death from me, or Hans Roeder who swallowed my poems. I only like this blindness that protects me, this darkness that resembles a huge gate that the Creator closed on me to make it possible for me to do as I please, far from spies and the curious.'

At some point I ended the conversation, but the voice stayed close by, as if Al-Firsiwi were standing behind the disintegrating wall of his old family home.

'Are you here?' I asked him.

After a moment's silence he replied, 'Yes, I am here in the heart of darkness.'

I jumped into the house through the collapsing window and ran in all directions, entering rooms without doors and ceilings and making formless birds fly away in fright. I asked him again, 'Where are you, are you here?'

His voice reached me from afar, through the phone held tight to my ear. It said, 'I'm in the courtyard of the mosque where Bacchus is hiding, lying down after having spent a long time standing on hard stone. One day my remains will be mixed with his: me, a representative of the human race in its eloquent rags, and him a representative of forgotten imagination, of the relationship between dreams and granite. Don't forget to visit me from time to time. Not for my sake but yours, for the sake of the frail thread that mocks us.'

When the call cut off, I was in the middle of the ruined house. I was overcome by a feeling of fear and desolation that compelled me to quickly head out to the nearby field, to collect my strength and get away from the place as fast as possible. I wanted to get rid of the phone, but I felt as if it were stuck to my ear and had become part of my facial features.

I walked in the road that ran through the village all the way to the cemetery. As I got in my car, I felt I was looking at this place for the last time.

When the storm surrounding the manhunt for Al-Firsiwi abated, I was able to see things somewhat realistically. He had put an end to a period of struggle and violence, both overt and covert, replacing it with a period of calm that was suitable for a time when so many people were scheming and profiting silently, with a kind of belittling indifference.

The Zaytoun Hotel reopened during the tourist revival when it did not matter who benefited behind the scenes. What counted were the newly opened roads around, outside and within the city. Guesthouses multiplied, as did business in traditional crafts. Buying power grew and property revived. Troupes to perform religious songs and chants were formed in this forgotten city. There might have also been some hidden scandals that made people pronounce the *hawqala*, appealing for God's help, without the sparks of anger in their eyes disappearing. Eventually, Al-Firsiwi's disappearance marked the withdrawal of the tragic from public life. There was also a large-scale movement in the city to please those who whimpered and whined. Yet I was not tempted to return to the hotel, despite my half-sister and her husband's insistence. I could not forget the sight of my mother sitting in the hotel lobby nor get rid of the sense of Al-Firsiwi's spirit controlling the place. It seemed to me that a return to the hotel under its new direction would put me in direct confrontation with two gigantic beings I would be unable to face.

Reality, however, is not always as simple as expected. In this flood of changes that brooked no challenge or opposition, the state saw fit to submit Al-Firsiwi's mosaics to forensic examination in Italy. A delegation of well-known archaeologists travelled to Rome, taking Al-Firsiwi's bag with them. There the pieces were individually examined, and the final report categorically concluded that each of the 13,624 pieces was from a genuine Roman mosaic that had originally represented Hylas, the companion of Hercules. It was different from the mosaic currently located in Walili, which showed Hylas in a struggle with two nymphs, one holding his chin and the other his wrist. In this mosaic, one nymph gave him a drink from a decorated cup while he embraced the other and looked angrily at a tiger about to pounce on the two nymphs. The design also showed a scene similar to the mosaic visible to this day: the creeping hunter, the dead bird, the trial, and the hungry tigers savaging the guilty hunter. About 2,000 pieces were missing to complete the design and assemble it again.

I called my father many times on his mobile phone in a desperate effort to talk to him. My purpose was not to inform him about the report, nor to express my tremendous happiness at this miraculous achievement, but to beg him to reveal to me the unique personality that extracted from Hylas's mosaic, the mosaic of Abd al-Karim al-Khattabi and Al-Firsiwi struggling against the serpent of the Valley of Death, as well as all the other designs he used to decorate the Zaytoun Hotel. If he was that unique person, why did he not tell me? Why did he spend years changing the course of this archaeological imagination to direct it into his own personal legends, without ever saying anything about it?

I sent Fatima an e-mail and attached that story with the relevant questions. She replied that Al-Firsiwi had done nothing but repeat what humanity had been doing since time immemorial – reproduce a single creation in different scenarios and personalities. I considered her answer a philosophical ploy to be done with a topic that did not interest her. I began having nightmares in which I was standing in the middle of the crumbling house, surrounded by dust, smashed ceilings and frightened birds, while Al-Firsiwi's face kept appearing and disappearing in the midst of the ruins, his voice getting louder and then weaker. In the distance I could hear the sound of collapsing buildings or explosions, I could not say exactly which. Every time I woke from this repeated nightmare, I felt immense regret for having failed to get close to Al-Firsiwi and understand him. I was sorry for merely considering him a colourful persona, a callous acrobat who knew how to step on words and emotions while maintaining his own balance and calculated chaos. Then I saw the paradox in a journey like Al-Firsiwi's. I had considered it confused and disconnected, while in reality it was extremely coherent and methodical, its links connected by flawless logic. I came to the conclusion that the true meaning of any life was this mysterious logic and nothing else.

In an effort to put an end to the confusion that overwhelmed me, I went to Al-Firsiwi's house and tried with my sister's help to find something there: papers, poems, a will. We found nothing but an open box with a single piece of mosaic inside it and a copy of the poetry book published in Frankfurt. In another room we found one of the letters I had sent to him from Germany, in which I accused him again of having killed my mother. In the wardrobe we found nothing but a rustic *djellaba* he had kept from his teenage years. As I pushed the *djellaba* aside, I felt a solid object behind it. When I took the *djellaba* out of the empty cupboard, the statue of Bacchus, as I had known it, was clearly visible, with his dull gaze and the bunch of grapes hanging over his shoulder.

My amazement and joy did not last long since I soon discovered that the statue was a copy made of brittle pottery and barely strong enough to move. It was impossible to know under what conditions it had been made, or by whom, with this amazing degree of accuracy. It consisted of a hollow clay body, its redness blackened by firing. When I examined it closely, I realised that Al-Firsiwi's obsession had gone as far as his making a replica with a broken foot to resemble the original statue after it had been removed from its plinth. I wrapped the copy in a white robe, as if I were placing it in a shroud, and carried it, in a kind of determined ceremonial, to the old abandoned house in Bu Mandara inhabited by forlorn birds and scorpions. I dug near the foundation of the western wall that was all that remained of the impressive room where the great Al-Firsiwi, the father of the first immigration, had stayed. There I buried the clay Bacchus, the statue remaining from mysterious thefts, itself considered in its clay condition an exemplary theft, in perfect harmony with this eternal wasteland.

On our way back from Bu Mandara, my sister asked, 'Why did you bury the statue?'

'I don't know really. I didn't know what else to do with it.'

When I got out of the car at the entrance to the Zaytoun Hotel, she turned suddenly before closing the car door and pushed into my hand the piece of mosaic, the only one left from all the chaos. I was moved by this gesture, but I did not know why. I was elated to have this tessera in my life, and I felt for the first time that the woman who had showered me with this happiness was not only Al-Firsiwi's daughter but my sister as well. Even though I was certain that I was leaving the city for good and without regrets, I knew we would remain attached to it by the strong bond of gratitude and brotherhood.

2

I WENT DOWN THE ROAD covered by shade and silence, and then I saw the blue hills stretching like lazy animals and the buildings that began to crawl from the Sidi Mohammed ben Qasem neighbourhood towards the mountain. The buildings, like their people, were crowded together and mysterious, and only characterised by their provocative white colour. When I turned left towards Meknes, I cast a cold look at Walili, as if I wanted to be sure there was not another car in the parking lot. I again felt depressed, as if the difficulty I found being nostalgic about places triggered it anew. I fought that black moment by thinking about Havana, about the seaside and nightclubs, about words that cropped up in the dark not because we needed them, but because the main street, the anxious souls and the song rising from the depths of the sea all needed fleeting words, words that flared like a match. We did not express anything with them, but we used them to build stairs towards rapture.

This thinking saved me from the onset of depression. I felt I would do something wonderful and exceptional if I went to Havana and shared a funny chat about Hamuniya with Bustrofedon. Why not? We could consider Hamuniya a vari-ation on Estrella Rodriguez. The former collapsed with her weepy *'aytah* in Casablanca and the second was swallowed by the night of Havana . . . Here I am here, where am I from? Where are you from? Ah, where. Let's go Havana, hava, here I am, here she is, hava. I am a mouth, he is a mouth, hafah, hafaha, Havana, Havana all of us, fahani, fahuni, hafuni, hafac, hafac, ha, ha, ha, nana, fana, Havana, ha, ha.

I called Fatima, who had returned to Madrid, but she was busy talking on another line. She asked me to call her later, but I insisted we talk then and told her, 'We have to travel together to Cuba.'

She exclaimed, 'Do you know what the weather is like there at this time of year?'

I had no idea, but she told me. 'It's simply a watery hell!'

'What about the idea?' I asked.

She replied, 'It belongs to a time in the past. It would have been a beautiful idea if it had happened before, but it's too late now. I went to Havana without you, or rather with someone else, and my illusions about it are over. Can we talk later?'

'Yes, yes, we'll talk later,' I said, and then put the phone down. As I drove I thought about 'before' and 'after', about the right time that no one had succeeded in setting since the beginning of creation.

In the days that followed that phone conversation, Fatima would talk to me in a somewhat rude manner, as if she were settling a score. I could not find a positive sentence to include in our phone calls or a pleasant way to end them. One evening she left a message on my answering machine, telling me she would accompany a Spanish journalist on a two-week visit to Morocco to investigate the case of the devil worshippers and Essam al-Khayati's disappearance. She did not include a single affectionate word, as she used to do, which I considered a virtual declaration of war. When I told her that later, she laughed and said she had stopped fighting years ago. But she remained aloof during her whole visit, which gave a sharp edge to all her comments and reactions. This upset Layla and led her to make some rash assumptions, most significantly that Fatima was expressing repressed jealousy and was unable to recover from her failure to have a relationship with me. Layla yet again asked about the true nature of my friendship with Fatima. I repeated to her the details of the story, including the feeling of loss that sometimes overcame me when I realised how important Fatima was in my life, yet there was no possibility of a sexual relationship between us. Once again Layla was upset because of my feeling of loss, and she considered it a lurking danger that might surface in our relationship one day. She also interpreted Fatima's present anxiety as a sign of the imminent eruption of that volcano.

The events that ensued put an end to Layla's sedition. It so happened that we spent an evening at my house a week after the arrival of Fatima and Joaquin, the Spanish journalist. There was an ambiguous rejoicing during our get-together that clearly reflected a waning in Fatima's ire and an increase in her affection for me, and for Layla as well. But I soon understood that the reason for this change was the visit she had paid to Ibrahim al-Khayati in Salé prison, particularly something Ibrahim had said. When the conversation turned to that visit at the end of the evening, Fatima admitted that she was very angry with the way we had given up on Ibrahim's innocence, or at least his presumed innocence, and the ease with which we had eliminated this important man from our lives. Layla said that the matter had nothing to do with innocence or guilt, and that even if we assumed that Ibrahim had in fact killed Essam, that did not make him a different person. 'He's still the same man who inundated our lives, yours in particular, with unusual feelings.' The forgetfulness surrounding Ibrahim, his wife and his son Mahdi, and his friends and acquaintances, was painful. 'He feels like it's a miracle that you remember him from time to time,' Fatima said.

After we dropped Fatima and Joaquin at their hotel, Layla said that the journalist seemed pleasant enough and wished that something would happen between him and Fatima. I said that what mattered was for Fatima to wish it, which made Layla say, 'I feel that she is searching for him but she probably does not dare desire him.'

I replied, just for the sake of bickering, that she was a few years older than him.

'Don't worry,' Layla said joyfully. 'He will grow old very quickly and then she will be younger than him.'

Fatima and Joaquin's investigation concluded that the musicians in the groups that were considered devil worshippers were simply budding amateurs. Not one of them was a professional musician or had a true understanding of song and dance. Most of them were university or school students who liked hard rock, heavy metal, death metal, black metal and grunge. Although many named their groups in imitation of international bands, especially those from the Scandinavian countries, such as Arthritis, Busted Eye, Polluted Mind, Cemetery Air, Orgasm and Snake Blood, they had never travelled abroad or participated in any international music festival. They only performed their work in the hall of the Secular Institute, FOL, located in Ibn Nussair Alley, and in other fringe venues in Casablanca. Most members of these bands lived their passion on the TV channels VIVA, MTV and HCM. Their role models were some of the groups that had preceded them, such as Total Eclipse, Immortal Spirit and Carpe Diem.

Despite the state of high alert that accompanied the arrest of these musicians, the police only confiscated some hard rock and black metal CDs and some black T-shirts with pentagrams, skulls and inverted crosses. They also took some magazines such as *Hard Rock*, and posters for Western bands. The young men mostly did not understand the meaning of the English lyrics they sang. The songs they composed were about issues such as Palestine, the chaos of Casablanca and the difficulty of living on a low income.

One thing stood out in the information gathered here and there: all the young men, including Essam and Mahdi, frequented the same clubs as a group called the Ravens, so named because their members dressed all in black, including black leather overcoats and black combat boots. The Ravens wore metal sleeves around their wrists and rings with pointed claws, and had their ears, noses and eyebrows pierced. They adopted sullen expressions and went to all the clubs and cafés high on drugs or alcohol, accompanied by young women with strange names and who wore low-slung pants that revealed their navels and a large part of their hips.

The leader of the Ravens was a man called the Vampire. He organised parties at his house, where he reiterated some of the ideas found in black metal songs, such as mocking Jesus, encouraging sexual freedom, and advocating pleasure, violence and death. But that was not a call for anybody to join in devil worship. It was simply a form of exhibitionism that sometimes prompted him to take his friends to a nearby cemetery and organise a drinking session around a plastic skull with a candle stuck in it. He was once accompanied by a girl called Bish Bish, and he encouraged her to kiss Essam in the presence of his friends and then lie with him on a grave and move in time to a noisy song in imitation of sexual intercourse.

Mahdi avoided talking about this time, probably because he was not fully involved in the groups' activities then, and possibly because he knew things he did not want to reveal. Fatima believed that the developments no one knew about were those that took place during Essam's friendship with the Vampire. No one knew how far the cemetery nights went, or the nature of the relationships between Bish Bish and Essam, and Bish Bish and the Vampire.

Joaquin concluded that it was not inconceivable that Essam had been the victim of one of the devil worshippers' rituals, thanks to direct instigation by the Vampire. It was also possible that this ritual had combined with a settlement of scores based on jealousy, revenge and even simple goading under the influence of alcohol and music. I tried to address those assumptions by eliminating the elements of prurience and exaggeration that were normal in this case. My words upset Fatima once more, and she answered me nervously, claiming that the fixation with incriminating Ibrahim al-Khayati was a political solution.

When I smiled at her, she said grimly, 'Yes, like I'm saying. The decision to downplay the seriousness of the case and release the guys who were arrested came after the media frenzy, the questions in parliament and the solidarity demonstrations. This explains why they couldn't go back and make it serious again by putting a murder at the heart of it. True? Right?'

'If you say so,' I replied.

That same evening we went back to the subject in Layla's presence. She poked fun at Fatima and Joaquin's theory, stressing – somewhat hastily I thought – that it was preferable for Essam to have been killed by Ibrahim and possibly buried in the garden, as the police believed.

I didn't know how it happened, but later I found Fatima crying bitterly. Anxiety had settled in our midst and controlled everything. I could not calm Fatima. Her crying fit took over her whole body and reached such a pitch that she paralysed us all; we could not do a thing for her. Layla convinced us, with unusual calm, that the best thing to do was to let the fit run its course.

Once we got in the car Fatima had regained her composure. She sat next to me and apologised for what had happened, saying, 'I don't usually collapse like a child. The point is that I find Ibrahim al-Khayati's case painful. It hurts me if he did it and it hurts me if he did not. It hurts me because he smiles like an idiot and asks me if I visited Mahdi and whether he has said anything, and why no one visits him and why Ghaliya does not visit him the way she did with the others in the old days. It hurts me that we accepted what happened as if it had to happen and moved on to something else as if we were not ourselves or as if the others were not themselves. Then what? What next? I return to a city that I know but find insipid; I find myself in an apartment like a teenager's. I feed a colleague, just a colleague who won't become anything more. There's friction with Layla, so sure of herself, happy with what she does, and you, I put you especially in the position of bringing me back to reason. What a shame. Why don't we run away to Havana?'

'You said it was too late.'

'I'm talking about the Havana nightclub in Casablanca. It was the last nightclub Essam went to before he disappeared.'

I told her I had been there once with Mahdi and I did not think it a suitable place for us, just a vast bubble of unmelodic noise performed by unattractive people.

I stood in the hotel doorway facing Fatima. Joaquin next to us was like a child past his bedtime. The night was desolate. I looked into Fatima's eyes, transparent after the tears. Then I moved close to her and kissed her on the lips.

She said, laughing, 'That's nice, even if too late!'

Layla's sharp voice and rapid sentences woke me up at three in the morning. She wanted to know if Fatima was with me.

261

'Why would I do that?' I asked her.

'I don't know. I either felt it or dreamed about it.'

I replied sleepily, 'Check for yourself. Do you see how tiny I look in this large bed? There is no woman here.'

She asked angrily, 'Did you wish there were?'

'No. I just want to sleep actually.'

Layla felt sorry for me and said, 'Sleep well and sweet dreams.' She was sorry for her behaviour and asked me if I did not want her to appear out of the phone, and I said yes. She then said she loved me.

Fatima and Joaquin went on collecting news from various sources about Essam's relationship with the Vampire. They wanted to know if he had seduced Essam into some kind of satanic relationship that had brought him back, even after the court case and what was considered the betrayal of Arthritis. According to Fatima, this suspect relationship might have created the sort of dramatic tension that could lead to a crime. But when, two days later, I took her and her Spanish colleague to the airport, she had distanced herself from the story. She considered Ibrahim's arrest before the trial a sensible measure as it would protect him from any foolish act on the part of Mahdi or his mother. She added that Ibrahim was totally convinced Essam had crossed to the other side and might now be in a training camp somewhere, a member of a sleeper cell. I shuddered when I heard her talk so casually about the issue, as if engaging in this tragic destiny was a simple possibility among many others.

I wanted to ask her not to pay any attention to that possibility and to keep up her correspondence with Ibrahim, to help him remain strong. I wanted to convince her to abandon the idea of publishing her investigation in the Spanish press, because of the anxiety some Moroccan officials experienced whenever something was published in the foreign press. I told myself that, after all, the investigation only had limited importance because it did not go beyond the buzz generated by that kind of trial.

As if Fatima had heard what was going through my mind, she said unexpectedly, 'What could create excitement in this kind of investigation is the possible relationship between black metal bands and the Islamist groups.'

'That would be playing games with no connection to the truth,' I said.

She then asked me to stop wasting the little time remaining before her departure talking shop. I did as she asked and dropped the subject. She urged me to take care of myself, to remember my yearly tests, especially my prostate exam, and to watch my blood pressure. She wondered why I didn't devote more time to writing, and why I didn't go and see her in Madrid. 'You need a city that has real nightlife,' she said.

She also asked why nothing in my relationship with Layla was clear.

'What do you want to be clear about it?' I asked.

'I mean everything,' she said. 'And most of all, whether it's a love story.'

'How do you want me to know? I know there's a story and I know more importantly that I am very comfortable in the relationship.'

She asked if I dyed my hair. 'Never,' I said angrily.

She adjusted her attitude and said, 'You have some grey hairs here and there.' She put her finger on the places she meant.

I said, 'If I'm still alive and my hair hasn't gone white, I will come to Madrid.'

She stood up to go to the boarding gate and hugged me quickly, as if she were getting rid of an annoyance. As she was collecting her things, she said nervously, 'Don't ever say "if I'm still alive". It's a phrase that upsets me.'

On my way back from the airport, I was anxious because of this lousy goodbye. I found myself engaged in a remote argument with Fatima, about the way she implicitly blamed me for something I had not done. What did she want me to have done? I should have betrayed my wife with her on the first day. Had I done so, our relationship would have ended perfectly many years ago. But we did not do that and left the matter open to missed opportunities. Meanwhile, for each of us this friendship grew stronger and even more complex. What did she want me to do? Was it possible to build something on top of ruins? Even Al-Firsiwi could not do that. I ended this angry monologue with a torrent of choice swearwords that I addressed to myself and Fatima for obvious reasons, and then to Al-Firsiwi for no obvious reason.

3

I CALLED AHMAD MAJD TO ask him about an apartment Layla
had bought in a project he was developing in Rabat. She
had requested minor changes inside the apartment, but the
work was not yet completed. While discussing this issue,
Ahmad asked me if I was interested in valuable information
regarding a new real-estate scandal.

I said jokingly, 'Does it concern your group or the
competition?'

He did not laugh and told me that he preferred to discuss
the matter in person.

I went to Ahmad's huge construction project in the suburbs
of the capital. It comprised luxury apartment buildings, social
housing – to justify the very low price he had paid for the land
– and an area of villas. All of this was built on the site of the old
hospital and the social work facilities of a number of ministries.
The land was close to the city's green belt, where building was
forbidden. But the state went inside the green belt with its
construction projects, citing their social role. Layla had bought
a small apartment in one of those new buildings, putting all her
savings into it. She would also be putting half her monthly
salary into it for the next ten years.

I wondered whether I too should buy an apartment in the same building. This would bring us close to a semblance of family life without the restrictions of living under the same roof. I liked the idea and immediately discussed it with Layla. At first she seemed distracted, but then she showed an over-whelming enthusiasm that made me embark immediately on a property venture with unforeseen consequences.

It was the first decision I had taken for Layla's sake. Previously, we had talked about the things that would help us build a rela-tionship, when Layla had admitted she missed terribly some elements of daily life in our liaison, for example bringing a gas cylinder and installing it nervously like someone not handy in such things; or my preparing breakfast or using the wrong toothbrush by mistake; or her shouting at me because I had left a wet towel on the bed, knowing very well that that upset her. There was also the issue of socks. She hated men's socks even if they were clean, in fact, even if they were brand new.

'Do you sometimes leave the fridge door open?' she asked me.

'Yes,' I said. 'And the wardrobe door and the kitchen tap.'

'My God, those are things I could kill over!'

I told her that we'd better avoid sharing anything that might lead us to a bloody end. She then said something that surprised me. She said that what delighted her in our relationship was that it had been a source of amazement from the first day. She wondered how she had met me and how we could continue to be together. She was surprised how we hadn't met for years and then how we hadn't missed each other on the way, although everything around us called for that. She was particularly surprised how we lived a love that we did not declare, that we did not expect and that we did not need to manage.

My heart pounded when she talked about love, like a teen-ager thinking about it for the first time. It was the way I had felt when I regained my sense of smell, my face buried in Yacine's shirt. I had the impression that Layla was pouring over me all at once, as if she were water that had been dammed for a long time behind a huge boulder, but had finally managed to displace the boulder and come streaming over me. I had no choice but to put myself at the mercy of the raging water and let it carry me, not knowing where I would surface or go under as I released myself from time, since time was condensed in this torrent.

That evening as we were leaving Layla's house I told her that I loved her. She said simply, 'I know.'

Quite disappointed, I said, 'But I never told you that before.'

She insisted, 'Yes you did. A million times without uttering the words.'

'No, no, no,' I said. 'There's a terrible misunderstanding here. The feeling itself, I mean the feeling of love, never occurred to me. You know, I felt that the person I am, who does not experience the feeling of love, does, in fact, love you. But this feeling was nothing but a cold awareness. It has nothing to do with what I feel today.'

We got into the car, and when I started speaking again, she stopped me and said that the subject did not interest her at all. She then took my hand, placed it on her chest and said that she wanted to sleep a little while I drove to the Japanese restaurant. Then she said, 'Look how beautiful the sky is, the clouds, the melting colours. And the light, oh my God, do you see the light?'

'I do, I do.'

'It's a sky just for us.'

I laughed, surprised, but she insisted, saying, 'Really, it's a sky for us. Every time we make love, it gives us this gift.'

I drove in silence while she held my hand and I felt her breathing. When I stopped near our restaurant, Layla was fast asleep. I switched off our mobiles and lay down without removing my hand, unconcerned by the curiosity of the passers-by.

Layla had told me many times that all her life she had looked for an easy-going man and that I could be that man. I attributed that to my total inability to ask her for anything. And the pain I had endured liberated me from many aspects of myself without my planning it or making an exceptional effort to that end. Therefore I began watching what was happening to me as if it were happening to somebody else. This distance gave me the capacity to act with a satisfying generosity that I did not clearly understand until I sensed its delightful impact on my surroundings.

Layla, however, understood everything. She knew how I worked and exactly what my weaknesses were. She knew that at a certain moment in my journey, which resembled the steps of an acrobat, there would be a momentary loss of balance that could push me into a precipitous fall. She was very concerned that this moment would take me by surprise in a dangerous place or that my fall would dent my dignity. I, on the other hand, dreaded having one of my fits while with her. I didn't care at all whether it happened on the train or in the street. But not with her. Then one day it happened. I begged her to keep talking to me, not about anything in particular, but with unchecked words as if I would breathe with those words. She did that with amazing skill, as if she had trained for it for years. After that I never needed to suggest to her what she had to do. She would know the fit was approaching before I felt it myself. She would take my hand and help me get over the dark moments, as if leading me to a comfortable chair.

Layla also knew that I loved her and clutched her back from the talons of savage loss. I ran after her absent face in details that happened in my life, or did not happen. She became an unalloyed possibility from the first day. She was always possible, and if she did not materialise at a specific moment, it was not because she was not there but because the moment was not the one, and now she was at an infinite moment and so was I. There was a desert that I had to cross, and I knew that paradise was at a certain turn in this immensity. She knew that, too, and responded to every situation that upset us by saying, 'It's a matter that does not concern us, it's happening to other people.' In so doing she borrowed an image that she knew represented precisely my relationship with the world.

We received our apartments the same week. But I spent a whole week getting rid of my belongings in my old home. I had told Layla that this apartment would be meaningless if I did not use it to fulfil a wish going back to my adolescence of an empty white house with hardly any internal walls. And so it was. One of Ahmad's contractors helped me realise my dream.

I reserved the space for the bedroom and the bathroom and left all the rest open with a huge balcony that ran along the side that faced west. The kitchen was on the right from the entrance, and the remaining space extended to the blueness of the ocean. All this white expanse would be filled with nothing but white curtains, a large low black table, and four white poufs for sitting on. In the kitchen I placed all the utensils in a wooden black frame made to measure, which turned them into a neutral barrier that did not disrupt the sense of emptiness. I had a single bookcase with very few books that I had kept from my desert days, which I put in the kitchen out of a conviction that books belonged to the realm of spices, oils and preserves. In the lower drawers of the kitchen I stashed the documents and photos that I did not have the courage to burn. Two days before I moved into my new apartment I sold all my paintings, taking advantage of the huge rise in their value, and I donated my library to an association in the Yacoub El Mansour district in Rabat. I gave my furniture to the first old friend willing to take it. I had a single large key for the apartment made out of pure red copper.

No one liked my home. All my friends found it cold and desolate, and made fun of the minimalist decor. Even Layla said that I had imported Japanese emptiness to a culture that finds itself only in clutter. Despite all that I stood my ground for fear I would relapse if I went back on my decision. I later realised that I mainly used the bedroom, while the white void was inhabited by mysterious souls.

One evening Layla and I were sitting in this spiritual space, taking our time to eat dinner. We could see our shadows, the flame of the candle and the wild fish – as I called Al-Wazzani's carving standing on the table – reflected in the glass of the balcony, while the sky was still lit by a soft sunset. I was coming and going to the kitchen without interrupting my conversation with Layla or going out of sight. She found this situation practical and appreciated having the whole kitchen open to the living room.

'The surprise comes in how the food tastes, nothing else,' she said. 'I saw from the start that you were preparing fish, but that only doubled the surprise of tasting the tang of saffron in the slices of sea bream. Both the place and the meal will forever remain two sides of a single coin. The relationship between places and tastes is truly amazing.'

When the horizon turned totally dark, Layla asked me to draw the curtains because she always imagined that someone was watching us. I did as she asked, knowing that the flowing white drapes would give the glass façade a cottony dimension that would totally change the sensation of the inner space. As soon as the lights of the city disappeared and the white drapes fell over the transparency of the glass, something blossomed in the ambiance. The light and the emptiness became like a mad wind playing in the mind and planting a fiery desire in everything. Layla said that if she had not been so shy, she would have walked around naked in the space.

I got close to her and began seeking her nakedness, in submission to my fingers and a desire more powerful than I had felt in years. I felt as if I did not recognise my own movements, which seemed to be guided by something that rose freely within my body. The details of her body seized me by surprise, without passing through the mind's filter that used to guide me to her. They reached me through her neck, her chest and the smoothness of her back. I closed my eyes and submitted to her fingertips exploring my features and prying inside every shudder that passed through me. I heard for the first time her innermost sounds rising between my hands, reaching me from a cavernous flow, not a language but a straining musical performance. Then I found myself inside her breath, her sweetness and a closed oyster, where I transformed into the scent of the sea scattered far by salt and seaweed. She resisted my incursion with nervous pushes, a mixture of rising and ebbing, until she succeeded in creating a small breach in our wave. She said she wanted to walk naked. I followed her gradual rise with my hands and lips until she placed her two small feet with long toes, the nails carefully painted, on the same marble that I was warming with two burning cheeks. I saw her toes move when I touched them with my lips, then I saw the feet move like glowing objects. I remained lying down and could not see her walk in the white space; I saw only her feet leaving the shiny surface of the marble and then returning to it in breathtaking harmony.

When the cold stung I sat up and asked Layla to stand against the curtains, which she did with exciting compliance. I saw her expression for the first time and I was enveloped with what looked like thick clouds as a result of what I saw. Her face had become filled with the emptiness she was walking in and had acquired a metaphysical dimension, as if the effort she had made and the secret dance she had performed had poured infinite distance into her expression. I stretched my arms to her for a long time. She did not move, but remained standing in front of the curtains in all her desire. I begged her to touch her body. She moved her hands in unison, starting with her face and then descending over all her body until she reached the bottom of her tummy with one hand. With her other hand she pulled part of the curtains over her body, covering movements that made the cloth ripple and her face fill with the glow of total pleasure.

I fell in love with my apartment that night. After that night I felt clearly that Layla would fill the place of the mysterious souls. She would live in this house the way she lived in my skin. She liked the idea of the books placed in the kitchen, and she would even help me get rid of books I used to consider essential in my life, such as the complete works of Hölderlin and Rilke, Henri Michaux and Pessoa. She said that poetry was not beautiful when it was easily accessible, and that when I wanted to read it, I should go to the library and read only one poem.

She developed a theory of minimalism and applied it to my music collection and my clothes. I was happy to find myself freed of the weight of the years that had made me attached to the insignificant things piled around me, in the belief that I was preserving the years themselves. I even felt that this renewal in the material domain gave objects a new soul. It was as if another person had come as reinforcements in the battle that I had been waging for survival.

4

M Y DOCTOR NOTICED A general improvement in my condition, and recommended that to fully recover I take up a sport that would exercise body and soul. He suggested a yoga club that offered Pilates. I welcomed the advice with childlike enthusiasm. But I couldn't stand the fact that the club was in the basement and that the regulars made fun of my jerky movements. I discreetly withdrew, but not without going through a transformational experience.

In the yoga club I met a young man who looked very much like me. He and Yacine were as alike as two droplets of water. When I told him that he said, smiling, 'You might well be my father. I am the illegitimate child of a woman who died single. If twenty years ago you knew a young teacher from the city of Khenifra and you might have had a child with her, then I'm your long-lost son. From now on you have to make room in your life for me.'

When he noticed my anxiety and nervousness, he burst out laughing and said in a friendly tone, 'Don't worry, I won't harass you. I don't want a father that I'm supposed to kill in order to live at peace.'

His concise, joking sentences made it clear he was quite unaware of the bomb he was throwing into my life, for one summer, twenty-four years earlier, I had had a passionate affair with a woman called Zulikha. It ended, naturally enough, at the beginning of the new school year. There was nothing special about the story except that she looked like the French actress Romy Schneider.

Remembering her, it was almost like the only real tragedy in my life had been her disappearance one distant autumn, followed by her sudden death, which I knew nothing about. Then our potential son turned up – a broadcast engineer who liked yoga and comedies.

I was overcome with questions about whether Zulikha might have been the woman I had lost but could not remember. Perhaps news of her death had reached me without my realising. I charted all the accomplishments that might have been expected in her life and turned her into a vague object of loss. A suspicion tormented me: I had finally found an explanation for my being emotionally lost, yet I had not found the woman, not even as a distant memory.

Al-Firsiwi, if he were to reappear, could rest assured about his offspring. No matter how much we tried to get away from our seed, they plotted their own course, which, sooner or later, snared us in the net of paternity.

I spent a few weeks in a spin at this striking discovery. When I told Layla about it, she commented sarcastically, 'You'd be stupid to think that being a father is simply sowing your oats!'

Fatima, on the other hand, advised me to take it easy and ask the young man if his mother's name was Zulikha. I returned to the club for that reason, and when he left the hall I went up to him and asked.

He replied, smiling, 'Of course her name is Zulikha.' Then he asked me quite seriously, 'Do you want to put your doubts to rest?'

274

I nodded, so he said, 'Let's do a DNA test. If it confirms that I'm your son, everything will be clear. You'll have to pass by the club as soon as possible and pay my monthly membership!'

He walked away and then turned to look at me and laughed, his face joyful. I did not think then that he resembled Yacine or me to the degree I had imagined when I first met him. But I said to myself that he probably looked like Zulikha, whom I didn't remember then, and never would.

On the way home I thought long and hard about what was happening to me, and I told myself that this was also one possibility among many others that could come along. Devastated by the loss of an only son, we suddenly find ourselves a father in a different story. We await the birth of a baby girl with great joy, and then she is born with a handicap; we think our life is over with the arrival of this baby, only to discover that life has become meaningful. No one could know which possibility might bring the greatest comfort. I told myself this because I felt calmer about the tragedy of Yacine's loss than about this new story.

I shared my thoughts with Fatima, and she suggested that we adopt a child together. I tried to avoid the subject but she insisted. 'The baby would only need you to be a father from a distance. You'd see, helping to shape a human being would only require a few years – perhaps less time than would be needed for a tree. That person would then become your heart's delight.' She also said, 'Just imagine how many things we would put right with such a venture, even those things that time has spoiled.'

I told Fatima that I did not have the energy for such things any more. Her silence on the phone made me feel guilty, because I realised that her suggestion was a desperate cry for help.

At the end of the day I was walking in the crowded Al-Akary market, where all the activity connected to food reduced my anxiety, when I found myself face to face with the young man who resembled me. The first thing I saw was his wide smile, his happy expression. He surprised me with an exaggerated greeting. With a generous sweep of his arm, he stretched to embrace an embarrassed man walking past him.

He said, laughing, 'This is my father, the one and only person legally responsible for this calamity,' and pointed to himself proudly.

I too felt like laughing, but I controlled myself and said reproachfully, 'That's a cruel joke!'

He tapped me on the shoulder and said, 'Let go. Life is good. Let's laugh.'

I lowered my head and left defeated, unable to pinpoint the nature of my feelings, which were a mixture of disappointment and boundless joy at my escape.

I told Layla part of the story in a somewhat humorous manner, but she found it very moving. She said she loved the young man as if he were my son or our son from a past relationship that had happened years ago. She liked the light-heartedness of the young man, who should have been burdened by the responsibilities of beginnings. When she asked me his name, I was surprised to realise I had neglected to ask him, as if I wanted the matter to remain a mere possibility. Layla – God knows what her feelings were – burst into tears and said she was very sad because we could not have a baby together. At that point, unaware of what made the issue so easy for me, I perpetrated the worst theft imaginable. I suggested to Layla, very simply, that we adopt a baby, with me as a hands-off father. I told her with neurotic insistence to keep the matter a secret, as if hoping secrecy would be tantamount to revoking the suggestion completely. She immediately busied herself with the most minute details of adoption, its rules and regulations and institutions, all the while asking the reason for my insistence on keeping it a secret, and wondering if I thought that revealing it would matter to her.

That was how Mai came into our life. We did not tell anybody that she was our daughter, but all our friends, including Fatima, understood. They refrained from commenting, except Bahia. She broached the subject indirectly with me two or three times, talking about Layla, expressing her strong admiration for her. She said that Layla had a certain purity that freed her of any doubt and that Mai was a symbol of that deep purity. On another occasion she asked me if I was convinced that a child could play a constructive role in a relationship. I told her that this might happen in reaction: when two people form a human being together, they indirectly re-form themselves. She told me that she had never felt that way either with me when we had Yacine or with Ahmad Majd and their baby daughter, Ghaliya. On another occasion she asked me if Mai had filled some of Yacine's void.

'No, never,' I said, and I confessed to her that Yacine had not disappeared totally from my life. He had stayed with me for many years, taking part in some of my daily activities. When I saw her dumbfounded expression, I told her I did not mean it metaphorically, but that I really used to see and talk to him, before he disappeared again for good.

During this period of her life Bahia had settled into her new persona, a calm, relaxed woman who gradually put on weight until her body matched her new status. She put up a barrier of carefully studied interests, all dealing with charitable work, social ventures, and conservation of the *malhoun* heritage. There were also all the related social events, consisting of soirées in friends' houses, in *riyadhs* and hotels, and everything else that burnished the halo around Ahmad Majd. Bahia did not seem enthusiastic about what she was doing, although she defended her husband and the real-estate boom that reflected the country's excellent health. I saw her once adopt that position in her new house in Marrakech, and I was struck by how stridently she backed him. After the guests departed, I told her that nothing had called for such a response, especially seeing that Ahmad Majd was, as usual, countering the arguments with his usual caustic wit and sneering at his adversaries' intellects. She nervously explained to me that she was not doing it for him but for herself.

Meanwhile, all Marrakech was talking about Ahmad Majd's relationship with his private secretary. Going with her to hotels and restaurants was not enough any more, and she had started to accompany him on long trips to the UAE and Saudi Arabia. She had returned veiled from her last trip to Saudi Arabia and had described at length and in a pious tone her *umra* with Hajj Ahmad.

Some of our friends were convinced that she was a second wife and that the concerned parties were keeping it secret. But Bahia did not reveal, either in her conversation or comportment, anything to confirm the existence of another marriage. Every now and again, all the players in the story – with its real and imagined aspects, the open and the hidden – would meet over couscous for Friday lunch, but no one seemed to know any more than anyone else.

The Butterfly

I

AHMAD MAJD TOLD ME about a real-estate scandal engulf-
ing a luxury housing project in Tétouan built by the Sour
al-Watani Group on land they had bought from a known drug
dealer. After the project was inaugurated amid much fanfare, it
was discovered that the land belonged to the state and had been
sold using fake title deeds. This led to sweeping arrests in the
ranks of the administration and courts ruled in favour of the
state. The property developer had to pay for the land twice.
That the elite inaugurated a project based on stolen land, as
well as the involvement of numerous parties in underhand
dealing, fraud and forgery, made the scandal blow up in public.

I said to Ahmad Majd that he must be happy with this turn
of events, since the scandal involved his biggest competitor. He
said quietly that he was not in competition with anyone, and
added that his life and that of generations to follow him would
not be enough to manage the success he had achieved. He said
he had mentioned the issue because he was aware of the danger
such corrupt deals posed to the future of democracy in
Morocco. I could not help but bring up, laughing, the four
hectares in the centre of Marrakech that he had bought from
the state at a very low price, on the understanding that in

return he would cover the cost of removing the inhabitants living on it. Once it was cleared, he sold the land at a price five times lower than the market value to a powerful group that did not dare acquire the land directly from the state. He did that in return for other sites in Marrakech and other cities at a token price. Was that not also a fraudulent deal? I asked him.

Nothing made him flinch. 'In this arrangement,' he responded, 'is there a hint of forged contracts, legal skulduggery or hush money? Do you want to criminalise buying and selling for obscure political purposes, or stop human intelligence from breaking into the property market?'

I said, despondent, 'I don't want anything of the sort. I only want to save my skin!' He laughed from his belly and said that I was the last person in this town who thought all that was done or not done aimed only at getting his skin.

I told him that I was not like that, but I understood that I could be that way, because this general mood of confidence disturbed me. The feeling that we had all made it to safety and that nothing threatened our negligence was a stupid feeling with nothing human about it.

Around this time Ahmad Majd was finishing what he said was the apartment building of his life. It was a huge structure close to the new main road, where buildings were not supposed to be higher than four floors to avoid blocking what was left of the view of the High Atlas mountains from inside the medina. But Ahmad Majd had fought a bitter war to go up nine floors. That battle forced him to buy, at market price, a nearby lot that allowed him to move his apartment building a few metres away from the first location, which would have blocked the view of the Atlas entirely.

Ahmad Majd used to say that the city was a city and the mountain a mountain, so why did anyone want to drink their coffee in the street as their sleepy eyes roamed over the High Atlas? 'Plus, my brother,' he would continue, 'no one looks at the mountains when they're walking or driving in the street. That's just tourist nonsense summed up in that stupid photo of someone lying under a luxuriant palm tree, smelling the orange blossom and gazing at the snow on the Atlas. Bullshit! All that's left to do is add a Tanjia pot to the scene to conjure up stewed kidney from under the ground.'

Despite all that was said about the apartment building, Ahmad Majd pushed ahead with the project. He said that what Marrakech needed was a building that would free it of the spirit of the distant past and bring a bit of frivolity into the city, to break the grip of the ubiquitous brick colour, the palm trees and the general appearance of a stop for desert caravans. He shaped his building in the form of a giant butterfly, with a nightclub below the ground floor and restaurants at ground level. A vast banquet hall and shops were located on the first five floors, while luxury apartments occupied the remaining floors. An amazing apartment would take up the whole of the ninth floor, where the residents would have the Koutoubia in the palm of their hands.

Foreign companies competed to be awarded the interior design on all the floors. Ahmad Majd did not specify any features for the interior except for materials and shapes. The external decor consisted of a soaring butterfly, and the inhabitants of Marrakech did not wait long to nickname the building the Butterfly, which became the official name used by city residents as a reference point for appointments and on maps.

People were struck by this building with its provocative shape, located in the heart of the medina, whose ancient character was protected by an army of conservatives, informants and the curious. But few of them knew that the apartments on the top four floors were the ones that had allowed the building to sprout without anyone seeing it. Whenever I asked Ahmad Majd in total innocence about the owners of those luxury apartments, he would mention a number of rich Gulf Arabs, and a world-renowned French perfume maker on the top floor. He did not mention the name of a single Moroccan. I would smile at that, and he would smile back and say, 'The building will remain a mystery. There's no point in insisting.'

On the ninth of May that year, Ahmad Majd organised the opening of the Butterfly. It was a celebration exactly as he had planned for many years and it surpassed everything people had imagined about celebrations, even the reopening of the Hotel La Mamounia in the 1980s. The echoes of those festivities had reached the landings of Kenitra central prison where Ahmad Majd had been incarcerated. He had never suspected then what would happen less than a quarter of a century later. Even those celebrations with all their splendour did not amount to one tenth of what Ahmad Majd designed for the inauguration of his new building.

At the opening of the Butterfly, hundreds of young men wearing the same traditional red costume and the same striped Marrakechi hat stood on both sides of the building. Thousands of butterflies, guided by invisible threads, and thousands of multicoloured birds, pigeons and doves invaded the Marrakech sky. Hundreds of guests were transported from their respective hotels to the Butterfly on the backs of white camels. A waterfall gushed from the top of the building to its marble courtyard. For years to come people would remember the philharmonic orchestra that came all the way from Berlin and the dozens of male and female singers who performed. Behind the stage where they were singing was the largest butterfly, revealing the colourful and brightly lit balconies of the building. People would especially remember that for the first time since Marrakech started having festivities, dancing and partying till late at night, hundreds of men and women roamed the city from one end to the other, carrying plates of dates and glasses of milk. Ahmad Majd had had the drink glasses made especially for the occasion. He'd engraved the name of the building and the date of the opening of its huge shopping mall on the glasses, along with a picture of baby Ghaliya with a sentence below it reading: '*This is by the grace of God.*' The crowd partied to the early hours of the morning.

The official celebration ended about midnight. Ahmad Majd said after the opening party ended he would go up to the dream apartment on the ninth floor as a guest of the French owner, the perfumier, who had paid cash for the apartment without seeing it. I asked if it were possible for me to know the price of the apartment, but Ahmad Majd laughed, saying, 'Can you just enjoy yourself and keep quiet?'

Fatima, Layla and I joined Ahmad. The apartment opened into a circular hall in the style of the Andalusian domes, and in the middle was a fountain of intertwining horses made of white marble, jets of water spouting from their mouths. A group of guests hovered around this piece of art, talking at length about the well-known British sculptor who had made it especially for the apartment. I had the impression I knew the sculptor, having seen him in a catalogue Fatima had brought me from an exhibit of major European sculptors a few years earlier in Strasbourg. Fatima confirmed my guess. She was open-mouthed in amazement: the sculpture cost more than all our apartments put together. Layla said she found the hall vulgar, and she was right. But her opinion in no way affected the mood of this second festivity, and I was surprised by Ahmad Majd's anger, for he heard the comment as he was making room for himself among us. Nevertheless, I decided to stay in a good mood for the party and refrain from any cheap jibes. The most amazing thing in the apartment was the swimming pool. It stretched to the end of the balcony and gave the impression that the water was flowing in the street. Layla and I stood there for a long time admiring the illuminated swimming pool, which revealed a huge mosaic mural. We were looking at it in awe when our happy host approached us and explained that the mural was a Byzantine mosaic that had followed him for thirty years, from one house to another. He added, 'I think it has finally settled down in this suspended paradise.'

Layla asked, 'Where was it thirty years ago?'

'I don't know exactly. My business rep bought it at a British auction. So I imagine it was somewhere in the Middle East.' Then he asked us if the reflection of the light on the mosaic bothered us from this angle, and Layla assured him there was no reflection at all. 'Good,' he said. 'I just wanted to make sure. We placed a glass cover on the mural to protect it, and I feared it would reflect the rays.'

Layla said, 'I'm just trying to imagine the void that the removal of this masterpiece left behind.'

Our host replied in a friendly tone, 'It would be like any other void, my lady. A mere void.'

We spent a long time admiring the apartment, which felt like a museum. There were sculptures from the Far East, Persian miniatures, Turkish glassware, and a mix of textiles, leather and silver and copper vessels. There were also works by the major Orientalist painters, including Delacroix and Jacques Majorelle. Layla jokingly suggested stealing them. I told her there was certainly an electronic security system in place to protect the treasures, which had already been stolen once during their lifetime.

There was a large wooden gallery and huge plants in the massive bar that overlooked the Koutoubia. Fatima, Layla and I sat at a small table near the counter and away from the noise of the guests who had spread around the swimming pool and filled the apartment's balconies. We were discussing our common preoccupations when I felt that someone was looking in my direction; or, to be more precise, I felt a presence that was overpowering me. I expected someone to appear suddenly. This terrified me and I was unable to move, as I thought about Al-Firsiwi, my mother and Zulikha. Layla wondered what was wrong with me. I asked her to check if there was someone behind me or on the other side of the counter watching me. She told me she couldn't see anyone.

I looked to the right, where the refrigerators and the shelves of cups and glasses were, and I saw him standing there, looking over the city with his dreamy expression and the bunch of stony grapes over his shoulder. I saw his broken arm and his adolescent size. The statue had all the dullness of granite dating back to the first century BC. I stood up trembling and approached it. I examined its right foot and found it had lost four toes, the same ones that were still on the statue's plinth at the entrance to Walili.

'It's Bacchus! The Bacchus of Walili,' I yelled in excitement.

A number of guests gathered round. Ahmad Majd arrived, clearly upset. Layla held on to me as Fatima examined the statue and took photos. I was overcome with a feeling I could not define, a mixture of joy, madness and fear.

Ahmad Majd shouted at me, saying, 'Bacchus, Bacchus! And so what?'

I said, 'Nothing, but we must take it. That's all there is to it.'

Our host approached our group and asked, a smile frozen on his face, what was the matter. Fatima explained that it was simply an unexpected encounter with a person we knew. The Frenchman said, 'I always like to play a role in unexpected encounters.'

Fatima pointed to Bacchus, saying, 'He has been our friend for about a quarter of a century. In other words, ever since he disappeared from his family home in Walili.'

The Frenchman did not make any immediate comment, but his face rippled with a mounting tremor. He said this adolescent Bacchus was not considered an exceptional artistic achievement, despite the lyricism deriving from the lack of harmony between the age of the young man and the delicacy of his movements, which almost stripped the statue of its unworked feel. 'Despite all that,' he said, 'I loved it at first sight when I saw it in Frankfurt. I must confess that it did not cost me much. I can honestly say it is the cheapest piece in my collection.'

We left the apartment after an extended argument over what to do. I insisted on staying to wait for the police to arrive so I could make a statement regarding Bacchus's recovery. But the French host, Ahmad Majd and other guests suggested otherwise, so as to avoid ruining such a beautiful evening, especially since the owner was not denying the fact or distancing himself from the matter. They all said they knew nothing about the origins of the Bacchus statue, and they wondered if it would be possible to wait until the morning for the guests to leave and the festivities to end. Then we could do whatever was needed, quietly.

Ahmad Majd asked me whether I was more interested in Bacchus or the scandal.

'Both,' I said, and to be honest, I added, 'I'm interested in the scandal, first and foremost.'

Finally, dragging my feet, I left the gallery, went in the direction of the swimming pool and then to the circular hall, and finally to the lift. I was unable to fully recover from the in-between condition I had experienced. I had the feeling I had found Bacchus and not found him; I was happy at this and not happy; I was surprised and not surprised. I thought of calling Al-Firsiwi but I wondered what I would get from doing so. I would probably succeed in destroying his legend regarding Bacchus, and then what? Wouldn't it be better for him to continue believing that he had fooled us all? Was there something closer to the truth than lies, since both revealed each other?

People in front of me were getting into the crowded lifts, and whenever they became a single mass of heads and apologies, the doors would shut and a mysterious abyss would swallow them. I was about to derive a certain lesson from this evocative image when Layla pushed me into the abyss.

I surrendered to an enjoyable descent, wishing it would never end, when the lift doors opened to a large commotion. At the centre of it all, I saw Fatima bleeding from her nose and shouting. It took me time to understand that two men had grabbed her as she was leaving the lift, attacked her and taken away her camera.

We went straight to the police station, where I reported that I had found the statue of Bacchus that had been stolen a quarter of a century before, and named all the witnesses who had been with me. Fatima reported that she had been attacked and her digital camera stolen. She was convinced theft in such a luxurious place would not be for the money but because she had taken pictures of Bacchus in the ninth floor apartment, in the presence of prominent guests and the owner, the most famous perfume maker in the world.

I no longer had any desire to get anything out of this storm. All I wanted was to return to our room in Ahmad Majd's house and hold Mai in my arms. I urged Layla to hurry home, assuring her that I did not want anything from this situation, neither a court case nor a victory. All I wanted was to embrace Mai. This sudden upheaval made me easy prey to a destructive fear. My heart constricted, and I imagined that I would not find Mai in her bed or that I would find her swimming in a pool of blood. I had a fit as I fought this fear. I did not know why the fits occurred at my moments of fear in particular.

Layla began spooling the lifeline of words that would help me breathe, throwing it out to the depths that had started to swallow me. I stretched out my arm to grab the rope, but my hand was going crooked and bending back. I tried to return it to its normal position with my other hand, but it too froze against my chest. I was totally tied up while Layla continued to talk about Mai, who had taken her first steps, unexpectedly, the previous day. 'She stood and looked at me. I told her: come on, come to Mama, and she took one step, then another, and then walked all the way to where I was, without smiling or crying, as if she were doing something she had been doing for ages.'

I then saw a face looking at the car window. I saw a garden and a person running with a dog or away from it. Then I could not see anything except a white light, an overwhelming white light that gradually faded away, revealing objects and sounds. I saw Mai extending her tiny hand towards my face. The moment she touched it, I understood everything.

The police called us in the following day. They told us they had found no trace of a Roman statue in the apartment. I told the officer that we should be taken to court for making up a crime. He said amiably, 'We don't see any need for that. There's no complaint against you.'

I smiled dumbly at the faces that surrounded me. Fatima led me out by the arm. I felt a heavy burden lifting off my chest. I might have been worried that Bacchus, in the event of his glorious return, would become a lawsuit that I would have to manage in connection with many things that were beyond me.

'OK. The best thing is for all of us to retire to their corner, isn't it?' I asked Fatima.

She turned towards me and asked me with teary eyes what I meant.

I said that it was normal for such things to happen at the end of a muddled party, where one sees people and things that no one else sees.

Fatima said, 'It was simple theft. Why are you trying to give it wings?'

'I was a stone's throw from achieving my only victory over Al-Firsiwi, but I failed. His story about the courtyard of the village mosque will remain the most plausible.'

We got in the car, and Fatima hurried to wipe her face and get ready as she always did when she was overtaken by anger. She said, without any trace of hesitation in her voice, 'I will never return to this country to live. I cannot live in a place I do not understand.'

I wished, deep inside, not to believe her, but I failed. Then I quickly felt better because her decision not to come back had nothing to do with me.

When we returned to Ahmad Majd's house and I told Layla what happened, she reacted by quickly and determinedly packing our suitcases. We did not even need to discuss the matter. We put the suitcases in the car and left. She insisted on driving. I gave in, not wanting to upset her, but she begged me while I was sitting in the back with Mai never to drive again.

'Promise me, I beg you, never to drive again.'

I told her frankly that I would never give up this poetic machine, and if a fit did not kill me while I was driving, it

would while I was doing something else. 'What's the difference?' I asked.

'The difference is that you won't be around for me to
hate you.'

Layla drove in her deliberate, restrained manner while I
played with Mai, teaching her sounds made by birds and
animals and play-acting roles from cartoons that only the two
of us knew. Mai was excited, and after more than an hour she
became tired and began rubbing her eyes. Still she did not give
in and concentrated her efforts on making me sleep, placing
her cheek on my head the way her mother would do for her,
then passing her fingers through my hair, insisting with her half
words that I rest. Whenever I moved to evade this obligation,
she got upset like a true mother and quickened the stroking of
her fingers.

When Layla said we were approaching Settat, Mai said,
'Shustt, shustt.' The last thing I heard was Layla's laughter. Then
I woke up and heard her say, 'We've arrived.'

I put Mai to bed and helped Layla get everything in order
before going up to my apartment. I entered the large, empty
space illuminated by the city lights, and took a deep breath.

2

I WOKE UP EXHAUSTED FOR unknown reasons and thought: no one can do anything for anyone else. At that stage in my life, or that moment of the morning, I had the impression that I was a prisoner of situations I was not responsible for and was unable to get away from. Even when I had all the best intentions in the world to do something, I could not do it. I could not do anything for Fatima, I could not do anything for Al-Firsiwi, I could not save Bacchus and I could not go to Havana. I could not run away to a far-off island with Layla, yet I could not stop thinking of escape as the only way to start a new life.

I said all of that to Layla and she answered sharply, 'A few months ago you could not think about a new place to live, and here you are now living in it and according to the ridiculous Japanese style of your dreams. Before that, there were loads of things you could not do, but sometimes they happened without a huge effort on your part.'

'Like what?' I asked.

'Our relationship, for example. Many lives had to intersect before you could find the way that led you to me.'

I asked her angrily, 'And you?'

'I always knew what I wanted.' This seemed to me the ideal expression of human happiness: to wake up or not wake up and be able to define exactly what you wanted without random additions and gaps, to say 'I want to get up now and go to a park' and to walk with a strong feeling that serenity would certainly be found where the row of eucalyptus trees ended.

For many years I had carried Yacine on my shoulders, and every time I laid my head on the pillow I would decide to bury him. In the dark I would rehearse the rituals of the delayed funeral: I would carry the bier by myself and proceed towards the hole, but when I looked at it, it appeared bottomless. As soon as I lowered the bier into it, I would see Yacine come out and run through a vast cemetery with headstones made of flesh and blood.

Ahmad Majd called me one day. He was in a pitiable condition, searching for words to resume our friendship as if nothing had happened. He said Bahia was very ill and he was taking her to Paris for treatment. His words did not sink in and I did not ask him for explanations. I was not worried about her. I felt as if something were happening to a distant person, and no matter what occurred I would be unable to help. I felt better about that and I realised that powerlessness was, after all, comforting, because it freed you of guilt and always made you the victim.

I called Fatima many times to tell her about Bahia's illness, but she did not answer and did not contact me. I thought that she too might have disappeared, like Al-Firsiwi and Ibrahim al-Khayati and Essam. I was overcome with a deep fear and called Layla. I told her I wanted to see her immediately because I was afraid she would disappear. She was busy, so we agreed to meet in the evening, though this did not spare me from being troubled the whole day by black thoughts about her disappearance. When we met and I told her that, she caressed my face with her hand and said that I was merely upset because of what was happening around us. She also said that the quarrel with Ahmad Majd had opened a door to fear that we had to shut quickly. I was very happy that she said this, and said it for my sake, knowing full well that Ahmad Majd did not deserve this effort. I wanted to comment on the matter but she begged me not to. We ate quickly and went to a modern dance performance at the French Cultural Centre.

The show was fast and frenetic, the tempo high and athletic. It shifted all the burden on to us, as we shrank back into our seats under the pressure of that devotion of the body that toyed with violence and seduction. I told Layla when we left the show that words were the best means of expression for human beings. There was something too intimate about the body and movement, or a limitation, that prevented the act of expression from making unexpected stupid mistakes.

She said, 'We are able to do that with violence or love.'

I agreed with little enthusiasm and continued walking, feeling something hot rise from my guts that absorbed me in a kind of material absence. I thought it was the sign of a new fit, but soon realised that part of the show's choreography had seized my body, which felt possessed by a violent inner storm. We got into the car and Layla ignored me as she drove, and I heard Yacine confiding to me in a clearly stern tone, 'Now. Now!'

'Now what?' I asked.

He repeated insistently, 'Now!'

I shouted angrily, 'What now?'

Layla said, scared, 'What's with now? What's with you?' She pulled the car over to the side of the road, confused.

'Nothing, it's nothing. I think I'm tired, that's all,' I said.

We continued on our way. Layla had regained her composure and tried to justify the confusion that had taken hold of me. According to her I had internalised the scene of violence in the show, and the slow and clean movements depicting mutual seduction and pleasure had led to a sudden desire to kill.

I said, 'Yes, it might have been that.'

As a special consolation, she suggested that we sleep in the same place, an idea I deemed a good ending to a trying day.

So here she was on the snow-white bedding, bathed by the glow of a distant lamp, her hand resting on my chest as she slept curled up in the foetal position. I asked myself what love was. For many years I had been unable to identify a feeling connected to this emotion. As I watched her face, radiant in peaceful sleep, I told myself that perhaps love was being with a woman at the right time.

As we were eating breakfast the next day Layla said, 'You must visit Bahia as soon as possible. It isn't Ahmad Majd who will make her feel at peace.'

'No one can do anything for anyone else,' I said.

'I don't like to begin the day in a bad mood,' she said angrily.

Whenever I travelled from Rabat to Marrakech, I would look out the train window and see places I had known for years, barren fields, square patches of cacti and a scattering of withered eucalyptus trees. Nothing had changed in these poor landscapes, where every now and then I would spot somebody crossing these badlands with the assurance of someone living in paradise. One day the motorway would pass through that arid poetry, and we would have to draw another landscape to put in train windows. The motorway would extend all the way to Agadir, and the journey from there to Tangier would take only eight hours instead of the two days it did before. We would become a small country that could be crossed from north to south in less than a day.

Bahia quietly greeted me when I arrived. She did not look like she was suffering from a fatal illness or the devastating anxiety linked to it. We sat in the garden and she talked to me with amazement about the war waging between her husband and his rival. The latest chapter involved land that was open for development on the mountain road, land that was on the books as security at one of the banks before the ferocious rival got hold of it through scary pressure tactics, fraud and byzantine manoeuvres.

Bahia knew the tiniest details of what she called the new scandal. She was trying to deduce what should be deduced, in the form of a pessimistic analysis of our general condition, which did not seem about to be cured of rampant illnesses like those.

I said, joking, 'But the wheels are turning, or so I believe. There are no breakdowns, and I only hear stories about the huge fortunes being made here and there. I have not heard so far about a bankruptcy declared or about to be declared.'

'Bankruptcy is like a terrorist operation,' Bahia said. 'Nothing on the horizon predicts it, and then suddenly you hear about it on the news.'

She asked me if I knew about her illness. I nodded and said, 'It's an illness like any other illness.'

She was moved for the first time and talked about young Ghaliya. 'I don't worry about leaving her alone, but it hurts not to have spent more time with her.' She said that she had not noticed any emotional attachment on my part towards the child, and added, 'You don't like her very much.'

I defended myself, saying that I considered her our baby, but Bahia was not convinced. But said she understood and did not blame me. Human nature was supremely complex, she said, and oddly enough she did not see any logic in all that was happening to her except her illness, because it was the only thing in total harmony with her human condition.

Bahia confessed, without overdone emotion, that she sat every day in the garden and cried. She did not cry for a specific reason, but out of abstract torment where nothing was obvious except her tears. Every time she asked herself why she cried, she would cry even more without finding an explanation. She added, 'I did not get the life I dreamed of when I was young.'

'No one gets the life they dreamed of,' I said to her.

'I did not imagine that. I was convinced I would get from life exactly what I dreamed.'

I tried to explain that life was better when it remained capable of surprising us.

She laughed and said, 'As far as surprises go, I got my share and more. Imagine, I marry someone who loves opera and sculpture, and one day I see him cover the walls of our house with photos of the housing compounds he has built, his inauguration ceremonies and meetings to sign financial agreements.'

3

Fatima called from Madrid that evening. All I could detect in her conversation were bits of self-pity for her life and convulsive crying that made her sound drunk. I found it in me to ignore her crisis and face it with some firmness.

'Why this silly crying?' I said to her. 'You're in good health and able to enjoy music, theatre and cinema. You have a job you love and you live in a European capital. You can sleep with any man you choose. What more do you want from life? Do you think that life is as generous with everyone as it is with you?'

My anger calmed her down a little, and I seized the opportunity to tell her about Bahia's illness. But when I felt she was about to resume her crying fit, I said loudly, 'I spent part of today with her and she seemed fine, maybe better than us.'

Fatima insisted that I visit her in Madrid. I told her I would because I too needed space to help me reorganise this mess. I had the impression that as we talked about our plan of action, she got completely over her crisis. When we ended our conversation I was still anxious, though, but then came a text message from her: 'Thank you, I love you.'

I spent the evening in a small Italian restaurant not far from the tombs of the Saadis. The friends I met were very worked up about rumours concerning the arrest of a gang of drug dealers who controlled the city. One of them said that this would certainly lead to the formation of prostitution rings and sex tourism, and many guesthouses might be shut down as a result. Since we were close to the general elections, the only beneficiary from these security measures would be the religious movement. Marrakech, with all its magical treasures, would then fall victim to the pincers of the Taliban.

Another well-informed friend said, however, that big business would be the real beneficiary of the situation, big business organised as a political and social force. It would use the income it provided, the jobs it created, the publicity it produced and the foreigners it pleased as bargaining chips to obtain comfortable seats in the political arena. He said no one could counteract the religious movement except that group. There would be a new leader of this kind in every major city, and if there was not, one would be created, until this blessed commodity became available all over the country.

Someone else suggested handing the major cities to the Islamists as a solution, in order to make peace with the terrorists. I laughed at his suggestion and told him these two options had nothing to do with each other, because terrorism worked for its own account. If the cities were handed over, they would become psychologically devastated, with explosions as their only amusement.

We quickly abandoned this discussion that lowered our spirits and agreed that our country counted among its leaders geniuses who knew how to manage matters without help from our rotten moods. At midnight we timidly went to one of the city's hotels to see a famous transvestite from Casablanca, who had come to Marrakech to belly dance.

I was awakened the next morning by the sound of Ahmad Majd's insistent banging at my door. When I opened it I saw his worried expression, and he told me that Bahia's condition had deteriorated suddenly. He was taking her to Paris.

We all met in the middle of the big house. Bahia was preparing to leave. She was smiling, playing with young Ghaliya and running her fingers through the girl's hair. I assumed she was in pain, but I did not have the energy to say anything. I took a cup from the table and poured coffee, unaware in my distress that I was spilling it. I heard Ahmad Majd say, 'We mustn't be late for the flight.'

I walked them to the door, hoping they would ask me to stay there for a little while. Bahia did, saying as she hugged me that it might be better for young Ghaliya. I returned to the breakfast table and watched Ghaliya spreading butter on a piece of toast, acting like her mother with her hurried movements and small bites. She had Ahmad Majd's eyes and Yacine's round face. Her features revealed a certain joy hidden behind a serious expression. I wondered if this would be my last breakfast in the big house, and the thought upset me. I wondered if the feeling of devastation would be the same at the death of a person I had no relationship with any more. I was surprised by a fit of tears I felt rising from my guts. I withdrew to the bathroom and splashed cold water on my face, while thinking about a way to breathe outside the big house.

On my way to the railway station, I called Layla. She was not at all nice to me.

'This is a story you have to put behind you,' she said, 'and not immerse yourself in it again as if you had never left. Since you have changed your life, there is nothing more to go back to. Why do you insist on keeping everything in tow for ever?'

'But I'm not keeping anything in tow. There is only a painful situation that I cannot face in an unemotional manner,' I said calmly.

She replied angrily, telling me that I walked with my head turned backwards, like a person looking towards the past.

I tried to find a way out of this anger but failed. She then asked if I had spent the night in the big house. When I told her I had, she said, 'I was sure you would do that. It's disgusting and vulgar, but you cannot do otherwise!'

I asked her about Mai. She put the receiver in the child's hands and left us to talk with our voices and first words, not knowing how to end the call.

I finally went to Madrid, but I could not have gone at a worse time: Bahia was undergoing chemotherapy, Layla was angry with me and with everything, and my life was in suspension over something unknown.

I spent happy days with Fatima. We enjoyed Madrid by night, talking nonstop during long dinners. It was all very good for our spirits, as if she and I were undergoing group therapy. We talked about books, films and music. We dug into our small problems and our memories and found forgotten details and treasures that we soon placed above all our other feelings. We did not feel how quickly time was passing till the first week of my visit was over. I called Layla to gauge her mood. I found it was still sullen, and nothing helped change it, neither my talk about the city, its restaurants and its theatres, nor even an offer for her to spend the remaining time of her spring break here with the two girls. Her refusal was categorical and rude, so we ended the conversation under dark clouds.

I patiently tried to recover some warmth in our relationship during conversations over the following days, but I failed. When I was fed up with the situation, I asked her if she still loved me. She told me she did not even love herself. I tried to pursue this thread, but she closed all avenues and said she did not want to talk about the subject any more.

I was constantly thinking about our estrangement, trying to find a way back into the world we had built with a great deal of passion and effort. But I always faced Layla's insistence on enveloping everything in mysterious silence. I talked with Fatima about it, and she said that maybe things had happened that frightened Layla. I wondered what they could be. She said, 'I don't exactly know, but my instinct tells me that something you did or did not do scared her.'

I was disconcerted that Fatima considered me so scary. It made me recall the details of my relationship with Layla as I searched for that fatal moment: how I loved her, and how I lived a terrifying schizophrenia split between two time periods, how the threads of our story were woven from a vague past and a troubled present; my fits, my relationship with Yacine, my work, my risk taking, my family, Al-Firsiwi, Diotima, Bahia, Essam, Mahdi and Fatima. I could not find anything that did not play a direct or indirect role in building our story.

Fatima noticed my depression and said, 'You will see that it is only a passing crisis. Don't forget that age too lands painful blows, hitting women especially hard.'

I swallowed my voice and realised fearfully that returning to my apartment in Rabat would be a difficult test of my ability to remain alive.

I then remembered all the lovely moments I had spent with Layla, and I felt that if I did not make love to her as soon as possible, I would die of sadness. I immediately called her number and told her that.

She said angrily, 'You have to come back first.'

'I'll come back immediately,' I told her.

'I must still tell you that I have become as frigid as a block of ice!'

I did not tell her that she was the sweetest block of ice in the world. I did not tell her how desolate the world would be without her, nor did I tell her that for some incomprehensible reason I expected something bad to happen but did not know what it was.

That evening I needed to bring back the feeling that had followed our conversation. I was surprised that Layla's voice was sleepy, and she begged me to call her later; she was exhausted and wanted to eat and go straight to bed. The conversation upset me, and I was overcome with a sudden anger at myself. I had failed to protect this last chance in my life, because, completely unfairly, I was being mistreated by the woman for whom I had given up Marrakech, with whom I had adopted Mai and for whose sake I had read, despite myself, a novel by Saramago five times. As my anger grew, it was evident to me that I deserved better, but since there was no better alternative, I went back to being hard on myself. I felt that everything happening to me was due to the unhappiness I had inherited, passed on from father to son, and that would stay with me to the very end.

To explain to myself what was happening, I imagined a person standing on the bank of a large river who cast his hook and line into the calm waters. Suddenly the line went taut, and the fisherman sensed from the violence of the movements the struggle he would have with the fish. He felt the resistance of the fish, its anger, refusal to submit, sudden thrashing and then compliance, as if the fish was not hooked but had decided to swim towards him. It arrived, floating over the water and jumping in frenzied movements as if to say it was not dead. Then all movement stopped and the line went limp, lying still on the surface of the water, the fish gone.

All the sadness in the world now overwhelmed the man. It chewed him up before spitting him out as wreckage on to the shore. What would the man do? What would he do with all the despair? Suddenly he looked at the flowing river and the reeds bending in the wind, he listened carefully to the rustling of the leaves in the nearby trees, and he became aware with a joyous conviction that this was the best thing that had happened to him in a long time. He understood that the fish getting away was the most deeply pleasurable event in his life, and that this sunny day where there was still a river, a sky and trees was exactly his lot in life and there would not be any other. If there were another chance, he would be overwhelmed by all the despair in the world because he would not get a sunny day, a river and trees.

Layla's sudden distancing in this dramatic, painful and destructive manner was the best thing that could have happened to me. What did I want from this story? To spend the rest of my life in exhausting disagreements in order to learn how to escape the clutches of old age? To devote myself to suffocating the fish? To sew a life tailored to our measurements, which would undoubtedly become too small for our bodies and we would be obliged to rip it up?

What did I want beyond what I had achieved? That first shiver, the response of the fishing line, the beating of the whole body as it welcomed another resisting body, the pleasure that went as far as the desire to kill, the peace offered by pain? And then what? Did we have to spoil the impossible with the crumbs of the possible?

I walked in a street unknown to me, and once I realised I was lost, I went further. I talked to Fatima on the phone, and told her I did not know where I was and did not want to know. If I found a restaurant I liked, I would call her back.

When we finally sat at a table in a noisy restaurant, one that took Fatima more than two hours to find, I was at my best. I was elated by my new condition, happy to have escaped certain death if the relationship had flipped over due to excessive speed. I shared this with Fatima, but she was upset because the hard-to-find restaurant was located in a dangerous part of the city.

'Since you're talking about an accident, I will tell you what is usually said in such situations. Wait until your blood cools down, make sure your bones aren't broken and you're not suffering from internal bleeding,' she said.

I laughed at the comparison and then showered Fatima with a flood of jokes and funny stories. I ate and drank like a happy man. At the end of our dinner I said to her, 'Are you reassured now? Nothing is broken!'

We went back home. As soon as I entered the lift I was overcome with cold shivers. I lay down on the sofa bed trembling, and Fatima covered me up, concerned. I begged her to go to sleep, explaining to her that it might be only a cold because I had walked for a long time in the bitter weather. She agreed with me and decided to give me something for my cold. When she went to fetch the medicine, I thought to myself that it was my body punishing me. I wondered why I risked pretending to have escaped danger when I still consisted of bleeding shattered pieces in a topsy-turvy relationship. I might be sad to such a degree that I wouldn't stay alive. I would die immediately. I couldn't bear the idea of living without Layla for even one second. I had known from the first day that with her I had found eternity.

I felt excruciating pain throughout my body, but could not pinpoint its exact source until I realised that my soul had fallen victim to an unbearable agony. At that moment I felt that I was suffocating and losing consciousness, but my pain did not subside. I wanted Layla with me in that bed that was soaked with my sweat, and I wanted her to tell me that she loved me for ever, like she had never loved any other person in the world. I wanted her to threaten me, to say that she would come out of the phone and tell me that she hated me, making sure, however, that I knew she did not mean it.

I opened my eyes to a room full of natural light to see Fatima sitting close to the sofa. She had just returned from the office and was very worried about me. I pulled myself up and asked her the time. She said it was past two in the afternoon. I went to the bathroom and apologised for all the trouble I had caused her.

'You didn't stop moaning all night,' she said. 'Does anything hurt?'

'Yes. Everything hurts, but what hurts most, what hurts me to death, is losing Layla.'

'But you haven't lost her,' replied Fatima.

'I felt something bad in her voice,' I said.

Fatima told me that she found my delayed adolescence annoying. Her words made me really angry. I quickly shut the bathroom door for fear of doing something crazy. Raising her voice over the sound of the running water, she said, 'You must first know what happened.'

When I did not reply, she said, 'I'm sorry, I'm leaving.'

I packed my suitcase and booked my return ticket on the Internet. As I was walking along the cold street looking for a restaurant where I could still eat lunch, I called Layla. I did that quickly, like someone diving into water. In a calm and friendly voice, she said that she missed me very much and that I must return quickly, that this trip and Madrid were meaningless. I discovered that under the influence of her new tone of voice I had changed and become an exhausted person with only one wish: to rest and enjoy the chances for peace with oneself and with others that life has to offer.

4

Before I left Madrid, Spanish newspapers announced the discovery of a link between a Moroccan detainee and the group responsible for the Madrid explosions. Once more, there was an extensive debate about Al-Qaeda in Morocco and whether there weren't preparations for a terrorist campaign on the Mediterranean's northern shore.

I was with Fatima in the airport terminal casually discussing these matters, as if we were avoiding talking about personal matters. A man whom I felt I knew but did not recognise approached me. He greeted me warmly and said that he was from my village. To confirm this connection, he mentioned the names of people from Bu Mandara as if they were shining stars in the human firmament. He paused in particular at Al-Firsiwi's name, and when he mentioned his own father's name the resemblance I had noticed from the start became apparent. I greeted him anew and wished him a happy holiday in that city that had no connection to happiness.

After he went off, Fatima asked me if I was bothered by his Afghani outfit. I told her that it was national dress by now. She laughed, and once again asked me to take care of myself and to take from life whatever it was willing to grant me and avoid ruining its mood with endless requests. She said, 'Life is like a woman and does not like that. How long will it take you to grasp this simple principle?'

I objected, saying, 'Aren't you ashamed to use the same advice I gave you weeks ago?'

She hugged me for a long time while the departure call concealed her crying. When I entered the gate I raised my hand high without turning back and then walked towards the plane, submitting to an unexplainable feeling that I too did not like even myself.

When the plane levelled off at cruising speed, the man from the airport, my townsman, joined me, invading my privacy with a flood of stupid comments on immigration, life in the West and Islam's innumerable enemies. I answered him, agreeing to things I had never thought about. All I wanted was to see him return to his own thoughts and leave me alone. But he seemed to like my reactions, and would go away every time the hostess needed room in the aisle and then come back. He found a solution and asked the passenger next to me to exchange seats, which the passenger did gladly to my great annoyance, thus putting my mood, with all its sudden and permanent weaknesses, at the mercy of this man.

During the hour of the flight to Casablanca, matters moved extremely fast. He talked to me without any preliminaries about Yacine, whom he'd known. He said that although he had only met him once, in Paris, he was the kind of person you did not forget.

'Do you know what happened to him?' I asked.

'Of course. Otherwise I would not have talked to you about him,' he said.

All my intellectual powers were on alert, and I besieged him with hundreds of questions about Yacine, convinced that an exceptional coincidence had finally provided me with an opportunity to find out the truth about what had happened. My voice rose whenever he gave me ambiguous or incomplete answers. I asked him personal questions, such as why he had been in Madrid, whether our encounter was a coincidence, or had he known we were on the same flight.

He was flustered by the unexpected questioning and lost the confidence with which he had talked to me earlier. Even his bearing lost its force and harshness, which had been in harmony with his clothes and severe features. The plane had started its descent to Casablanca airport when he begged me to leave him alone, and told me that he had introduced himself to me spontaneously and should not have done that. But he had been unable to resist the opportunity to talk about Yacine, never expecting his decision to lead to this interrogation.

He went on, 'Now, I beg you to calm down. I did not know the Yacine who did what he did. I just knew Yacine, period. I can appreciate the fact that nothing in the world interests you more than knowing exactly what happened to him and led to his death. Fine. Do you want us to close this subject the best way? OK, here is my phone number. I'm going to Marrakech tomorrow. Call me there. We might be able to meet a friend of Yacine's who travelled with him to Afghanistan. Please understand that I have nothing to do with what happened. Beware of getting carried away and drawing conclusions, thinking that I'm involved in any of those things. I'm only trying to help you, because we met due to divine providence, and only God knows the reason. Why are you looking at me like that? Perhaps you think some group has arranged this encounter. But how could any group, no matter how shrewd, co-ordinate all your doings with all my doings? Try to remember the details of your trip and then try to find something that could be considered pre-arranged.'

I said, as if talking to myself, 'Life as a whole is a pre-arranged story!'

'What? Do you mean to say that everything is governed by divine will? It is indeed so. If you only knew where I was going before I decided on this direction.'

I looked down at the runway and saw it surrounded by high vegetation. I was absent-minded to the point of thinking that the plane was taking off for Madrid. It sometimes seemed to me that life required that we listen again to some of its elements by replaying the record. Then, when the plane reduced speed and banked right towards the airport, many scenes came to mind.

My neighbour was getting ready to leave the plane and said nervously, 'Don't forget to call me. A coincidence is better than a thousand appointments. We might never have met. One of us might have died without ever having known the other existed!'

I thought that would have been much better than this suspicious encounter.

I called Layla many times, but she did not answer. That evening I knocked at the door of her apartment, but she was not there. She called me late and told me her daughter was spending part of her vacation with her father in Marrakech. She had had to take Mai and stay there, to be close to her.

I said somewhat stupidly, 'I'm back!'

'I know. I too will be back in two days. Do you know, Mai cannot stand being separated from her sister? Here, we all go out together, like this evening. It would be very nice, were it not for the attitude of the "first lady".'

'I'll come to Marrakech tomorrow,' I said.

She replied angrily, 'That's all we need! Listen, I can't see you here anyway.'

I was angry as well. 'I can't see you either. I will be busy with another mess!'

WHEN I arrived in Marrakech, I went to see Bahia. She had lost her hair due to the chemotherapy, but she dealt with the situation with studied elegance. I had the impression that she was on her way to recovery. Even more than that, she had regained her confidence in her ability to defeat the illness. As we were eating lunch, she said that she talked to Ibrahim al-Khayati by phone, since new rules allowed this. The three of us talked at length about what should be done for Ibrahim now that the date had been set for the start of his trial. Ahmad Majd said we would ask for his temporary release and then see what would happen.

Bahia returned to her conversation with Ibrahim and told me privately, while we were drinking our coffee, that he wanted to talk to me regarding an important matter related to Yacine. My heart convulsed, and I would have told Bahia about my appointment with the man from Bu Mandara in the afternoon if Ahmad Majd hadn't interrupted to tell me it was better to visit Ibrahim in person than talk to him on the phone.

I left the big house for the Nahda Café, but as soon as I got into the taxi, I realised that there was still a whole hour before the four o'clock appointment. I decided to walk a while before going to the café. As I walked I remembered Ibrahim's message and wondered what he could tell me about Yacine. I imagined he might have met someone in prison who had known Yacine, or that he had obtained information from someone who knew me. I imagined that someone was using him in a case related to Yacine's friends. Then I considered how these separate elements had coincided by chance, one in Salé prison and the other in the Madrid airport, and whether there was any possible connection between the two stories. Or rather, how there could not be a connection between them.

At that moment I thought that my encounter with the man from my village would be more productive after I had talked with Ibrahim. I might learn from Ibrahim something that would help me in my meeting with this person. I returned home, but unfortunately was unable to reach Ibrahim on the phone, no matter how much Bahia and I tried, and I was almost fifteen minutes late for my appointment. When, out of breath, I arrived at the café, I did not find anyone there. I sat down, depressed, and waited half an hour, then I got up heavily and left the place, preferring to think he had come by earlier and, not finding me there at the agreed time, had left.

By seven o'clock in the evening I had called him over and over, reaching only his answering machine. I thought a thousand times about Layla and wandered the streets aimlessly for more than two hours. I was convinced that what remained of my destiny on that difficult day was for a car to hit me and put an end to my inadequacy. At that very moment Layla called.

'Tell me please,' she said, her voice loud over the phone, 'I beg you, say you are in Marrakech.'

'Let's meet immediately,' I said.

I needed time to get ready for this encounter – not to make the logistical arrangements but to prepare for those first moments when we do not know whether we are about to begin one thing or resume another. There are those other moments when we have to submit every gesture to a precise test to understand what is coming back to us whole, unabridged, and what might have been diminished or exceeded its familiar limits, or has simply become the gestures of a different person.

We were in a room in a quiet tourist hotel and every now and then we heard the mumbling of people drinking around the swimming pool. We made love with shy movements as if we were doing it for the first time, but also with a devout intensity, as if we were apologising for something that had happened to us or something we had done. At some moment of our pleasure, I was overcome with a desire to do something more than love, something that would make Layla seep into my breath and my pores, into every part of my existence and settle there for ever.

I was kissing her, looking deeply into her eyes, following the vibrations of this desire to its end. I did not notice in the eruption of passion that she was crying. It might have been because she detected everything that raged within me, or maybe because she had found me again after a temporary loss.

I got a call from the man from Bu Mandara around midnight. He apologised for missing our appointment, but Yacine's friend lived very far away. I was certain I would apologise to him as well and tell him I was not interested in this encounter any more – which I had not wanted in the first place – but he suggested meeting at ten the next morning at the entrance of the Club Med Hotel. I agreed reluctantly. After my experience with Layla that evening, I did not need anything else. When Layla asked me about the matter, I told her about it, purposely filling it with humour and irony. She got upset, wondering whether I was aware of all the dangers lurking in a contact of this kind.

'Consider this,' she said. 'By chance you meet a young man at Madrid airport, and by chance he becomes the intermediary for an encounter with a possible friend of Yacine's. Don't you smell a trap of sorts?'

I told her, 'I don't have any logical reason to suspect that.'

Sleep allowed us to resume something that had nothing to do with the strange meeting. For long hours, no dream, no tossing or turning, no stray movement succeeded in separating us, until daylight bathed the two of us under our veil of anxiety.

As I was getting ready to leave, Layla asked me, 'What do you expect from this encounter?'

'Nothing,' I said. 'I only want to hear from someone who knew Yacine what happened. How he adopted this cause and how he lived in its worlds, how he was exposed to what he was exposed to, how they handled his corpse and what they did with it. I want to hear all those details and more. I want to be filled with them and with the truth those details represent. If this happens, I will go through true mourning and the subject will be closed for ever.'

Layla took Mai from me and went to the other room. She called back, 'I don't know what will be closed, but I'm not reassured at all.'

Mai cried nervously. Layla scolded her and gave her to me, almost throwing her into my arms. This made her crying worse, so Layla came back to take her, apologised for her actions and for acting more childishly than Mai. I waited until the small storm had passed, and then I moved close to Layla and begged her to spare me an argument. I couldn't stand that and I truly wanted to get out of the tunnel I was in.

'You won't be able to get out of the tunnel if you keep going back and forth inside it,' she said.

'It's not like you imagine. I see a distant light but I'm not strong enough to reach it.'

Layla started gathering her things, getting ready to go back to Rabat, and I took advantage of this to say, 'I'll go to my appointment, then catch up with you.'

She replied as she buried her face in the open suitcase, 'If you don't tell the police before you go, don't bother catching up with us!'

I stood at the door, hurt by this uncalled-for remark. I turned my back to the noise that Mai created as she tried to follow me. I left, confident that I would arrive at the light I could see in the tunnel.

5

I ARRIVED AT JAMA AL-FNAA square half an hour before my appointment. I went towards one of the entrances of the medina and walked in its morning calm, before the shops opened and calls and shouts filled the air.

I was moved by something I could not specify, a combination of apprehension for what was coming and pain for what had happened. I felt light and free, contrary to what I expected. I stared at the faces of the passers-by, almost certain they could not see me, as if I had become a mere vision checking the conditions of the city. I saw a dark, lowly person arguing with an olive seller, assuring him that no one would buy this acidic product so early in the day. I heard the seller tell him, calmly, that if he knew how early in the day Tanjia was prepared, he would not open his mouth with stupidities. This seemingly unnecessary dialogue cheered me up. Despite its uselessness, the alley would have been desolate without it. A woman came out of a side alley and mumbled a series of swearwords I could not make out, before a young girl who did not seem to have had time to finish dressing caught up with her. She bent over and kissed the first woman's hands and head, trying to placate her with words that would have softened a heart of stone. I tried hard to grasp something from this incident, but to no avail. I was saddened by all the tenderness bursting from the sleeping city, as if I was eager to have a part of it but failed to grab hold. Then I found myself face to face with a child who appeared to be able to see me.

'What did the man mean?' he asked.

'Which man?' I said.

'The one who was looking from the roof.'

'What did he say?' I asked.

'He said, "Has the beneficiary of the trust arrived?"'

'Does the matter concern you?'

'It does not. We just want there to be something understandable this morning!'

I resumed my walk, pleased by the child's curiosity, then I retraced my steps so as not to miss my appointment.

Two buses were parked near the Club Med Hotel, whose façade was almost totally covered by a poster announcing an international film festival. Nearby were a large screen and a stage that seemed huge in the empty square. I glanced at the entrance of the hotel and alongside it, but I did not see the man from my hometown. I tried to imagine the features of the young man who was Yacine's friend, but failed. I noticed a person walking hesitantly in front of the hotel. I expected him to be the man I was meeting, but when I got close to him he asked me the way to Bab al-Jdid.

The man did not show up at the agreed time, nor more than an hour later. This hurt me, and I wondered if I had fallen victim to the games of heartless teenagers. Perhaps they were watching me from their hiding places. I remembered the young man who had let me believe I was his father from an old relationship, and I thought that maybe at a certain age we become the victims of such games, and their catalyst. Right then, I was willing to put up with the abuse of the world in exchange for a meeting with the two young men, to save me from this wasted morning. I saw the person. He was facing the buses, wearing a Pakistani shirt, a dirty *taqiyah*, a counterfeit Nike tracksuit top, and sports shoes of the same brand. I thought he was the same man I had met at the Madrid airport, who had been willing to connect me to a thread that would lead me to Yacine, for no reason other than that he too was a son of Bu Mandara and wanted to do a good deed for me. Well, for God's sake first. There was nothing behind this except lessening the world's misery and losses. But where was the expected friend, the cornerstone of this story and the justification for its existence in the first place? Why hadn't he arrived? Could he have been too scared of this strange encounter? What would scare him? Maybe he thought I would contact the police, as Layla had suggested. He would be right to think like that. Even if we discounted that possibility, there was no place for a relationship between us not built on fear. We would fear each other to eternity.

The man turned suddenly and I realised it was not him. I noticed his Pakistani shirt bulged out slightly at both sides, which forced him to hold his arms away from his body, as if he were about to pick something up off the ground. I noticed his ferocious expression, as if he had just finished a violent fight. He was watching me. When I got close to him, assuming he was the young man who had known Yacine and who had been sent on his own by the man from my hometown, he turned like a robot and walked towards the street behind the hotel. I could think of nothing better to do than follow him, in the belief that there was something fatalistic and inescapable about this act of submission. I walked behind the man thinking about Layla; it seemed extremely strange not to be thinking about Yacine and Yacine alone. I sent her a short message on my phone: 'No one turned up for the appointment. I love you.'

The man was walking leisurely towards the Koutoubia, and I was forced to run after him. Then I slowed down, waiting for him to get further away before catching up again. Koutoubia Square was filling up with pedestrians, traders and loiterers. The number of men who looked like my 'friend' increased, and I strained to keep him in sight. At one point he stopped by an open-air bookseller and started leafing through old books and some magazines, which, to my surprise, were women's magazines. When he resumed his walk it was almost noon and the sun was strong. At that moment I saw him walk in the direction of Bab al-Jdid. I remembered the other young man who had asked me the way to Bab al-Jdid a little earlier. Did he have anything to do with this man? And why?

The man quickened his pace, and I did the same until we reached the Hotel La Mamounia. There in front of the main entrance he stopped beside a taxi and bent down to talk to the driver through the window. He then crossed the street and walked towards a garden that belonged to the hotel. I stood waiting for him without knowing whether he would come back, without knowing whether I would follow him again. He came out suddenly, turned right, and then exited through the gate in the railings and crossed the street, heading towards the pavement that led to the big hotels. I followed him quickly, struck by a crazy idea about the strange fit of his shirt. I wondered if he wasn't getting ready to blow himself up with a suicide bomb in a specific place, and was looking for a significant mass of foreigners to carry out his task. No sooner had this idea become clear to me than the man disappeared. I ran with all my force along the long pavement until I reached the entrance leading to the hotel district. I went through it, moving fast and thinking about the hotel I had gone to, where I had not seen the person I was supposed to meet. I went then in the direction of Al-Saadi Hotel, then the Kempinski, then the Atlas.

I thought of calling Layla and asking her to warn the police about the possibility of someone getting ready to blow himself up imminently near some hotel. I was afraid to alarm her, though, about something that might not be true. I was soon convinced that the man must have gone to the Conference Centre and the Meridien Hotel, where the guests and organisers of the film festival were gathered. At this hour most of them would be eating a leisurely breakfast after a long night and too little sleep, or eating a light lunch while basking half-naked in the sun.

I moved to the other pavement and dashed towards the triangle of death, as I imagined it, not knowing what I could do if I arrived to find the man about to detonate his deadly belt. Once again I thought about calling Layla or Bahia or Ahmad Majd, but was unable to access their numbers in my state of confusion and fear. I reached the door of the Conference Centre and found the place suffused by the calm of the noon hour. I was swimming in sweat, looking with shifting eyes for the slow-paced man who was not wearing socks with his trainers and could not let his arms hang down in a natural way. But he was not there or anywhere else I could see, where I could meet him and see his face turning yellow as the moment of action approached.

I returned to the Olive Gardens near the Hotel La Mamounia. I wanted to get away from the places where I might meet people I knew. I wanted to return to the starting point where I had an appointment with a person I did not know, who was supposed to tell me about the mysterious time that had swallowed Yacine. Who had arranged these impossible appointments? Why was I following a man with whom I had no connection, and about whom I did not know anything that gave me the right to expect all of this evil from him?

I arrived at the Olive Gardens exhausted. I sought their humid shade and walked aimlessly, thinking. what would happen if I took a taxi and heard the breaking news about a faceless and nameless suicide bomber and the carnage he had inflicted. I shivered when I remembered that I could have informed the police about him.

At some point, still stunned by that possibility, I felt something oppressive behind me, as if someone were breathing heavily. I turned in a panic, but there was no sign of anyone following me. I turned to look right and left, and noticed a body moving between the trees. When I moved quickly to catch up with him, I had the impression it was Yacine chasing someone. I ran after him and called his name every time I saw him, but he neither responded nor stopped. I was upset with him for not answering, and for betraying the promise he had made to me to disappear for good. I was burning with anger and ran faster, forcing him to quicken his evasive movements. I wondered why he had come back at that moment and why he was concocting this stupid chase. Was he the one who had organised this story down to the last detail? What was he enticing me towards? I wondered if Yacine was planning something for me, pushed by some group. And who was that group? I then remembered the scenario in which I imagined Yacine still alive after his death notice, shedding his identity with an imaginary death in order to reappear with another identity and another plan. I was confused by what was happening around me, and I was scared to have Yacine participate, before my eyes, in a bloody event where I would be a victim.

I returned once more to the Olive Gardens, looking for the person I thought was Yacine. I had used all the strength I had left to chase a ghost that had appeared and then disappeared. Then I was overcome with a great fear, lest the vision turn out to be a devilish manoeuvre to distract my attention and involve me in a false chase, while another person was preparing his attack perfectly. In the midst of all this overwhelming confusion, I heard a beautiful voice chanting Qur'anic verses. The voice sounded familiar and close, and I realised I had heard it more than once before this day. But I was unable to recall whose voice it was or the circumstances in which I had heard it. I thought of Ibrahim al-Khayati. What did he know about all this? Had he received a message from Yacine about the dates in Marrakech? I said to myself that this was the missing link. There was something that had not reached me, something that had got lost on its way to me. There was a thread connecting all these separate events that I had not seen until now. I was thus at the heart of a story that I did not understand and where I was not in control of my own role.

I reached the end of the Gardens, right in front of the iron gate leading to the lighthouse. No one but me came out of the shade of the olive trees. Had Yacine been no more than a vision born out of my confusion? Had the person I followed been simply an externalised inner image that I had let loose in the city? I was about to give in to those desperate suppositions when I saw him at the end of the inner pathway of the lighthouse, walking very slowly with the steps of an exhausted man, defeated and desperate. I headed towards him once more, trying to convince myself that it was not him and that he did not resemble the man I had lost. It seemed to me that his shirt was no longer bulging as it had been and his arms fell normally to his sides. There was only a muscular pride to his walk. But when I got close to him, I changed my mind; when we were a few steps away from the basin, I was sure it was him and that something under his shirt was making him walk like a robot.

He reached the edge of the basin, raised his face towards the sun, turned to face the *qibla* and prayed without removing his shoes, like in a war. This detail in particular was what changed me into the force of a tornado; I could hardly recognise myself or what I had been until that moment. I remembered nothing but a word I had heard from Yacine months ago on our way back, Layla and me, from a dance show – 'Now, now, now.'

Now, I said to myself and I took off like an arrow towards the person who was praying fervently, his eyes closed. I surrounded him with my arms and pushed him towards the basin.

At that critical moment when he took off from the ground, the man turned his head directly towards me, and, for an instant, behind his thick beard and fierce look, I saw the face of Essam, more terrified than he had ever been, moments before a cold white cloud took us in its awesome detonation.

A NOTE ON THE AUTHOR

Born in 1951, Mohammed Achaari is a Moroccan poet,
short story writer, journalist, former Minister of Culture
in Morocco and head of the Union of Moroccan Writers.
His work has been translated into English, French,
Spanish, Russian and Dutch. *The Arch and the Butterfly* is
his second novel.

A NOTE ON THE TRANSLATOR

Aida Bamia is professor emeritus of Arabic language and literature at the University of Florida in Gainesville. As well as being a literary translator she is the author of *The Graying of the Raven*, and was the editor of *Al-'Arabiyyah*.

A NOTE ON THE TYPE

The text of this book is set in Bembo. This type was first used in 1495 by the Venetian printer Aldus Manutius for Cardinal Bembo's *De Aetna*, and was cut for Manutius by Francesco Griffo. It was one of the types used by Claude Garamond (1480–1561) as a model for his Romain de L'Université, and so it was the forerunner of what became standard European type for the following two centuries. Its modern form follows the original types and was designed for Monotype in 1929.